Praise for

THE WINNOWING

"This is a fast-paced and exciting murder mystery for teens."

—Historical Novel Society

"I liked this book even more than the first one. There is so much happening in St. Louis; The depression, a crazy Veiled prophet and a secret society trying to wipe out half the population. Hazel and Stanley's relationship is thrown through some tough situations. I love this book because even with all the bad things happening, the characters never lose their witty spark. The characters are so fantastic…

I highly recommend this series. You can't go wrong with a good detective mystery with a little bit of romance!"

—Megan, Book Wife Reviews

"…quick and snappy with excellent pacing, and all the same characters we loved before back in a situation with higher stakes and more to lose. It was EXCELLENT."

—Hannah Michaels

THE WINNOWING

STANLEY AND HAZEL
BOOK 2

JO SCHAFFER LAYTON

OWL HOLLOW PRESS

Owl Hollow Press, LLC, Springville, UT 84663

The Winnowing: Stanley and Hazel Book 2

Library of Congress Cataloging-in-Publication Data
The Winnowing / J. Schaffer Layton. — Second edition.

First Edition — 2019 by Month9Books.

Summary:
Darkness descends over St. Louis, a city already rocked by the Great Depression. More and more people are disappearing, and some have turned up dead. A sinister secret society is putting forward their plan known as "The Winnowing," designed to wipe out those they consider undesirable.

ISBN 978-1-958109-24-3 (paperback)
ISBN 978-1-958109-25-0 (e-book)

To my stalwart, loving parents who did the best they could.

Ta-da!

CHAPTER ONE

A black-hooded figure hovered over him and brandished a long, curved knife. Stanley shut his eyes tight, an unseen force held him down, and he couldn't move. The knife pierced into his eyelid, pushing further into his skull. Stanley screamed in agony.

Shouts reverberated in his ears, and Stanley sat up in bed, heart hammering in his chest. It took a few moments and shuddering breaths to realize it had not been real. It was still dark outside, and his bedroom was only illumined by the streetlamp outside his window. The dim outline of his dresser and the darkened mirror over it startled him a moment. But the movement in the shadows was his own reflection.

Just a dream, Stanley reminded himself. *Just like the others. That's all.*

The hairs on his arms prickled. No. That wasn't all. Stanley shivered and folded his arms across his bare chest. Something dark lurked in the room, staring at him. Like what he'd felt at the St. Louis Statue when Evelyn was killed, and in the caves when he found Hazel tied to a chair at the mercy of that maniac. His "street sense" rang like alarm bells in his head.

With the yank of a string, the bare, bulb lamp near his bed lit up the small empty room. The ordinary sight of the leaky ceiling and peeling paint grounded him. Stanley blew out a slow breath to calm himself. His eye stung. Lifting a shaking hand to his right eye, he winced and then looked at his fingers. A small drop of blood.

"What the hell?" he rasped. Stanley turned around and saw it laying on his pillow: a spiny, black, tree branch.

He threw off his covers and scrambled out of bed, tripping over his clothes as he reached for the baseball bat propped against the dresser. He stared at the black limb as if it were a huge spider about to scuttle away. How did that thing get in here?

Wrenching open his bedroom door in case he needed a fast escape, Stanley squeezed the bat in his hands and checked the bedroom window. The lock remained fastened. Just to make sure, he reached out to touch the glass, which remained solid and unbroken. Holding his breath, he crept out of his room with the bat raised. The floorboards creaked under his bare feet, and he froze, eyes darting to the darkened stairwell. He swallowed, but his mouth had gone dry.

Legion. Whatever or whomever that was, watched me sleep. They could have killed me. Did Charles escape the asylum? Something is here...

Fighting the rising panic, Stanley crossed the hallway to check his uncle's room. Seamus went out on his beat early in the evening, so an intruder could easily lurk in there. He wiped his hands one at a time on his pajama pants and gripped the bat.

"All right you rat bastard, show yourself, and let me hit you like a home run," he growled through the door.

No answer.

Stanley opened the door and flipped on the light switch. He blinked as his eyes adjusted, then he looked under the bed, in the closet, and checked the windows. Nothing. No evidence of forced entry. No sign that anything had been disturbed.

Moving into the hallway, he looked down the stairs into the darkened living room. Ears straining for any sound, Stanley gripped the bat, trying to gather the courage to go downstairs. Anything could be down there waiting for him, ready to kill.

If they wanted to hurt me, they would have done it while I was sleeping, not wait for me to have a baseball bat in my hands. The thought didn't make him feel any better. The blackness at the bottom of the stairs took on a life of its own, creeping along the floor and reaching up for him.

Taking a deep breath, he charged down the stairs, jumping over the last two steps. He landed with a thump, the bat held in front of him. Stanley did a quick scan of the room, half expecting a horde of hooded figures to emerge and stab him to death.

He flicked on the light. Nothing looked out of the ordinary. The clock on the mantel ticked away with tiny, metallic clicks. He searched the room, looked into the kitchen, and checked the doors and windows. No splintered wood from a forced entry or jimmied locks. Nothing.

Stanley dropped the bat to the floor. His hands shook, and he closed them into fists. Ashamed of his cowardice, he willed his body to stop trembling. *Get a grip, Fields.* Tea, he needed to make himself some tea.

In the kitchen, he filled the pot with water and turned on the stove. Hovering over the burner, he watched as the flames danced around the bottom of the kettle. He had no idea how Legion or whoever got into the house. They obviously wanted to intimidate him. Stanley touched his eye and winced; it was swelling shut.

The black stick was a message.

He didn't want to touch that stick, investigate it, or wonder about it. Burning it seemed like a good idea, turning it to ashes so he could pretend he'd never seen it.

Waiting for the water to heat, Stanley's mind tried to process what had happened to him in the two months since Hazel, Sandy, and he had emerged from Lemp Caves into instant stardom. Father Tim praised him from the pulpit during multiple masses, and the whole of Dogtown wanted to shake his hand. Even worse, the Ghosts of Smooches Past kept jumping out at him, giving him "eyes" in class, and a few even suggesting marriage. In the life before he met Hazel and all of the Veiled Prophet stuff happened, he would have eaten it up with a spoon, fork, and knife.

Stanley just wanted everyone to let him alone. He forced himself to hang with the Knights, go to school, and be social. In the confessional, to Father Timothy, he admitted to being afraid, but would never admit it to anyone else. Still, some people knew he wasn't okay. Uncle Seamus had been drinking more than usual but hiding it from Stanley so as not to worry him. Sister Mary John asked him if he was ill, and Hazel suggested he should see a psychotherapist. Arthur said that Stanley's new-found commitment to chastity of the lips made him grumpy and crabby, so he should do everyone a favor and plant one on Hazel.

At the moment he was more concerned about the deadly message left on his pillowcase. He was reluctant to go back upstairs and examine it. Stanley walked over to the bookshelf by the sunken, shabby couch in the living room. On a low shelf was a small statue of St. Michael, patron saint of cops and defeater of the Devil. Stanley knelt down. Crossing himself, he prayed the St. Michael Prayer Seamus taught him when Stanley was old enough to speak:

St. Michael the Archangel, defend
us in battle.
Be our defense against the wick-
edness and snares of the Devil.
May God rebuke him, we humbly
pray, and do thou,
O Prince of the heavenly hosts, by
the power of
God, thrust into hell Satan, and all
the evil spirits,
who prowl about the world seek-
ing the ruin of
souls. Amen.

Crossing himself again, he stood and climbed the stairs with determined steps. Setting his jaw, Stanley entered his bedroom. It was strangely cold, even for this time of year. He stooped down and grabbed a white t-shirt from the floor and pulled it over his head and tattooed chest. With a scowl, Stanley leaned over his bed and carefully picked up the branch between two fingers.

The bark had been stripped before the branch was painted black. He held it up to his nose and sniffed. The paint smelled fresh, probably only a few hours old. Holding the branch up to the light bulb by his bed, Stanley noticed that the twigs had been twisted off, leaving sharp, splintered points. What is this thing? The tea kettle screamed from downstairs, and Stanley jumped, fumbling the stick. One point pricked his finger and drew blood.

With a nervous laugh, Stanley dropped the stick, wiped his finger on his shirt, and went back downstairs. He poured hot water into a chipped mug, and bobbing the tea bag up and down, went to sit on the couch. Leaning back, he shut his eyes, the faint smell of dust and whisky coming from the faded cushions was familiar and comforting.

Ever since the World Series game with Hazel, Stanley waited for something like this to happen. But there'd been nothing, not even the sense that he was being followed. Even Arthur's pigeons stopped disappearing from the streets. Sometimes, Stanley doubted what had happened.

Now, the black painted stick, a declaration of war, a warning that the time of peace was over.

To steady his nerves, Stanley slowly finished his tea and tried to think of things that calmed him. The prayer made him feel a little better, but he needed something more to drive out the rest of the darkness. Stanley pulled out a Louis Armstrong album, set it on the battered phonograph bought from a second hand store, and lowered the needle. Satchmo's trumpet blew like the Archangel Gabriel on the Day of Judgment, blowing away the minions of evil.

Stanley leaned back into the couch and rubbed his face. He wanted to go back to the time when all he had to worry about was when the Raven's palookas tried to shake down school kids for money, and scrounging up food for hungry folks. Not that he regretted getting involved and saving Hazel and Sandy, but …

Hazel's smiling face appeared in his mind. In the past weeks, he'd been at her house, they'd gone to a movie or two, with an escort this time, and had listened to the final game of the World Series together on the radio. They'd been interviewed for papers and on the radio together. In all that time, there were no kisses or anything like that, but it was nice all the same. Considering his past, it seemed like the right way to do things. He was a reformed gentleman now.

Despite his efforts, he sensed a reserve from Hazel and her family. Frowning with frustration, he thought about how he'd proven his character over and over. It seemed like somehow his position of birth was the only thing swells really considered. "He's a great boy… for a Dogtown kid." He stared down at the black tinge of newsprint on his fingers. Washing them didn't help much. Didn't change who he was.

He wasn't really looking forward to the party at Hazel's house tonight with all the swells. She went on and on about it being for her birthday and also as a "reward" for him. But it sounded like pure torture.

As the needle on the record hissed the end of the music, Stanley stood and looked at the clock. 5:15 a.m. The newsies would be gathering at the street corner. He needed to find one of Arthur's pigeons. Fast.

He grabbed his hat and coat on the way out the door and jogged down the slowly wakening street to where the newsies gathered. It was December, and many of the shops sparkled with Christmas tinsel. The chilly air nipped at his face. Stanley eyed the mob of shabbily clad newsies, many of them scrawny and underfed, living off cigarette stubs and handouts. Teeth didn't seem to be among them, so he would need to get someone else.

"Jacksie, hey, I need you," he called to a slight, brown-haired boy who'd just reached down to get his stack of newspapers for the day.

"What's up, Stanny? I gots to get these papes over to Lindell."

Stanley reached into his pocket and pulled out his last two bits and held them out to the scrappy kid.

"I need you get ahold of Arthur and sell my papers at my spot today."

The boy looked at the money for a moment. "I'll do it, but I won't take yous money. What should I tell him?"

"Tell him to come to The Castle."

The scruffy kid stared at him for a moment. "Is this Knight business?"

"Never you mind, bud. Just do it."

Stanley turned around without another word and headed toward Forest Park, his thoughts swirling around what the black branch could mean. A threat? A warning that he was being followed? Would more kids be disappearing from the streets? Was The Winnowing finally in motion?

He stopped at the edge of Forest Park and patted his coat. A few weeks ago, he'd carefully ripped the inside lining to store the diary of Evelyn Schmidt. He never went anywhere without it, not even trusting his own house as a safe space. He'd been right.

After a few minutes of walking, he reached the edge of the Hooverville in Forest Park. The normal crew of homeless people in tents milled around, doing laundry, cooking whatever kind of breakfast they could lay ahold of over fire pits, and some looked at papers hoping to find nonexistent jobs.

A group of about ten college-aged kids were circulating among the tents. They carried colored flyers, handing them out to everyone they could find. Furrowing his brow, he walked to the nearest person, a pretty, college coed with carefully done up blond hair, puffy red lips, and a friendly smile.

"Hi, handsome, what's your name?"

Turning on the charm, Stanley smiled and said, "Well, that's secret information. Don't just give that out to everyone, you know."

She held her hand out for a shake. "I'll tell you mine if you tell me yours."

"Nah. You'd be shortchanged." If she recognized his name from the papers and the radio, he might never get rid of her. Plus, he could tell she was trying to snare him.

She looked a little offended and began to lower her hand, so Stanley reached out and shook it anyway. "You're not from around here." He gave her big smile.

The girl had to smile back. "What gave me away?"

"You've got a bit of a New England accent."

"Guilty. I'm here to help at the new Family Care Clinic. It offers health care for the poor."

Stanley narrowed his eyes with interest. "That's nice of you. What kinda things does the clinic do?" Hazel volunteered there, and she seemed convinced it was the best thing for the poor since FDR's New Deal.

The blonde handed him a flyer. "Basically just trying to give street kids a healthy life, you know? Inoculations, take care of injuries, all of that."

He took the flyer. It seemed on the level, inviting people in with little or no cost. But something about this clinic run by swells made his skin crawl, something he couldn't put his finger on at the moment. His street sense, or Second Sight, as Uncle Seamus called it, seemed to be on overdrive lately.

"Huh. Well, I could spread some around."

"That would be helpful. We'd appreciate it." She handed him the stack in her hands and gave him a smile full of white, straight teeth.

Stanley nodded at the good-looking girl. "Sure."

"You know, I'm going to be doing an internship at the clinic after the holidays. You should come see me there. And maybe show me the town?" the girl said, playing with the lapel of his jacket.

A month ago, Stanley would have said something like, "How about tonight, dollface?" But now, he couldn't. He was too stuck on Hazel. Even if this New Englander was a looker.

"I might see you around," he said, not wanting to be rude.

She winked at him. "I'll be around the park or Gaslight Square handing out these most days until Christmas."

With that, she walked away, joining another cute dame. They whispered and turned to wave at him. He gave them a wave back and then headed toward The Castle.

He wondered why out-of-towners would come to St. Louis to hand out flyers for a new health clinic. Looking at the flyers again, he looked for the organization sponsoring the clinic and found the small print at the bottom.

Funded by the Society for Fitter and Healthier Families.

Maybe he was being paranoid after finding the black branch. Everything in the world wasn't sinister, after all. Who wouldn't want a fitter and healthier family?

He made his way to The Castle, an abandoned, red boxcar in the middle of the woods in Forest Park. He'd found it one day while exploring the woods and figured it would be a perfect hiding place for a gang. From here, his Knights of St. Louis launched their raids on the abundant trash cans of the fancy Lindell set, in order to help feed the poor and needy. Now, The Castle was a sort of war room to figure out what to do next. Which lately, had been precious little.

He heard the voices of the Knights from inside the boxcar.

"Mine was left in our milk bottle on the doorstep this morning. Ma was sore at the milk guy, until I told her it was probably some kinda prank."

"Bastards left mine in my hat on the kitchen table."

So, they all got one too.

He lifted himself into the rusty boxcar and stood up. The interior was dim and cluttered with old blankets, an old sofa full of holes, and a small three-legged table with several lit candles on it. The Knights turned to face him, each of them holding a painted black branch. No one spoke for a moment until Arthur, ever present bowler hat and cigarette in place, said, "Took yous long enough."

"You guys got here pretty quick," Stanley said.

"It was an emergency," Anino piped in, holding up his own black branch.

Stanley nodded and then motioned to Arthur and the pack of cigarettes he held. "Can I have one of those?"

They all looked at him, not bothering to hide their surprise. Even Arthur, who often badgered him about smoking a pipe or something, hesitated before shaking out a cig and giving it to Stanley.

He put it in his mouth, grabbed the matches from his coat pocket, lit it up, and said, "What are you all staring at?"

As a response, Shuffles said, "Nothin', boss. Are we gonna talk about these here fancy, painted sticks or we just gonna use them for firewood?"

Stanley coughed a little as the smoke entered his lungs. "What's there to talk about? It's a declaration of war or intimidation or something. They want us to know everything is about to begin. And, unlike all of you, mine gave me a nice poke in the eye."

Jakob rubbed his chin. "Yeah, but why black branches? What does that even mean?"

Arthur sneered. "Does that even matter?"

The Knights argued for a moment, and then Stanley held up his hand. Something scratched at the back of his mind. He had noticed a couple of pages stuck together the last time he'd looked at the diary. Suddenly he had to see what they were. "Wait a tic. Might be something in the diary about all of this."

He reached into his coat and pulled out the diary. Flipping through it, he found the stuck pages. He slipped the blade of his pocket knife between the pages and carefully eased them apart. The heavy, black ink had acted like glue. After some tearing, the pages opened to reveal a drawing of a tree with branches spreading out over the two pages. Stanley let out a breath. He'd sensed right.

Across the trunk was written the word "Eugenics," and on each of the gnarled roots expanding below the tree were written words like "genealogy," "biology," "genetics," and "mental testing." Stanley noticed several broken branches falling from the tree, painted black.

Stanley held it up for the Knights. "This is it. And look what Evelyn wrote here, 'The dead branches shall be pruned in The Winnowing.'"

No one spoke for a moment; every one of them stared with mouths slightly open.

Arthur took a puff and blew out a slow stream of smoke. "Guess we're the dead branches, eh?"

"What's that word mean?" Anino said, pointing at the page where "Eugenics" was written.

Stanley didn't answer for a moment; he wasn't sure what it was, but he was starting to guess. He took a last puff on the cigarette and snuffed it on the ground. "We need information, especially about eugenics and what it means to The Winnowing. Looks like they're connected. Anino and Shuffles, hit the streets to see if there is any talk. Jakob, go to the library, see what you can find out about eugenics. I'll talk to Seamus and see if he'll tell me anything. Arthur, we'll need your pigeons."

They all nodded.

"Not sure I feel very cozy about the swells right now," Shuffles said, turning the black branch in his hand.

"Hazel's party should be a real gas, eh?" Anino said, frowning.

"Yeah. Chances are, we'll be watched. Be aware. Don't say anything boneheaded or stupid, get me? Try to blend in as much as possible with these swells. Right now, they're gonna treat you like their own personal pets, but I'm guessing they tend to kick their animals when they get mad. So, be nice, little, lap dogs."

The Knights murmured and frowned at that.

"I feel hunted. Like an unacceptable element," said Jakob, touching a nervous hand to the yarmulke he wore on his head.

"Nah. These people are screwy. Nothin' wrong with yous or any of us." Arthur scowled.

"I'd like to see them try to weed us out. We can't let them get to us. So, let's get cracking. And I'll meet you all back here around six, and we'll go to Lady Bananas. All right, amscray, you mugs." He was shaken, but Stanley tried to sound stronger than he felt.

All of the Knights filed out except for Arthur who lit another cigarette.

"So, you got something else, boss?"

Stanley smiled. "How'd you guess?"

Arthur shrugged his shoulders. "I'm magic."

Snorting, Stanley pulled out the flyers and dropped them on the small table. "I want to know about this place. They were handing these out to people in Hooverville."

"I've already checked this place out; your little trinket works there. Richies trying to feel good about themselves and all. They do this crap all the time."

"She's no trinket." Stanley scowled. "Anyway, I want the pigeons to keep an eye on the place."

Arthur frowned and tapped the ashes from the end of his cigarette. "I'm missing two. Might be happening again. I'm getting short on birds to send around the city."

"Then all the more reason to see what the hell is going on at these clinics. I can't prove anything yet, but something doesn't sit right in my gut." He snuffed his cigarette on the table and handed it back to Arthur.

He slipped Stanley's partially smoked cigarette back into his pocket. "That gut of yours ain't ever wrong." Arthur nodded. "But we's gonna need more recruits. Pigeons and Knights."

Leaning against the door and staring outside, Stanley rubbed his forehead. "Yeah, I thought about that. But where am I going to get them?"

"Try that slick Italian you pal around with. See if he's ready to leave the gangsters. Time to lower your standards and all. This is war."

"Yeah. Yeah, you're right. And by the way, that cigarette was disgusting." Stanley wiped his mouth.

Arthur grinned. "You better put some raw meat on that eye." He jumped down from the boxcar, straightened his bowler hat, and walked slowly off, whistling "John the Revelator," his new blues song of choice.

Stanley was unnerved. What if something happened to his Knights before they could figure out all this business? It weighed on him how much they trusted him. He wanted to be tough, but this black stick development had him thrown off. He reached up to his eye and gently probed it. Swollen for sure and he could barely see out of it. Maybe that's why everything seemed dim.

Well, this is just great. Going to Hazel's party looking like I've been in a street fight or like a girl slapped me or something. That's all I need right now, for that whole set to think I'm more dangerous than I actually am.

He let out an exasperated sigh and wondered if he should just skip school and get some sleep. The eye would be a good excuse. Sister Mary John might understand. He could tell she'd been worried about him.

He walked slowly back to his place, taking in every sight, scent, and sound of the city coming awake. Men and women with tired faces shuffled down the streets, wrapped in coats against the nippy, early morning. Vendors at their carts shouted out what they were selling, while kids in packs wound their way to school. Part of Stanley felt he could stay in St. Louis forever;

it was the only place he'd ever known. And yet, he knew he would never stay here, even before all this Veiled Prophet business happened. If he lived through it, he would get the hell out of Dodge.

Then he thought about Hazel. How could they ever work out? Dogtown boy and rich girl. This was America after all and not snobby England. But what did he have to offer her? What kind of life? Shaking his head, he pushed those thoughts away. He had to focus on the problem at hand. That drawing in Evelyn's diary disturbed him.

When he got home, he found Vinnie lounging on the porch, his dark hair hanging in his eyes, and a smirk on his face.

"Where ya been, Irish? We were supposed to walk to school together. Say, did Maggie belt you one in the eye?"

"Funny, you Italian bastard. You should be in comedy picture shows."

Vinnie stood and looked closer. "Nah, someone poked you, but good. Let's skip out today."

Stanley shrugged. He was too tired to face school anyway.

They went inside, Stanley found a piece of meat in the ice box, and placed it on his eye. They sat at the table, cracking peanuts in silence for a moment, and then Stanley said, "I want you to join the Knights."

"Ain't much for small talk today, are ya?" Vinnie grinned.

"No time for it anymore. Things are getting crazy." Stanley told him what happened in the night, leaving out that he shook like a boxer in his first fight.

Vinnie whistled. "Now you want me to join. Ha."

"Sorry. I know it's the worst time to ask. But even The Raven says it isn't a safe place anymore."

Vinnie sighed. "Yeah. The Raven is getting out. He released us, which never happens. We're having a final thing at the

Rookery tonight. He's scared. And that's a fact. And so am I, to tell it true."

Stanley nodded. "Yeah. The lights are going out all over St. Louis."

They looked at each other for a moment, and then Vinnie grinned. "I'll tell you what, I'll join your do-gooders if I can borrow the fancy shoes you got from the paper."

Few things filled Stanley with pride more than the shoes he'd earned by setting a record for the most papers sold for the St. Louis Post-Dispatch in a year. And he never let anyone borrow them.

"Nah. Can't. I need those for Hazel's birthday party tonight. I already look bad enough as it is with the eye. Hell, they already think I'm a thug who'll rob and beat them. I have to wear that smart suit and my best shoes, and that's a fact."

Vinnie leaned over the table. "Please, Stanny. I'm taking Patricia to the little shindig at the Rookery. Want to look aces. I ain't got no fancy shoes or nothin'. I'll join your Knights if you say yes." Vinnie held out his hand to shake.

Stanley looked at his best friend. They'd been pals through some tough times, and without Vinnie, his job at the ballpark would have been half the fun. Vinnie might be a lazy good-for-nothing, but when it counted, he always came through. He owed him. If it wasn't for Vinnie, they never would have found Hazel in the caves. Stanley could just wear his old shoes, shine them up good, or borrow Seamus's.

Stanley shook his friend's hand. "All right, ya palooka. They're upstairs under my bed."

Vinnie ran up, got the shoes, and with a quick "see ya later," went out the door. Stanley bolted and locked the door.

Exhausted, Stanley dropped onto the couch and closed his eyes. He hoped to get a dance in with Hazel at the party. He just wanted to forget everything and hold her. She was warm and soft and had that special Hazel sweet smell. Even with all of that moxie, when he held Hazel, she melted into him like she needed him. Feeling her wrapped in his arms by memory, his skin warmed and his heart slowed. Within minutes Stanley sunk into sleep.

CHAPTER TWO

Hazel dozed at the desk where she'd been filing papers. Cocooned and cradled in warmth, the slow thump of a heartbeat sounded in her head. Floating peacefully over the darkened city, the sparkle of St. Louis far below, Hazel gazed down at the roofs of Dogtown. Stanley was somewhere down there…

The shrill ringing of a phone across the hall startled her awake. Back in the hard, wooden chair, she placed the last few files into the correct drawers and crossed the hall. Hazel smoothed down her apron and tucked a stray curl behind her ear before pushing the door open. She was met by a sterile waft of rubbing alcohol and a bright overhead light bouncing off white walls. Doctor Karl Galton sat at his desk, bent over a stack of patients' files. He looked up at her, and a lock of wavy, blond hair fell across his forehead. The young doctor smiled and removed his round, reading spectacles.

"Well, Hazel. All done for the afternoon?"

She smiled, hoping her cheeks weren't as pink as they felt. "Yes. The storage closet is organized, and both exam rooms are spick and span. The new patient forms are filed, and Marie's medicine cabinet is restocked." Hazel took a deep breath, proud of the look of approval she had just put on the young doctor's face.

Dr. Galton nodded. "Terrific. You've been a great help these past weeks. Thank you."

Hazel grinned. "I'm happy to help. What you do for people... it's really swell."

"Doing things for other people is the best way I know of to overcome life's difficulties..." His eyes showed a flicker of sadness. Hazel wondered, as she often did, if he had a tragic past ... perhaps a terribly romantic and doomed love affair. She was a sucker for that. She snapped herself out of a sudden desire to put her arms around him and ask him to tell her everything.

"It's good to see you smile. You're a very brave girl." He had said this kind of thing before. "Some people would never recover from what you endured."

She swallowed, not wanting to remember. "Yeah, I worry about Sandy Schmidt."

"You're a good friend. I hope you don't blame yourself for anything that happened.

Young Chouteau was unwell."

Charles Chouteau. Her kidnapper. The man who had changed her sense of reality and nearly destroyed her best friend.

"Yes. I know." People were always talking about Charles as that poor, delusional boy. There was much head shaking and tongue clucking of regret and pity. Had he not been from a wealthy, elite family, Hazel was sure the attitude would be much different.

He gave her a bright smile. "Hadn't you better hurry along? Your big celebration is tonight."

"Yeah. See you there?"

"I wouldn't miss it." Dr. Galton winked.

Hazel left before she giggled or said something stupid. It was a silly crush, but he was delicious to look at and smart as a whip. He spent all day doing things for people who could otherwise never afford his help.

In the supply room, Hazel removed her apron and hung it in the locker. She grabbed her handbag, pulled out the powder compact, and glanced at herself in the small, round mirror. Her lipstick had worn off and her curls had gone astray as usual. It would be nice if she could just go home, snuggle up in a blanket, and read her fan magazines. She'd always loved motion pictures, but now she wanted to escape into the shimmering, silver world of Hollywood even more. It was safer. Instead, tonight she had to be social. Hazel's parents were throwing an immense party for her sixteenth birthday and to celebrate Stanley and his Knights rescuing Hazel and Sandy from their kidnapper.

They were local and international celebrities for a couple of months. Her best friend, Sandy, shied away from the spotlight. She'd been through too much. Sandy was no longer the sassy rebel who liked to be the center of attention. Cameras threw her into a panic, and she'd often wear a wrap that helped obscure the scar that ran down the side of her face. For the rest of them, it had been a heady time of newspaper stories and recognition. Stanley and Hazel were even invited on the Cracker Jack radio hour. They were "America's own, Cracker Jack kids!"

Hazel struggled to find footing in her new reality. It felt like the time she was a kid, and her family had gone to Florida. They spent the day at the sea; sparkling blue waters and warm sun, a picture of serenity and beauty. She had wandered too deep into the warm embrace of the waves, and an unseen power beneath the surface dragged her down and away from the shore. Tumbling under the water, she kicked and thrashed toward the surface only to find herself clawing at the sand. She'd lost her bearings and did not know which way was up. Then, her father's large hand had clamped around her ankle and yanked her out of the water.

There was no large hand to rescue her now.

The perfect, sheltered world she once lived in had been exposed as corrupt and unsafe underneath all of the glamor and gentility. During the day, she threw herself into fun or the diversion of volunteering at the Family Care Clinic, while at night she'd drown in nightmares: dark melodramas where she was tied to a chair, and a hooded madman sang while carving up her best friend in front of her eyes. Sandy's screams always woke Hazel to the disconcerting contrast of satin bedding and her opulent room.

Hazel paused outside of Marie's exam room. The door was ajar, and the nurse was speaking with a colored woman that Hazel recognized as one of the Sinclair's maids. Her name was Maxie.

"My guts are twistin' something terrible," the woman told Marie.

"How long have you had trouble digesting?" Marie asked with her slight German accent.

"Goin' on a week now."

"We will get you all fixed up. Let me just do some tests…"

"Thank you, ma'am. I just can't tell you what this means to me. You're a gift from Jesus." Maxie's voice was husky with emotion.

Hazel moved away from the door, smiling to herself. It felt right to be a part of something good after being so sickened by the evil that almost killed her.

A shiny, black Buick waited outside for her. Jennings stood on the rundown sidewalk in his suit, looking out of place. This neighborhood didn't see very many chauffeurs.

He nodded his gray head at her. "Miss."

"You didn't have to come. I told Mumsy I could walk fine with my guard dog." She glanced around to where she had tied Henri's leash.

"Your pup insisted on a ride." Jennings opened the door, and Hazel's young German Shepherd bounced around happily in the back seat of the automobile. "He's quite the killer…"

Hazel laughed. "Henri is still in training. He happens to be a fierce bodyguard. He got me here safe, didn't he?"

"No doubt. Your parents don't want any mishaps, with the party and all. You have a way of finding unexpected adventure." Her chauffer grinned. "Miss?" He gestured toward the open door of the Buick.

"Oh, all right. Thanks." Hazel slid into the leather interior, gratitude and guilt singing their duet in her heart. She knew how lucky she was, with an economic depression crushing the country, to be one of the fortunate few who didn't have to beg, steal, or borrow anything. Henri clambered into her lap. He was getting much too heavy and big for that.

"Down, you silly pup." Hazel slid Henri into the seat beside her and scratched him behind the ears. "Platz," she commanded, and Henri sat. "Braver Hund," she cooed, using the German the dog trainer taught her. Her parents had hired a serious dog handler named Mick who had experience with police dogs. The Malloys wanted Hazel's dog to be dangerous and threatening, but he was mostly goofy.

The Buick cruised through the rundown neighborhood, where men looking for work stood in threadbare clothing on the sidewalks. Some familiar-looking newsies wandered about with stacks of papers that hadn't sold in the morning rush. A couple of kids in ragged trousers tap-danced on sidewalk, caps in hand.

They glided past a long soup line of dejected and hungry-looking people, hoping to get a bite of food. There was not much to suggest that the holidays were coming in this part of town. Hazel thought of the abundant spread of fancy food Mumsy had ordered through a caterer for her birthday party. One tall man in baggy trousers and a flat cap turned to watch the Buick go by. His lined face and hollow eyes were a headline about everything that was wrong with the world: it wasn't fair.

Tonight would be the first society party since Hazel's life had been turned inside out. She wondered how to go back to pretending that the poor didn't exist and that everyone in her circle was safe. Even though the idea that there was some kind of evil conspiracy among the wealthy of St. Louis involving the Veiled Prophet seemed more fantastic as the days went by. She began to doubt the reality of any of it. But her best friend's sister, Evelyn, had wound up dead and had a diary full of cryptic accusations against some mysterious powers in the city. Hazel had been avoiding these things since her rescue.

Besides, Stanley still had the diary.

Stanley.

Hazel sighed. She still needed to sort out how she felt about him. They were friends and "America's Cracker Jack kids," but anything else beyond that seemed impossibly complicated. In the first days after their rescue, she felt so close to him, and she wanted to cling to him as hard as she could. Then slowly he became a reminder of everything she wanted to forget. But sometimes her heart would feel warm or she'd get a tickle in her stomach when she remembered the way his blue eyes burned so fiercely when he had found her tied to that chair in the caves; the smell of his skin and the strength of his body, even injured, as they helped each other escape from the tunnels.

Hazel's parents, though grateful to Stanley and willing to help get to the bottom of what possible corruption was growing among the elite, did not encourage Hazel to spend time with him. They still wanted her to focus on options in their own circles—providing they could figure out who was part of the conspiracy that killed Evelyn and who wasn't. They liked Stanley, but they saw more for Hazel's future than a lanky newsie with no money or real prospects.

While on the outside, she was now the darling debutante of St. Louis, Hazel's inner terrain had been permanently altered as if by a dark, swirling cyclone. Mumsy had her go to a psychotherapist to talk about what happened. He emphasized her need to realize that nothing that happened to Sandy or Stanley was her fault, and that Charles Chouteau was psychopathic. Maybe it helped.

Hazel knew everyone wanted her to be okay. She felt the need to be better and to make them all think she was fine. People treated her too carefully, and she hated to see her parents worry. She could be strong—everyone was depending on her to be the same girl full of moxie and smiles. She was a Malloy for Pete's sakes!

"How was your afternoon, Miss Hazel?" Jennings asked from the front of the vehicle.

"Just ducky, thanks."

Hazel sat on a satin, tasseled stool with her eyes closed as her maid, Peggy, brushed and curled her dark, wayward hair. She had awoken from a brief nap with a headache, and now it was show time.

Her silk slip, trimmed with lace, was cut low enough for the new gown that hung in her closet. Hazel had always loved stylish clothes, but tonight she felt as if she was playing dress-up. In a way, she was. Tonight she had to be the dazzling debutante, assimilating into the elite circles to discover their supposed secrets. If the Veiled Prophet was indeed some criminal mastermind, he would be watching, and his sympathizers were unnamed. Hazel needed to convince everyone that she had immersed herself into her rightful place. Pretty, carefree, and clueless.

She and Stanley had been careful to never mention the details behind their kidnapping when being interviewed in the papers or on the radio. The story went that Charles Chouteau was a psychopathic killer, out of his mind with jealousy, and on a rampage. There was no mention of the Veiled Prophet or Evelyn's diary, with its puzzling codes and numbers. Until they figured out more about The Winnowing and who was involved, they would keep it to themselves. It was too dangerous.

Peggy set the ivory handled brush down on the vanity. "There, now. You look lovely," she said with her soothing Irish lilt. She squinted at Hazel and frowned. "Let me get you some Bayer tablets. We can't have you scrunching up your forehead like that."

"Thank you." Hazel lightly rubbed the sides of her head. After Peggy hurried out of the room, Hazel turned around in her seat and gazed at herself in the mirror. Her eyes grew wide. Hazel's chestnut hair was tamed and glossy, perfect curls framing her face. Mumsy had lined her eyes with kohl, powdered her face, and painted her lips a deep red. Her brows had been plucked into slender arches, and pink rouge seemed to make the blue in her eyes sparkle. She looked like a starlet from the pages of Photoplay. The jaunty sound of the live band downstairs floated, muted in the background, and Hazel smiled at her re-flection.

Peggy returned with a glass of water and the pain medicine. "Aren't you the very picture of glamor? Stanley will fall over dead." Peggy winked at Hazel in the mirror.

Bananas.

Hazel waved a hand and tried to sound amused. "What do I care?" She popped the bitter, little pill into her mouth and took a sip of water.

She rubbed her lips together and stood as Peggy crossed the room with her long, satin, party dress. It was cream and pink floral and the very latest style. Mumsy had paid a pile for it. Now that Hazel was sixteen and a part of society, she had to so-phisticate her look.

Her maid helped to slide the slim cut gown over her head, chest, and hips. It slipped into place with the whisper of silk on silk.

"Well, Miss. That'll do," Peggy sighed.

Hazel nodded at the knockout in the mirror. "Yeah."

Her headache had faded by the time she descended the staircase. Music from the live band played "The Very Thought of You" as Hazel carefully chose her footing on each step in new, sparkling heels. The large foyer of her home was filled with finely togged people and the cacophony of conversations competing with the music.

She had just gotten to the bottom step, when a hand grabbed her elbow.

"Wow, Hazel. You're a dish tonight." Gabriel Sinclair grinned at her. He was the picture of a society boy in his tuxedo and slicked-over hair. His eyes gleamed behind his spectacles.

Here we go. Hazel took a breath and gave him a smile. "Why, thank you, Gabriel. You handsome devil." She winked, and his grin cracked wider, color rising on his cheekbones.

"Come dance with me." He held out his arm, and she took it.

"Lead the way." Hazel held her chin high as they made their way through the crowd. She felt the gazes of everyone following her. She was the favorite of the hour, and something inside of her began to glow.

The double doors to the spacious conservatory were open, and the music was loud and dreamy. Swags of flowers decorated the walls and chandelier. The elite of St. Louis bobbed and swirled around to the lively band set up at the far end of the room. Everyone of importance was there. This was the clambake of the season, and it was in Hazel's own home.

Gabriel Sinclair led Hazel to the middle of the floor and took her in his arms. His cologne and hair tonic filled her with a giddy feeling as a new song began. He steered and spun her with large, warm hands and confidant steps. Over his shoulder, Hazel noticed with triumph that Regina Peck and Brigitte Slayback were there like a couple of overstuffed geese with all of the trimmings, flirting with a couple of frat boys. They looked over and noticed Hazel dancing with Gabriel, and a look of panicked envy crossed both of their faces.

Let them eat that with gravy.

Hazel swayed to the music with Gabriel. He was a heel, but sometimes she forgot that. Whenever he came around, he watched her attentively and always tried to engage in conversation even when she constantly shut him down. He had confided in her one time when his family had come to dinner that he was broken up over Charles. They had been friends for years, and it really had shaken him when everything happened. Gabriel had looked into Hazel's eyes and asked her with all sincerity how she was doing and told her how glad he was that she was safe. He had even expressed admiration for Stanley's courage. It was the first time Hazel realized that Gabriel was an actual person.

Of course, the next moment he said something idiotic, but still… it was interesting. She didn't hate him now.

"Where do you go, Hazel Malloy?" Gabriel said in her ear.

"What?"

"I can feel you thinking hard." He chuckled.

Hazel smiled. "I like this song," she said, embarrassed as though he could actually tell that he'd caught her thinking about him.

"I do too." He pressed his cheek to hers, and she let him.

As the song ended, there was a slight disturbance from the far end of the room. Hazel glanced up, and her heart paused.

Bananas.

Stanley stood in the entrance of the conservatory, tall and suited up, a hard look on his face, one eye almost swollen shut. He was flanked by some of his Knights, looking rough and out of place in suits, smirks on their faces as they scanned the room. It was like Eliot Ness and his Untouchables about to raid.

The "good people" of St. Louis stared uneasily and made way as the boys stalked into the room. Hazel sometimes forgot what they must look like to everyone else. They were a tough looking lot, battle scarred, and imposing.

The song ended and in the pause before the next one began, Stanley took long strides across the room, toward where Hazel and Gabriel stood, still holding hands.

Stanley's eye twitched. "Heya, Haze." He tilted his head toward Gabriel. "If it isn't soft slugger trying to get to first base." His jaw flexed, and he breathed in through his nose, and Hazel knew he was counting to ten.

Gabriel released Hazel's hand and calmly replied, "Good to see you, Fields. You clean up nice."

Before Stanley could respond, Hazel laughed. She wasn't sure why. Nerves. But Stanley flashed a scowl at her. "Something funny?"

Uh oh. He was in a mood. She didn't want a scene. "I'm just happy to see you boys. What took you so long?" She reached out and straightened his tie and then lightly touched his swollen eye and frowned.

His face softened a little. "Took some time to get these mugs into monkey suits."

Music had started up again, and the Knights were mingling in the crowd and intimidating girls into dancing with them. Hazel knew the looks of dismay girls gave them were an act. It was expected of them. But really, the boys were a little bit famous, and the danger was exciting. It was like having Bogart or Dillinger ask you for a dance. Who would say no?

"What happened to your eye, Snoopy?" She wasn't sure she even wanted to know.

Stanley's scowl melted away. "Can we talk?"

Hazel looked over at Gabriel to see if there would be any trouble.

Gabriel smiled at Hazel. "Thanks for the dance, Hazel," he said before turning to Stanley and nodding. "Fields." Gabriel walked away tall and straight, smooth as can be.

"What an act," Stanley muttered.

Hazel bristled. "Look who's talking." She sniffed and made a face. "You smell like cigarettes."

Stanley ignored the remark, took her by the arm, and led her out of the conservatory through the glass, French doors onto the veranda.

It was a cool, December night, and the moon was high. Small lights and torches lit up the trees and flower gardens. A few party guests strolled the paths in the moonlight, some holding hands. The Jazz playing inside felt artificially cheerful at the moment.

"Well?" Hazel crossed her arms and shivered.

Stanley had a grim expression on his face. "They've been in my house. The Veiled Prophet is after me."

Before Hazel could respond to that unwelcome revelation, she heard footsteps.

"Hazel, there you are." Dr. Galton stepped out of the shadows. He was a stunner in a tuxedo.

"You came." Hazel's grin gave way to a giggle that she quickly suppressed. She was relieved for the interruption… also the doctor looked like a movie star.

"I told you I wouldn't miss it." The young doctor glanced over at Stanley. "Hello, I don't believe we've met." He held out his hand.

Hazel held her breath and gave Stanley a look, hoping he wouldn't do anything embarrassing.

Stanley pressed his lips together and shook Dr. Galton's hand. "Yeah. I'm Stanley Fields, and you're the good doc from the clinic in Dogtown."

"Pleased to meet you. You and Hazel are the pride of our city." Dr. Galton released the handshake and then ran his hand down the front of his jacket seemingly on reflex.

Stanley caught it and scowled. Dr. Galton took a slight step back and gave a smile.

Hazel saw the way Stanley's jaw tightened. She turned to Dr. Galton and said in a chipper voice, "Well, it is so lovely that you came. I wonder if I could bother you to bring me some punch."

Dr. Galton grasped the excuse to walk away. "I would be delighted. Nice to meet you, Stanley." The doctor disappeared into the shadows of the veranda.

"Well, I like that. Who does he think he is, wiping my handshake off?" Stanley fumed.

Hazel rolled her eyes. "He's a doctor. He washes his hands all day. I've seen him wipe his hands off after holding a pencil. Don't take it personally."

"Ain't the same, and you know it. That was meant to insult me."

"Isn't," Hazel corrected his grammar, noting he was sounding more like the other newsies tonight. "Anyway, that's ridiculous. You need to stop thinking everyone is against you."

"Said every privileged swell in the book."

Hazel's headache returned, and she rubbed the sides of her head. She was suddenly disgusted with Stanley. "Fine. What is it you wanted to talk to me about?"

Instead of speaking, Stanley stared at her, his one eye swollen and the other glinting in the torchlight. He tugged at his tie as if it strangled him and took a deep breath. "Haze… what's happening to us?"

She squinted in irritation; her head throbbed. "Us?"

"Yeah… you and me." He took a step forward and reached out to take her hand.

Hazel quickly clasped her hands together and raised them to her chin as if in thought. "What do you mean?"

Stanley flinched and put his hand in his pocket. He closed his eyes and breathed in through his nose then looked down at his shoes. When he looked back up at her, there was hurt etched on his face. "It's like you've forgotten who you are. You're acting like one of them." He jerked his chin in the direction of the elegantly togged gentry dancing inside. "Is this your act? To get information?" His eyes looked hopeful.

Hazel didn't know what to say. Her mind was clouded, and all she could feel was confusion and irritation. She rubbed her temples. "I am one of them. And I'm trying to figure things out…" She saw the pained looked on Stanley's face.

"Haze… remember? In the cave when everything was dark and we were both battered and broken?" His bright, blue eyes pulled at her insides.

Hazel pushed away the panic his words brought. "I don't want to think about that."

He nodded. "I know… but think of this… there we were, and everything was all wrong. But we helped each other out. We leaned on one another and got out of that mess." He swallowed and gave a tiny smile.

Hazel felt a glow start in her heart, and then a sharp pain shot through her head again. She squeezed her eyes shut. "Stop it."

"What's wrong?" he said in a low, concerned voice and took a step toward her.

"Nothing. I don't know what you mean. I'm fine." She just wanted him to go away. He was ruining her birthday. And she saw how all the others looked at him. How could she play the debutante and get to the bottom of this Veiled Prophet business if Stanley was there? Nobody would trust her. She shook her head in confusion, because more and more she doubted that the Veiled Prophet and any of her neighbors were somehow sinister. Charles was a madman after all.

"You're not fine," Stanley insisted.

Hazel pressed her forehead with her hand. "I don't need you to tell me how I am. I don't need you at all."

Stanley folded his arms across his chest. "I see."

The music in the conservatory was a joyous contrast to the growing darkness Hazel felt. She wanted to go in and dance, but Stanley's gaze kept her rooted in place. He had something to tell her, and all she could do was hear him out.

CHAPTER THREE

Stanley had never seen this side of Hazel. Maybe she really didn't want him around and this was her way of telling him. His insides were in knots. It was bad enough to walk in and see her in the arms of the stuck up mug he'd been in a fist fight with. It felt awful close to betrayal, and he didn't like it.

"So, who is your next man, Gabriel or the doctor? Get bored of me already?" He wanted her to laugh it off and throw her arms around him like she sometimes did when he was out of sorts.

Hazel frowned at him. "I don't know what you mean."

Stanley took a deep breath, trying to control his temper and a feeling he couldn't describe. He had no real right to feel jealous. Stanley tried to sound reasonable.

"Forget it. Look, I have a bad feeling about that doctor. Something is off about that clinic."

Hazel snorted. "Dr. Galton? He is the sweetest and kindest man I know. That new clinic he started up is helping the poor.

Volunteering there has really opened my eyes to the needs in this city."

Stanley stared at her for a moment and then pulled one of the flyers from his pocket. "Yeah, I know. Looks like they're really putting the word out."

She glanced at the flyer. "Yeah, I helped put that together. Isn't it great? We're handing them out all over the city. It's going to make a real difference, finally." Hazel smiled, but it seemed forced.

Stanley gazed at her and almost didn't say anything else. She seemed really convinced she was doing some good. Why crush her? Let her have this, whatever it was. But the tingling feeling he always got as a warning wouldn't stop.

"I can't tell you why. I don't know myself. But this whole thing bugs me. Just be careful, okay?"

"Oh, because you're Mr. Careful."

Stanley shrugged. "Okay. Sorry. Just…" He touched his eye. It had swollen to the point where he could barely see out of it.

"What happened to your eye anyway?"

"Haze, its Legion, or the Veiled Prophet or someone working for him. They snuck into my house, well, all of the Knight's houses." He described what happened.

Hazel wrinkled her brow and seemed annoyed. "Perhaps it was someone playing a prank. I mean, why would they go into your house and stir up trouble? I mean, even if 'they' exist, I doubt they want to expose themselves like that. We're safe, Cracker Jack kids and all. They wouldn't dare. Sandy and I didn't get any branches in our bed," Hazel said with her arms crossed.

Stanley didn't know what to say. He didn't expect this reaction at all. She didn't seem afraid or concerned. She was looking at him like he was nuts.

"Of course you didn't, Ms. High Society. Don't you get it? They can terrorize us at will. You two, on the other hand, are high and dry. You can't be touched. No one will believe us and would probably think we were trying to get more famous or something."

Hazel chuckled. "Maybe you are. More dames for you, the big hero and all."

Stanley took off his hat and ran his hands through his hair. Why was she throwing his past into his face after all they'd been through together? His temper flared. "What's the matter with you, Lady Bananas? Smooching on Gabriel mess with your brain? I saw you blushing when he had his hands all over you." The way that dress made her look, he knew exactly what Gabriel and any other man with eyeballs was thinking. She was a dish and how, but it made him hot under the collar that fellows drooled over her packaging without knowing what was inside.

Hazel scoffed. "As if you have any room to talk, Mr. Margaret-and-half-the-ladies-of-the-streets." She tossed her head back and eyed him. "Gabriel is being really nice after everything in the caves. I like him. He's being a gentleman, unlike some people I know."

His fists tightened. "Yeah, because he wants you to forget that it was his best pal in the caves carving up your friend. He doesn't know you, Haze… and he wants to kiss you and get his pansy hands on you. Did he, before I got here?"

Hazel stood her ground, and she raised her eyebrows disdainfully. "What if he did? What businesses is it of yours, Snoopy? Sure, he knows me. I knew him long before I met you."

Stanley shook his head. "Forever wouldn't be enough for a guy like that. He'll never know you like I do. Stop wasting your time with these jokes."

"You shopped around, why can't I? You're not the only good-looking fellow in St. Louis."

He didn't like the sound of that. "Look, Lady Bananas, what I did or didn't do before we met is over. I thought you and I had a thing."

She curled her lip a little. "Did you now? And why is that?"

"You know. The baseball game. Everything we've done together. Our talks. Holding hands. We're partners. We're in each other's heads."

"Is that why I have a headache? Look, none of that entitles you to telling me who I can dance with," Hazel said, brows pushed together.

He stepped closer to her again, wanting her to come back. Be who she was before. "I see you. You see me. Nobody has what we have, Haze… You and I, we got it figured out. Nothing that they threw at us stopped us. All this rich and poor garbage. We're over that. Our fight is good against bad. Right now … you're surrounded by sharks in fancy duds."

She squeezed her eyes shut for a moment as if struggling to think. "Maybe it's not all as it seems. Maybe Charles made it all up. I'm starting to wonder. He certainly was crazy like everyone is saying. I mean, he killed Evelyn and kidnapped us. Everyone around me seems really sorry about it all. I can't believe that any of them had anything to do with it."

Stanley stared at her. What was going on here? She totally blew off everything he had just said, while he was gushing away like some kind of lovesick fool. It was like she was a completely different person. It made him feel helpless and angry.

"Did you forget Evelyn's lousy diary? Everything we read? All the evidence? The numbers on Evelyn's body? The black branches now?"

She stood there, blinking but not saying a word, as if the things he was saying were not sinking in. He hated it. He would rather have her shout and be angry. But she didn't seem right, like she was sick or something. Hazel rubbed the sides of her head. Stanley reached out to touch her on the arm.

"Are you okay? You don't seem right."

Hazel shook off his arm and looked around the garden, as if she didn't want to be seen having street rat slime on her precious skin. Stanley's stomach dropped. Arthur was right. She really was no different from the other swells when push came to shove. The anger inside of him exploded, and he looked for just the right combination of words to crush her.

"Oh, I'm sorry. Would you rather have Gabriel touch you? Or Dr. Galton? Well, go ahead and be their debutante. You know what happens when they're done using girls like you. Cast off and beaten to a bloody pulp with a baseball bat."

"Get. Out," Hazel hissed. The look of disgust on her face shot through him like an arrow.

"Already on my way, my lady." He gave her a mock bow. "Happy birthday." He reached into his pocket and slapped a small, brown package into her hands before stomping away into the darkness of the garden, the anger inside numbing the devastation he felt. The bushes to his right rustled, and out stepped Arthur, a smudge of red on his cheek.

"Where's the fire, boss?" Arthur said, taking out a cigarette and lighting it.

"Nowhere. Want to get the hell out of here."

"Oh. Why? Ms. Hazel and you have a little scuffle? You'll make up." Arthur smiled.

"What do you care? You don't like her anyway. And where have you been? What's that on your cheek?"

Arthur took a swipe at it. "Nothin'. None of your biz."

Stanley smirked. "Sandy in the bushes with you?"

Drawing on his cigarette, Arthur looked down, almost ashamed. "She was. She wanted to get back inside and be with her friends or something. She's a little… I dunno…"

They stood there for a moment, and Stanley looked up at the house. "No matter what we do, Artie, they'll never accept us. This isn't our world."

Arthur nodded. "No. It ain't. Hazel too?"

"Yeah. She's starting to act like one of them. And somehow she's starting to believe all of this mess with the Veiled Prophet was only Charles being crazy and making everything up. I gotta say, it's making me start to doubt my own sanity."

"You know that ain't true, boss. You know it."

"Not entirely sure what I know anymore."

"You're just dizzy cuz you love that snooty dame." Arthur spat on the ground.

"Do I love Hazel? I mean, how well do I know her anyway? Maybe I just feel attached, because we almost died together." He scratched his head. "Although even before that … every other dame paled in comparison. She unsettles me like nobody else ever has. Does that mean something?"

Arthur snorted. "You's asking the wrong person on that one. And are we really gabbing about our feelings?"

Stanley laughed. "You're right. This is screwy." Stanley eyed his friend. "You're sweet on Sandy, though."

Looking at the lit end of his cigarette, Arthur said, "I don't mind her. I like her lips. And she's kinda like me. Hates the world too."

They stood there for a moment in the moonlit garden. Music and laughter from the party sounded in the background from the Malloy mansion. "I don't want to go back in there, but I feel like I should. Try to explain things to Hazel."

Arthur shook his head. "Nah. Not tonight. I can tell you're about to punch a wall. No point in losing it in a room full of swells. Ain't smart."

"God help us when you're the voice of reason, Artie." Stanley snorted. "I don't know. I want to shake her... I'm worried. It's like she's another person right now."

"You said that before. Maybe she ain't another person. She's in her real world, Stanny boy. Those are her people. Bound to happen. Come on, let's go to the Square." Arthur blew smoke out of his nose.

They made their way out of the grounds, when a small brown-haired kid, wearing clothes too big for him, ran up to them, huffing and puffing.

"Sirs... came as fast as I can... sirs... something..." The kid's chest heaved with the effort of trying to talk.

"Easy kid. Take a powder and a breath," Arthur said, patting him on the shoulder. "How ya been Dusty?" He dug into his pocket and pulled out a lollipop. "Here ya go, kiddo."

The boy grinned and took the candy, trying to catch his breath. "I ain't bad."

This, Stanley thought, is the Arthur that no one sees. He found himself wondering, again, what his friend was like before his life went down the sewer.

"But something... has happened at The Rookery. All the coppers of St. Louis are there."

His heart pounding, Stanley grasped the St. Jude pendant he wore around his neck. "What is it? Gang shootout?"

The kid shook his head. "Nah, the Raven is the only real gangster left in St. Louis. He was about to leave, by all accounts. Cops were letting him."

Arthur nodded. "What do you know?"

"I wasn't there. But from what I hear, it's not good, and one of the pigeons there said that Seamus," he said, nodding to Stanley, "said he wanted you there."

"What would that be about?" Arthur asked.

Stanley closed his eyes. "Vinnie. He's there. He borrowed my shoes for some going away party. Something isn't right. We gotta go, Artie. Or at least, I do."

Arthur nodded. "I'm with you. Thanks, Dusty."

With that, the kid sped off across the street and into Forest Park.

"It'll take about an hour. So, we better make tracks."

They walked fast through the historic, cobbled streets of St. Louis. Stanley and Arthur knew all of the shortcuts to the brewery, cutting through darkened yards and alleyways. They kept a sharp eye out for beat cops, but Stanley didn't see one the entire time.

Winding through a rundown neighborhood near the Mississippi River, they came to a wooden fence surrounding the old, abandoned warehouse that had become the gang's stronghold as times got bad. In the dark of night, it looked dilapidated and haunted. The Rookery was nothing like the mansions the mob used to have in their heyday. Something more powerful and frightening had moved into town and "cleaned it up." The gangs were a thing of the past.

Stanley counted ten cop cars with a brief glance, including the car of the St. Louis Chief of Police. Uniformed cops moved around in the dark with flashlights, patrolling the perimeter, and he couldn't figure out how to get past them without his uncle.

"What's our play, boss?" Arthur said, scanning the crowd.

"Maybe just walk right up to one of the gumshoes."

Arthur frowned and dropped his cigarette. "Worst plan I ever heard. But I don't have a scrap. So, lead the way."

Stanley scanned some of the policemen and breathed a sigh of relief. He saw Jakob's dad, Sergeant Kopan, walking about twenty feet from them.

"Look, there's our ticket," Stanley said.

"He hates me." Arthur scowled.

"Everyone hates you, Artie. Except me." Stanley elbowed him with a grin.

"Up yours, Irish."

They walked over to the short, paunchy cop. Stanley fought the urge to panic and tried to seem only mildly interested. "Hey, Mr. Kopan, what gives?"

The dark eyes of the Sergeant regarded him, narrowed in suspicion. "Why are you here? Shouldn't you be at the fancy party?"

"Jakob's still there kicking up his heels. I got bored with all the swells. Heard something was going on here. Is my uncle around?" Stanley said.

Levi Kopan sighed, rubbing his face, anxious. "I'll get him, but I'm not gonna guarantee that he'll be happy to see you."

"He's expecting me."

The old cop nodded. "Okay… but this isn't a party." He crossed the weedy, gravel lot and went into the Rookery.

Arthur paced, gazing at the building, mumbling to himself.

"What are you doing?" Stanley finally asked.

"Thinking." He tapped his bowler hat.

"Can you do it to yourself? You're making me batty."

Arthur walked away from him a little and lit another cigarette. The orange glow of it lit up his face, emphasizing his furrowed brow.

Seamus came out of the building and strolled toward them. "Boyo, I knew you'd be here quicker than lightning. Do you know what's goin' on?"

Seamus's manner threw him off guard. Usually, around other cops, his uncle kept up the gruff, commanding exterior that showed no one what he would call "weak emotions." But when Seamus finally reached them, he put his hand on Stanley's shoulder and looked him in the eyes.

"No. I don't. Where's Vinnie? I want to talk to that dumb, Italian idiot and get my shoes back."

Seamus frowned, his face pale in the dim light. "I dunno where your pal is. I think you better come with me, son. You best be seeing this."

CHAPTER FOUR

Hazel stared down at the small, brown package tied with twine in her hands. She tore it open and dropped the wrapping to the ground. A small medallion of St. Joan of Arc on a string glinted in her palm. Her heart squeezed, and she wrapped the string around her wrist. *Oh, Stanley.*

She fled into the conservatory. Hazel bit her lip and blinked back tears. Stanley had stormed away, and although she'd wanted him to leave, now that he had, she felt alone standing in the middle of a crowd of people dancing and laughing. It was her birthday party, and the maddening boy had caused a scene and left. How could he even complain about the doctor or Gabriel when he couldn't even walk by a dame without giving her goo-goo eyes? Things were so out of whack. What had happened to their friendship? She rubbed her head and took a deep breath.

Some of the things he'd said needled her. There was a growing feeling inside Hazel that these really were her people, and Stanley didn't have a right to judge them the way he did. Maybe Charles really was crazy with all of his talk about the

Veiled Prophet. Maybe the cops were dirty, and maybe the gangs were really the ones to blame for everything that was going on. The rich and privileged were always being blamed for everything.

Stanley was selfish and unpredictable. Things had been so confusing lately. She and Stanley clashed more now than they ever had. There was so much pressure from everyone else about how Hazel should behave and the stress of figuring out what was going on. More and more the whole ordeal seemed to be a bunch of hooey. Yet she wondered what the story of the black branch Stanley had found in his bed was all about. She just wanted to forget all about it and enjoy her life. She didn't know who to trust anymore.

Dr. Galton approached with a cup of punch. "Here you are. Happy birthday, Hazel."

Hazel took a sip of the cherry lime punch, glad to have something to do to keep from bursting into tears. She cleared her throat and forced a smile. "Thank you." She looked around at all the important people enjoying themselves and felt a rush of relief.

"Hazel!" Her mother's brash voice carried across the room. "Come here, and bring that delicious doctor with you!"

Hazel cringed and gave Dr. Galton an apologetic look. Half the room seemed to move away from where Mumsy danced in place, swaying her hips, her drink sloshing back and forth in the glass. She was drunk, of course. Mumsy had gone through her own change since Hazel was kidnapped. Mostly, it involved martinis and champagne at all hours of the day, not just at parties.

The young doctor smiled. "That's an invitation I have no intention of ignoring."

Hazel appreciated how matter-of-fact and polite he was about everything. A true gentleman. What a contrast to the crass and disrespectful way that Stanley behaved.

As they approached, Mumsy giggled and held her martini glass high. Her gown was cut too low and was covered with downy feathers that surrounded her shoulders and head like the froth on the top of a glass of beer. Hazel recalled how her mother had chosen white to be "boring like the other society dames." But nobody could look at Mumsy and be bored. She was a stunning woman, but also looked as if she would do just about anything for fun.

"Mm. Hello, you doctor, you." Mumsy teetered forward with a flirtatious grin.

"This is a wonderful party, Mrs. Malloy." He put out a hand to steady her.

Mumsy cackled and slapped him on the shoulder. "Karl, how nice of you to say."

Hazel loved her mother. Mumsy had become more affectionate and attentive since the kidnapping, but it still ashamed her when Mumsy got drunk and caused a scene.

"Um. Mumsy, father was looking for you. I think he's in the drawing room," Hazel lied.

Mumsy yawned without covering her mouth. "Oh, for crying out loud. That man. Ruins all the fun."

"Shall we find him together?" Dr. Galton offered his elbow.

"That would be the bee's knees." Mumsy's face brightened.

Hazel fought back the urge to object. She had hoped to steer the doctor away from the spectacle of her mother's crass behavior. But the look on his face told her that he was acting in kindness without judgment. Hazel smiled, grateful.

"Have a good time at your party, Hazel. Go. Find someone to dance with." Dr. Galton took Mumsy away.

Hazel wandered through the crowd. People smiled at her and gave birthday wishes. They were good people. Refined and educated. Many of them gave generously to charity and had expressed so much concern and support in the days since her kidnapping. For the first time, she had begun to feel like she actually belonged.

As her head began to ache, the music became too loud for her to bear. She made her way back out onto the veranda to take in the night air and to think. The cool air felt good on her skin and seemed to relieve her headache. Hazel stepped around a shattered champagne glass and leaned against the railing. The smell of the torches mingled with the sweet aroma of magnolias and spilled champagne. Hazel looked up at the moon and thought of how much her life had changed in a couple of months. She didn't feel like the messy-haired misfit anymore. But who was she now?

She ran her hands down the front of her silk gown and thought of the people she had seen in Forest Park dressed in threadbare, ragged clothing. Hazel knew that the best way to help them was to use her position in society, like Dr. Galton. Not by fighting the elite and chasing conspiracies.

Sandy emerged from the garden and came up the steps onto the veranda. Her lipstick was smeared, and her black dress was crumpled and slightly twisted across the bodice. When she saw Hazel, she ran a hand through her bobbed hair to tame it as if it were the long, honey mane it once was. "Hello, best pal. Happy birthday. I left your gift in your room." Sandy's usual sparkle had been gone for a while now, but Hazel was still getting used to the sardonic, flint-eyed girl who had once been her best friend.

Something was definitely off. It had been ever since the kidnapping. But tonight there was something new. Hazel hugged her friend, and the smell of cigarettes hit her. She stepped back to examine her face. "Thanks. Glad you came. Thought you were going to skip it."

"You know how I love a party." She gave a wicked smile; the scar down the side of her face crumpled like a poorly stitched seam. As if suddenly conscious of it, Sandy brought her hair forward to hang over the side of her face.

"What have you been doing out there in the moonlight?" Hazel gave her a little push on the shoulder, hoping to sound playful.

Sandy bit her lip, and a look of guilt flashed across her face. Something inside Hazel froze. Who was Sandy's beau? Hazel thought of how Stanley had smelled of cigarettes earlier, and now Sandy did. Stanley had disappeared into the garden after Hazel sent him away.

"Just taking in the night, you know." Sandy ran her fingers around her mouth to tidy her lipstick. "So what did I miss? How's the party?"

Hazel narrowed her eyes. "It's a scream." Hazel felt a little sick to her stomach. She had no claim on Stanley, but Sandy had been her best friend for years. How could they?

Just then, there was shouting from inside the conservatory. Hazel rushed in to see a crowd gathering around something. The band had stopped playing, and someone was calling out.

"Is there a doctor in the house?"

Hazel pushed her way past the silk dresses and tuxedos; the air was thick with perfume and cologne and the faint smell of sweat. On the floor in the middle of the gathering was Teeth Guido in a crumpled suit that was too big for him and an outdated tie. He was flat on his back, staring at the ceiling, his mouth gaping open like the wind had been knocked out of him.

"Teeth!" Hazel forgot about her silk dress and kneeled beside the scrawny kid. "You okay?"

He let out a moan and pressed his hands to his stomach. "My legs gave out, and now somethin' ain't right in my guts, Hazie."

She put a hand to his forehead; it was hot and covered with perspiration. He began to writhe around, his eyes squeezed shut.

"I'm here." Dr. Galton appeared, lowering himself beside Hazel on the floor. He examined Teeth closely, not saying a word. He put an ear to his chest then held the boy's scrawny wrist, looking at his wristwatch.

"Doc. Am I dyin'?" Teeth gasped.

"I doubt that very much." Dr. Galton tapped on Teeth's abdomen and then laid the back of his hand on his forehead. He quickly wiped his hand off on the knee of his pants. Hazel hmphed to herself and wished Stanley had been there to see it.

"Is he okay?" Hazel asked.

"I need to get him to the clinic. Up you go." Dr. Galton hooked his hands under Teeth's shoulders, and another man who had been watching helped pull the boy to his feet.

Teeth winced in pain, wobbling on shaky legs. "I don't wanna go unless Haze comes too."

Hazel stood and glanced around. It was her party… but she liked Teeth and wanted to see that he was okay. "Okay, let me grab my wrap."

Hazel stood beside Teeth where he reclined in the examination chair, while the doctor looked him over and asked him questions about his health, family, and past injuries.

"I ain't got much, doc, but my folks are hardy. The Guidos eat nails," Teeth said proudly. He was a wiry, tough kid. Hazel had seen how he held his own in a scrap.

"I have no doubt. You seem to be from good stock. But I'd like to keep you here for a while to run some tests and make sure there isn't a serious problem that might require an appendectomy."

"A what?" Teeth furrowed his brow and then squirmed in pain again.

"Surgery." Dr. Galton turned to his sink and began to wash his hands.

Teeth went pale. "Cut me open? But Doc, I gotta be out on the streets selling my papes, or eatin' won't come easy."

"If your appendix is infected, eating won't come easy either. We will need to take it out," he said, shaking the water from his hands into the sink.

Hazel handed him a towel. He nodded at her and dried his hands. "Thank you."

She smiled and felt very useful. In the spirit of that feeling, she placed a hand on Teeth's shoulder. "Don't worry, fella. You're in good hands. And Shuffles can help sell your papers if that happens."

Teeth looked doubtful. He chewed his lip and ran his hand over the nice suit he'd been given to wear to Hazel's party. "I can always hock this," he said.

"You won't need to." Hazel gave him a wink. She could buy his whole stack of papers if she had to.

Dr. Galton took up his notebook and jotted down something onto the page. "Hazel, I see no reason why you should miss any more of your birthday party. Have your driver take you home. I will take care of your friend."

Hazel searched Teeth's face. "He is in a lot of pain."

"It's okay, Haze. You gotta go back to your party. I shoulda thought of that," Teeth said.

"I wanted to come," she said.

"I will give him something for the pain. Next time you see him, he will be a new man."

Hazel felt reluctant to leave. She worried about Teeth, but she also loved helping the doctor and being a part of something. "Okay. Well, I'll check in on you later. That okay?"

"Sure thing, tomato." Teeth winked at her.

As Hazel made her way through the clinic, she passed by one of the other exam rooms. The door was ajar, and there was a light on. Hazel peeked inside and was struck with the metallic smell of blood mixed with the sharp burn of hydrogen peroxide bleach. The German nurse, Marie, was mopping the floor and did not see Hazel.

She raised her hand to say hello, but something made her stop. The nurse pulled the wadded sheet off of the exam table and removed what looked like a piece of clothing and dunked it into the mop bucket of bleach. Hazel backed out of the room, uneasy. Marie was busy and was not a terribly friendly woman. Best not to bother her while she was working.

On her way out of the clinic, Hazel felt the crackle of something underfoot. She stooped down and picked up the crumpled pamphlet. She had seen one like it on Dr. Galton's desk before. It had something to do with healthy childbirth or something. She opened it and read:

*Good genes make a strong man
strong and an intelligent man smart,
while bad genes lead to poverty,
prostitution, and criminality. Improv-
ing the human race requires ridding
the population of 'defective proto-
plasm' while encouraging the
superior stock to breed more.*

Hazel crushed the pamphlet in her hand, and another sharp pain shot through her head. She took a deep breath. It was good that there were people out there trying to better the world and eliminate suffering. It was great that science was making that possible. Which reminded her that she would have to take another Bayer tablet when she got back to the party.

She raised her hand to massage her forehead, and the St. Joan of Arc medallion from Stanley brushed her cheek. Hazel rubbed the raised image of the young, warrior girl and tried not to think about the hurt look on Stanley's face as he had walked away.

CHAPTER FIVE

Stanley's instincts burned to a feverish pitch the closer they got to the Rookery. Goosebumps raised up and down his arms. The entire landscape seemed to pulse with a warning of whatever evil lurked inside. His stomach rolled, and he fought back the urge to throw up.

"Stanny, you okay? You look as white as a banshee. Maybe you shouldn't go in," Seamus said, halting them before they reached the door.

Shaking his head, Stanley said, "I have to. Feel it." He gulped a huge breath of air just to get the words out.

Nodding, Seamus pointed at Arthur. "You have to stay here, boy. Can't get you in. Shouldn't even let Stanley in, but I need him to understand what we're up against. This ain't no game."

Stanley hated the sound of that. Something had his uncle terrified. In the last month, Seamus had tried to discourage Stanley from being involved in the Veiled Prophet mess. He said to leave it up to him, Mr. Malloy, and other trusted men to get to the bottom of things. Stanley had ignored every warning, insisting that he and his Knights could handle themselves.

His body began to tremble as he followed his uncle into the mildewed, shadowed interior of the Rookery. Maybe he'd been cocky thinking he could deal with all of it, because he suddenly felt like he was about to get in over his head.

Seamus led Stanley down the same hallway he'd walked not long ago to visit the Raven. The walls seemed to close in on him, and he took a few deep breaths. Some beat cops and two detectives talked in low tones.

"Gotta wait for the meat wagons to clean up this mess. Ain't never seen anything like it," one cop said as they walked past. Other uniformed officers clustered together, muttering and shaking their heads.

"They knocked out the lights in there."

"Suppose they did that before or after decorating?"

"Gives me the creeps."

Seamus and Stanley passed into the cavernous, main room of the warehouse, and at first glance he didn't understand all the fuss. It was dark, but for the large squares of light on the floor from the moonlight coming through the high windows and the lights in the hallway. Everything looked to be undisturbed and in place. The hissing of a record playing at its end came from one side of the room, but there was a heavy stillness that made his heart skip. It was the kind of quiet and void he'd felt in a cemetery. Where was the party? The back of his neck prickled and he looked up.

Row upon row of bodies dangled from the rafters by long, thick ropes. Men in suits and women in dresses. Some of them swung gently as if blown by an unseen breeze, while others didn't move. Each one's head was covered with a black bag.

"Saints preserve us," Stanley breathed out. He wanted to bolt for the door, but he couldn't move. He could not look away.

There were dozens of bodies just hanging like the branches of a weeping cherry tree, the ladies' skirts like drooping blossoms.

The last of the St. Louis gangsters.

Seamus shook his head, and his voice came out hoarse. "Not even sure the saints can save us now. How do you suppose anyone could take a whole gang by surprise like this? Not a drop of blood any place. No struggle."

Stanley stared at the rows of bodies and thought how much work went into stringing them all up like that… it was a deliberate display. This was dark work. Unearthly. The musty, still air seemed to have had all goodness and life sucked out of it.

A few tables near the walls were spread with playing cards and untouched food. Even the room was dead now. Seamus walked over to the phonograph and removed the needle to stop the hissing sound, ending the party for corpses.

Vinnie said he was bringing Patricia here. Stanley's stomach dropped. Vinnie. Where was he?

He looked upward and searched the hanging bodies, examining the shoes. When he reached the final row, he saw them gleaming black, swirling slowly in the dark.

"No. No. Please, God. No. Please. Not Vinnie." Stanley ran over to the body, reached up, and grabbed his friend's dangling feet.

"Boyo, what are you doing? We can't pull them down. Not yet. What's wrong with you?" Seamus shouted from across the room.

Stanley collapsed to his knees and crossed himself. He let out a guttural cry. Memories of Vinnie working at the ballpark with him, punching each other in the boxing ring, and laughing together on long trolley rides passed through his mind like a fading reel of film. The first time they met at the age of six, they'd shouted Irish and Italian insults at each other. And after a brief fight, they'd become fast friends.

Now, here was the end of Vinnie. Sobs heaved out of him in waves. It couldn't be real. He let loose with a string of Irish Catholic, dirty words.

"Stanny, Stanny…" His uncle clutched at his shoulders and shook him.

"Vinnie, Seamus. This is Vinnie." Stanley didn't recognize his own voice. It was broken and shrill.

"No. Can't be." Seamus let out a groan.

"Shoes. Let him borrow them. My shoes," Stanley forced out between sobs.

"I didn't know, lad, I'm sorry… I wouldn't have brought you in… Mary and Joseph, pray for us. Curse these bastards. Damn them to Hell." Seamus knelt down next to him. He put his arm around Stanley and whispered in his ear.

"The fat is in the fire now, boy. Understand? Look at them. This is what we could all be. They want annihilation, not just control."

Stanley wiped his face. Anger rose inside him. He stood and balled his fists. They couldn't get away with this. Seamus's plan to scare him off had backfired. More than ever, Stanley was determined to fight them. Vinnie needed to be answered for. He looked up at the body of his friend and noticed something strapped to his leg. Stanley reached up and removed the black, painted branch, just like the one he'd found on his pillow.

"The Winnowing has begun, Seamus." Stanley clenched his jaw.

"Yes, boyo. There's no safe place now, if there ever was."

They stood there for a moment. No matter how long Stanley looked, he couldn't take in the horror or process it. Something inside him blocked every emotion, and he just felt numb now.

"Listen. We need to get out of here. The Chief of Police is lurking around, and he's not to be trusted, understand?" Seamus took Stanley's arm and led him away from the horrible room of body piñatas. Arthur waited outside, standing in the shadows.

"Artie… I…" Stanley wiped the back of his hand across his nose.

Arthur squinted at him, and a look crossed his face that Stanley never saw there. Fear. "That bad, eh? Hey, the Chief is here. I gotta scram, Stanny. I'll be seein' ya." Arthur darted away before Stanley could say a word.

After Arthur melted into the night, a tall, well-dressed man with white, slicked-back hair in a trench coat came up to them. He eyed Seamus and sucked on his teeth as if he had food stuck between them.

"Interesting night, wouldn't you say, Fields?" He raised his chin to the dark warehouse.

"Guess so, Chief," said Seamus.

"And I know this young man. Our famous, hero newsie. How are you, kid?"

He offered his hand, and Stanley shook it out of polite obligation. It was hard and cold. All Stanley could think about was Vinnie's body swinging back and forth, the Post-Dispatch shoes gleaming with a recent shine. And the black branch.

Seamus straightened his fedora. "Chief, why haven't the meat wagons comes yet? We gotta start processing these bodies, collecting evidence, and it's too dark in there."

"Ah, well, Fields, I have another crew on the way. I'm going to relieve you of this responsibility right now. Take this young man home. He looks like he's about to fall over."

Seamus stood for a moment, looking as if he wanted to argue the point.

"Don't worry about it, Detective. You've done good work here. Now, let someone else take over."

Stanley would have bet money that under any other circumstances, his uncle would have fought tooth and nail. Instead,

Seamus smiled and said, "Well, very good Chief. Guess these rat bastards got what they deserved anyhow. Probably the mugs who did this are long gone by now."

"That's the idea, Fields. File your report with me personally. I'll let your captain know."

Seamus guided Stanley through the small crowd of policemen, which seemed to be thinning and not growing. *Nobody here but the dirty cops*, Stanley thought.

"Seamus, do you…"

"Shut it, boy. Not a word," Seamus growled. He obviously had the same thoughts. This was all wrong.

They found a waiting police car, and Seamus gave the patrolman orders to drive them home. As they wove their way toward Dogtown, Stanley sat in the back of the patrol car, shaking. He squeezed his eyes shut to stop the tears. It started when he found Evelyn's body and everything after that. Now, the stick. Hazel's strange behavior. Vinnie. Dead. Hung. Gone. His whole world turned on its head in the space of a couple of months. How much more could he take? Was he cracking up? Would he be in the loony bin like Charles?

The only thing that kept him sane was to realize, despite what Hazel said, none of this was made up. It happened. He hadn't imagined any of it, and his gut instincts were spot on. There was no explaining away the reality of Evelyn's buried body, and that there would be a funeral at Vinnie's parish with his family wailing and weeping.

No matter how locked in your head you get, death reminds you what is real.

Stanley didn't remember getting home or Seamus helping him up the stairs. But the terror of laying his head on the pillow where the branch had been motivated him to grab his blankets, throw them on the floor, and fall asleep curled up in a ball.

CHAPTER SIX

The party guests lingered into the early morning. Hazel sat in a cushioned chair, massaging one of her feet, watching the last few couples sway to a slow version of "I Get a Kick Out of You" in the dim ballroom. Stray balloons swirled and bobbed on the floor in response to the dancing, orbiting the bodies pressed together in a dance that seemed to be more of a sleepwalk. Hazel slipped off her other shoe and dropped it to the floor.

"Take anything else off, and I may blush."

Hazel smiled over at Gabriel. "Okay, wisey. That's enough of that. I thought you'd gone?"

Gabriel removed his spectacles and slipped them into the front pocket of his coat. His hair was a bit disheveled and his tie loosened. "I got roped into a stimulating conversation about government bonds…" He covered a yawn and lowered himself into a chair beside her.

"Sounds like a scream." Hazel was ready to crawl into her pillowy bed.

The music died down, and the band began to pack up their instruments. Gabriel let out a sigh and extended his long, muscular legs.

"Well, it was a grand party." He turned and seemed to study her face, making her cheeks warm. "Say, Hazel… when are you going to end my suffering?"

"Just as soon as this headache goes away. What suffering?" Hazel pursed her lips and gave him the once over. "You look healthy."

He flashed his perfect, white grin. "Why, I believe that was a compliment from Hazel Malloy. I may swoon."

Hazel laughed. But when she looked over at him, Gabriel's eyes were fixed on her face, and he almost seemed serious. Her heart skipped.

Bananas.

He let a slow smile spread across his face. "End my suffering, and say you'll come to the VP Ball with me."

Oh, that…

Hazel had avoided answering him for over a month. Her parents had encouraged her to accept him. Pops said it was a good way to infiltrate the inner circles of the Veiled Prophet … he seemed to still think there was some kind of conspiracy beyond the madness of Charles Chouteau. While Mumsy had just commented about Gabriel's fantastic backside. She had seemed strangely aloof about the drama surrounding the kidnapping and had instead pushed Hazel to join the debutantes. It was a complete reversal to her previous encouragement to defy them all. Maybe Mumsy was right …

Hazel smiled at Gabriel and thought a moment. She had to go to the ball. Stanley couldn't go. Anyway, Stanley was probably sweet on Sandy now. It seemed as if they had been mussing each other's hair out in the garden earlier. Her stomach dropped at the thought. Yuck. She wasn't sure if she even knew either of them anymore. Everything was changing.

"Yeah… why not? Let's make it a party." Hazel stooped to pick up her shoes and stood, coming up face to face with Gabriel. Startled, she took a step back.

"You mean it, Malloy?" His voice was soft and sweet.

"Sure." Hazel shrugged, trying to remain casual while her heart thumped.

Gabriel stepped closer and tipped her chin up with one finger. "You're one in a million. Happy birthday."

Hazel saw it coming, and a hundred things went through her mind. She was sixteen and about to get her first kiss. Gabriel was handsome, rich, smelled good… He was also a real heel sometimes. He'd necked with every girl in the Lindell set. What if she did it wrong…

Stanley.

Gabriel's lips were warm as he pressed them against hers. She held still, not knowing what to do as he moved his mouth. A tingling feeling swept her whole body. It was… nice.

Too soon, he pulled back, a slight smirk of satisfaction on his face. "That was your first kiss," he stated.

Hazel blushed. Was it that obvious? Mortified, she opened her mouth, but it took a moment before any words came out. "Says who?"

"You." He reached out and tapped her nose.

Hazel tightened her lips. "You're a regular gumshoe. Goodnight." She turned and exited the ballroom with Gabriel's soft chuckles following her.

"Don't be sore, Hazel. I'll be seeing you."

She didn't turn around or answer.

Hazel sat on her bed in a silky, white nightgown. She held the long, pink, wrapped box that Sandy had left on her vanity. She was tired, mixed up, and her face still felt hot from Gabriel's kiss and the following embarrassment. It wasn't something Hazel wanted to think about.

She unwrapped the box and found a new silver majorette baton with rose shaped ends. Hazel smiled. She would have to tell Sandy how swell it was. A folded piece of paper in the bottom of the box caught her eye. She unfolded it and read:

Happy birthday, Hazel. Because of you, I'll live to my next birthday. Slip this baton under your pillow. You never know when you'll have to bash someone's head in.

Friends 'til the end. Sandy

Hazel got into bed, keeping the baton beside her. She clicked off her bedside lamp and stared up at the glint of the chandelier in the dark. If she could only clear her mind, the exhaustion from the day would pull her down into sleep where she didn't have to think. Her head still hurt, and she didn't feel like herself. Maybe that was good, and she was finally going to fit in with the right people… They weren't evil just because they were wealthy. The Veiled Prophet was a symbol of power and benevolence… Charles was just crazy.

No. What about Evelyn's death? The numbers on her dead body that the police covered up. And all that strange stuff about the Veiled Prophet in the diary. Was it all true?

She rubbed her head as a sharp pain ran through it. Forget everything… think of something good. Hazel tried to think about her favorite movie stars and the latest fashions.

Sure… that's the ticket.

Hazel ran through a catalog of images in her head. Hats, gloves, rouge, the proper shape of eyebrows, silk stockings, Clark Gable's dimple… William Powell's smile… Ginger Roger's shoes… Myrna Loy's… everything.

Henri's barks echoed up the stairs, letting Hazel know it was time to get to school. The overgrown pup had made it a habit to ride along in the Buick. When she came down the stairs, Mick, the muscled dog trainer, was feeding Henri a biscuit. Mick had been working with the young German Shepherd in the yard since before the sun came up. He'd insisted on increasing Henri's sessions and making him a proper attack dog.

"Brummen." Mick used German to command the dog in a gravelly voice. Henri let out a fierce growl.

"Anhalten." Henri stopped, his big, chocolate eyes looking up for praise. Mick rewarded him with a scratch on the head. "Braver Hund."

Hazel was surprised out how well Henri cooperated for Mick. That growl was a new trick. The vibration of it still hummed against the high ceilings and gleaming wood floors.

"Say, Miss Malloy, good morning." His greenish eyes were sharp and hard. He wore his hair slicked back with pomade that smelled of cedar and tobacco. His wide face and cleft chin made him look a bit like Spencer Tracey. A scar ran across the bridge of his broad nose and another one split his left eyebrow.

"Morning, Mick. How's Henri doing?" Hazel bent to scratch her dog's head.

"I want you to start drilling his commands and taking him out more. He's a good pup. Needs practice in different places, see?"

Hazel nodded. "Thanks, Mick. I have most of them memorized myself. He just needs to learn who's boss." Hazel cupped Henri's furry face in her hands, and the tone of her voice changed as if she spoke to a baby. "Don't you, silly pup? Yes, yes, you need to listen to mommy." Henri happily licked her chin, his dark eyes soft, pleading, and eager for attention.

"That ain't how to make him a killer." Mick grinned.

"Aw… you little sap. We gotta make a killer out of you." Hazel chuckled, wiping away the dog's kisses.

"I've been working on a few things to get him there." Mick clapped loudly, and Henri quickly stood at attention. "Achtung." He pointed to a ragged, Scarecrow-looking dummy lying in the foyer. "Fass."

Henri galloped across the floor a bit clumsily, pounced on the dummy, and bit the neck. He growled as he dragged the body across the floor to Mick.

"Wow." Hazel watched as her sweet pup held the dummy to the floor.

Mick gave her a wink like there was more to come. He held out his hand and made a fist. "Vernichten."

At this command, Henri went savage. He growled and bit, shaking the dummy back and forth violently until stuffing came out.

"Aus," Mick commanded.

Henri dropped his victim but continued to stare at it, snarling.

Mick put his hands on his hips. "Ruhig."

The dog went still and silent, watching Mick with intense anticipation. Mick nodded and gave his head a pat. "Braver Hund."

Henri wagged his tail, red tongue swinging happily.

Hazel clapped her hands. "That was sensational. It's a little scary …" She put a hand to her mouth and whispered, "Vernichten?"

Mick nodded. "Use that command wisely. Your dad was insistent that I make this dog a bodyguard. He's getting there."

"I should take him everywhere," Hazel breathed.

Mick gave a half smile. "You should, Miss. You really should," he said, his expression turning serious.

All the girls at the Mary Institute were abuzz about the Veiled Prophet Ball. It was only a week away. Hazel tried to pay attention in her classes, but she had a feeling of impending doom that she couldn't shake. Even if the Veiled Prophet posed no threat and there was no conspiracy, something didn't sit right. Maybe it was just the trauma of everything that had happened and nerves about the ball. Especially with Gabriel taking her. Would he try to kiss her again?

It was good to have Sandy back in class. She had stayed away from school for a month after the kidnapping. The pleated skirt and neat, white top of the school uniform looked unnatural on her. Too normal. The costume of the all-American schoolgirl without a trouble in the world was the wrong label on the bottle. Sandy had a severe look that the other girls didn't. Her straight bob was a contrast to the curls and waves of the other girls. And that scar …

At the end of the day, Hazel walked beside her best friend down the polished halls of their school. The other girls swarmed past them. Some stared. They had gotten so much public attention in the last couple of months it was fine that the girls at school mostly ignored them. It was as if their celebrity made the other privileged girls feel the need to shun them to put them back in their place. Equality among the elite.

"Well, Hazel. Your party was sure a smash." The exaggerated, southern accent of Regina Peck sent a zap of irritation through Hazel's body.

"Sweet of you to say, Regina." Hazel forced a smile as the tall, dark-haired girl stepped in front of her with Brigitte Slayback attached to her side.

"Yeah… *sweet*." Sandy's tone was sour with irony. The way she popped the "t" at the end was like a slap.

Regina blinked and patted her hair. Nobody was used to the new Sandy yet. She had always been a comic and on the unpredictable side, but never acidic.

"You two ready for the VP Ball?" Brigitte said with a snooty lift of her nose.

Sandy snorted and rolled her eyes.

"All set to go with Gabriel Sinclair, and Mumsy picked up my gown ages ago," Hazel quickly said to smooth over Sandy's reaction.

The two socialites exchanged a knowing glance. "Ah. Yes. Your mother's *designer*. There might not be a bird with feathers left on them for miles." Brigitte laughed. Regina covered her mouth and joined in.

Hazel made herself laugh along. Fitting in with these geese was enough to make her want to lose her cookies. But she had to try.

"I am surprised about you and Gabriel… but then again, his family is wild about helping people. You work at their little clinic, right?" Brigitte made a face.

Hazel wondered what she'd think if she knew Gabriel had kissed her. "I volunteer there." Hazel swallowed back the words she wanted to say.

"Well, at least you aren't going to the ball with that ragged newsie," Regina sneered.

Hazel wanted to stomp on her foot but instead opened her mouth to ask about their dresses. She was cut off by Sandy's voice.

"Listen, dearie… that ragged newsie has more spine and class than either of you noodles." Sandy gave them a look of disgust. "What have you ever done to make the world a better place? You're parasites with bellies about to pop with the blood and sweat of other people. You're nothing," she hissed. "We're all nothing. Don't you get it? Bash us in the head with a bat, and the world moves on. Wanna know why? Nobody needs us. We're like makeup on a corpse. Just for show." Sandy's hands were in fists, but her voice was low and icily calm.

Hazel stared at her friend who sounded like someone else. She hadn't expected such a passionate defense for Stanley or such apparent hatred for her own class. How could she say those things? Many of the Lindell families created jobs and donated to charities. The other two girls had gone a little pale with outrage.

"Come on, Regina. She's obviously not feeling well." Brigitte took her sputtering friend by the arm, and they marched away.

"Alesandra Schmidt… you said a mouthful." Hazel wasn't sure how to feel about what Sandy had just said. Was this proof that she and Stanley were an item? It probably shouldn't bother her, but it did. This kind of thing was certainly not going to help either of them fit into society. Those girls were horrid, but they were part of the inside crowd.

"We all came from nothing, Hazel. Immigrants all fleeing to a free land just to get a shot," Sandy said, turning her dead sister's ruby ring on her finger.

"That's true. But not everyone who makes good is a parasite."

Sandy grabbed Hazel's shoulder and stared into her eyes. "That wasn't my point. I don't get you. I thought after everything that we'd be in the same boxcar. Are you just playing up to these snobs to get to the bottom of all this mess?"

Hazel's head suddenly ached again. She was beginning to wonder if she had a serious medical issue. "I don't know. I don't want to talk about it… I gotta go to practice." Hazel pulled her new baton from her bag and walked away from Sandy.

She made her way out to the field where some of the kids from the track team were running, and a few girls were playing catch with a baseball.

Hazel began to run through her routine, twirling and tossing her baton with increasing speed. She tried to clear her mind. Contrasting thoughts about her own class were driving her batty. Charles' actions had besmirched the whole set. His behavior was an isolated incident … not some broad, deeply rooted truth about the upper class. Was it?

Bananas. It all seemed confusing.

Stanley and his band of Knights were a tough group with good hearts, but they were by no means morally superior. Though in the end, they had rescued her and Sandy. Hazel's mind flashed back to the dark cave. The scent of copper, old beer, and a mustiness that reminded her of what an old coffin might smell like. Sandy lay broken and bleeding against the cave wall, and Charles had Stanley on the ground. Hazel had filled with rage at the sight, and the next thing she knew, she had a copper pipe in her hands.

"Say, Malloy! Is that a weapon or a baton?" Mary Cooper called out as she trotted by on the track surrounding the field.

Hazel realized she had been aggressively swinging and parrying with her baton. She let out a nervous laugh and waved at her classmate.

Anino had shown her some Escrima moves with the kali sticks he used in street fights. He was one of her favorite newsie friends of Stanley's. He'd been so impressed by how she had fought off Charles in the caves, that he had met with her several times to teach her some basic blocks and attacks. Turned out she had a knack for it. Wasn't that different from learning tricks with her baton. Just more violent.

Mary Cooper slowed to a walk and crossed the grass to Hazel. She was a tall girl with round spectacles and curly, reddish hair and freckles. Mary was an annoying know-it-all in class but was friendly otherwise.

"Heya. That's looking good." She nodded at Hazel.

"Thanks." She tucked the baton under her armpit the way Anino did when he wasn't striking.

"I'm a clumsy mess and would probably clobber myself if I tried that." Mary pushed her glasses up her nose and wiped some sweat from her forehead.

"Oh. Well, it does take practice." Hazel smiled.

Mary stood looking at her as if she wanted to say more. It was not unusual for Mary to shoot the breeze with Hazel. It happened often enough. Just small talk and gossip. But not so much since all of the kidnapping drama. Hazel had learned that most people didn't know what to say.

"So… I heard you actually beat up Charles Chouteau with a pipe," she finally said, a look on her face that Hazel couldn't interpret.

"I gave him a good smack. I'd be able to do a lot more now."

"I see that..." Mary shifted her weight and took a breath. "I'm glad. I'm glad you hurt him. He was a killer, but he was more than that." She bit her lip and broke eye contact. "I never told anyone because nobody would believe me," she rushed. "Everyone thought he was sweet, and he spoke so softly. His family is in such high standing... powerful."

Hazel nodded, suddenly aware that Mary was telling her something important. Something she'd never told anyone else. "Yeah. He had us all fooled."

Mary swallowed. "And I'm not a dish like you or Sandy. Never been the pretty one... so I don't think people would believe me."

"Oh." Hazel understood. "You're telling me he's a masher."

Mary's cheeks bloomed pink. "Last year at Edith's Halloween party. He trapped me in the music room alone. I was dressed as an Indian princess, and by coincidence, he was an Indian chief." She stopped and glanced around the field. A cold breeze swirled by, and she rubbed her arms. Mary spoke quieter now. "At first, I was flattered. He said such nice things ... but then he wouldn't stop putting his hands on me. He's strong, Hazel." Her voice wavered, and her eyes filled with tears that she quickly blinked away. "Anyway, at some point Gabriel Sinclair walked in and broke up the party. But he'd already hurt me and done things... After that, he pretended I was invisible."

Hazel watched as Mary's brave face melted. She reached out and hugged the tall girl while she sniffed back tears. "I'm sorry," she whispered, not knowing what else she could say. He had hurt so many people.

"Don't tell anyone, okay? I'll be disgraced—seen as dirty," Mary sobbed.

"He's the disgrace. Not you. He's the dirty scum." Hazel's heart felt like it was being pulled out of her chest. It was so unfair.

Charles was a monster. It was clear that other people were not even human to him. Just playthings to handle, cut up, or smash with a bat as he pleased. She wondered how many other girls had suffered by his hands in secret.

Thank God Charles was locked away where he couldn't hurt anyone now.

CHAPTER SEVEN

Stanley sat on the stairs in front of St. James and stared into space. He felt removed from his body, numb, and nothing seemed real. Nightmares of Vinnie's dead face kept him tossing and turning all night. He'd been grateful the black bag hid the truth from him at the Rookery. Otherwise, he might never sleep again.

Seamus tried in his own way to help at breakfast, but just ended up uttering old Irish platitudes that weren't all that helpful. Finally, Stanley couldn't take it anymore and told his uncle he wanted to talk to Father Timothy. To lend truth to the lie, he'd walked to his local parish church but didn't go inside.

He sat on the cold steps and looked up at the stained glass, gothic windows. The cloudy sky above the church looked like billows of ink spreading and fading in water. There might be a storm coming.

Stanley didn't want to talk to the priest. He didn't want to talk to anyone. Instead, he just wanted to scream at the top of his lungs then gather up his stuff and disappear. Where? He didn't know and didn't care. Just anywhere, where he didn't feel the ghost of his best friend on every street corner or feel Hazel's eyes staring up at him with disdain. The look she'd given him didn't seem like her, almost as if Charles had possessed her body.

He shook his head. Stupid idea, really. Arthur was right. Hazel just wanted to be a swell and forget about everything that happened. He couldn't really blame her, not really. She wanted to retreat into her safe, little world and not think about the awful things they'd seen. He wanted to do the same. Seamus had said he was a man, but he didn't feel like one. Right now, he was just a scared kid who wanted to run and hide.

Taking out the diary, he stared at it for a few moments. This stupid, little book caused all the problems. They knew he had it, and they wanted it. And they would make his life, and the lives of everyone he cared about, a living hell. Despite what he'd said last night, Stanley didn't think they would spare Hazel either.

Maybe it was just time to get out, get rid of the diary, and somehow send the message the Knights were done. The whole thing was too much for him, and no one would blame him, not really. Not after Vinnie.

Stanley shuddered as the squeaking of the rope sounded through his memory. But he couldn't let the bastards win. He should give the diary to someone older, more responsible. But who?

He ran through the list of alternatives and rejected them all. And then it hit him; Father Timothy. He was a Jesuit. Weren't they the pope's spies and all that? Most of what was said about them was dumb, written by people who hated Catholics. Still, Father Timothy often gave hints about some of the strange things he'd done. And he seemed to know more about what was going on in St. Louis than anyone else.

Stanley stood up, straightening his coat and hat. That's what he would do. Give the book to the Jesuits and Father Timothy. Let them handle this mess. And he would finish school. Maybe. Or just leave and go west. He'd read about the Civilian Conservation Corps and their work out west. He always wanted to go out there. Maybe Seamus would give him the thumbs up.

Letting out a breath, he turned and went into the church. Dipping his finger into the holy water, he crossed himself and said a brief prayer. After kneeling at the altar, he went to Father Timothy's office.

Just as he was about to knock on the door, he heard voices inside; one of them was Seamus's street-hardened Irish lilt. Unable to help himself, Stanley put his ear against the door.

"I'm worried about the lad, that's a fact, Father. I heard him moaning and thrashing about last night. I don't know how much he can take. He's a brave boy, but still a boy. That scene at the Rookery, well, it gave me nightmares, and I've seen it all."

"I agree, Seamus. But he's faced everything like a man."

Another voice cut in, and Stanley stopped himself from crying out in surprise. "I'm highly impressed with his poise and grace with my daughter. He is a bit rough around the edges, but Hazel adores him. And from Sister Mary John's report, his writing is exceptional. I would not object to him working on my new enterprise."

Mr. Malloy. What was he doing here?

"Mary and Joseph, forgive me, Father, but did you hear nothing I said? And as the boy is with me until he's old enough, I have a right to say what's what."

Stanley furrowed his brow. They all were discussing some kind of future or project for him. But what?

"When I was his age, I clerked for my father's firm and was starting to handle clients."

Seamus shot back. "And when I was his age, I was crawling around the bottom of a ship, shoveling coal. What's your point?"

Stanley wondered what was bugging Seamus so much. He'd always pushed Stanley to be a man, encouraging him work different jobs and be independent.

"Gentlemen, I think Stanley is old enough to make up his own mind. Maybe we should let him speak for himself."

Stanley took this as his cue and opened the door. "Yeah, I'd like that. So, maybe you all should tell me what this is all about."

Seamus and Mr. Malloy looked at him in surprise, but Father Timothy just smiled and motioned him to an empty chair.

"Come in. I'd admonish you about eavesdropping, but I suspect you would ignore that. I'm afraid you've discovered our little conspiracy."

Stanley took off his hat and eased himself into the chair. He crossed his legs, trying to look sophisticated like Mr. Malloy.

"Okay, so what's this all about then?"

"Perhaps I'll explain, as I'm the one who brought everyone together," Father Timothy said.

Mr. Malloy and Seamus said nothing. Stanley felt like he was about to get let in on some little secret.

"Stanley, it's not an accident that I was assigned to this parish. The pope and the Jesuits were concerned when they learned what was going on in St. Louis, and his Holiness instructed the bishop to place me here. Before I became a Jesuit, I acquired certain… skills, you might say. We've been watching the Veiled Prophet organization for years now. Sadly, because many Catholics in this city have joined without realizing the more sinister motives. But one of them has recently become a Benedictine monk, Brother Martin, who is partly the reason why I am here."

A monk. Stanley remembered the letter he'd read in Father Timothy's study before the whole thing with the caves.

"Brother has given us a treasure trove of information from his own experience inside the Veiled Prophet organization, and he has interviewed and recorded the accounts of others who have escaped Legion. We now have spies in their group. But we have to be careful with the information, as we don't want to jeopardize lives."

"Are they after Hazel?" Stanley asked, leaning forward.

Father Timothy shook his head. "I don't know. But Seamus, Mr. Malloy, and I have been meeting, along with some others, to figure out who is at risk. We can't go to press to tell the world about what's going on here, nor to the authorities, as many of them are in with the VP. And all of them have bought into the diabolical teachings of eugenics. The Church has raised its voice in protest, but we've been told we are backward and 'from the Dark ages,' conjuring up images of the Spanish Inquisition and the burning of witches, and so we are ignored, dismissed, or not trusted."

Stanley saw the whole picture show. The Veiled Prophet was the figurehead for Legion. They'd cast a net over St. Louis, and their point of view was embraced by the educated and the elite. It didn't matter if they were Democrats or Republicans. All of them drank from the same sewer.

He stood up and paced the worn, polished floor. "Then there's no hope. Only sane option is to get out. I've been thinking of going west anyway. Let this city go to the devil for all I care."

The three men looked at each other, and then Seamus said, "Nah, boy. We got plenty of hope. But we may lose our lives because of it."

"So, what's the point then?" Stanley said. "People get what they deserve. They're choosing this."

"The point, Stanley, is that evil must be fought by those with the means to do so. Not everyone who is affected has chosen this," Mr. Malloy said, taking out his pipe. "I've respected your honesty and courage in regards to my daughter. Are you still that young man?"

He always thought Mr. Malloy was a blustering idiot of a father, so preoccupied with business that he didn't have a scrap of smarts left for the real world. This new Mr. Malloy caught him flat footed, and he forgot his manners. "Yeah, all that got greased when Vinnie got a rope tied around his neck. And what do you care? You live in a rich pile of bricks, and nobody can touch you. What do you know about struggle?"

His words reverberated in the quiet room. Stanley wished one of them would yell at him about his sass mouth or something. He took off his cap and ran his hands through his hair.

"Son, you've had a terrible few months. Mr. Malloy is trying to help," Father Timothy said in a gentle tone.

Nicholas Malloy gave Stanley a probing look, puffing on his pipe. "Teach me. All I know are my own struggles and what I can learn from others."

Stanley nodded. "Okay, I'll tell you my secrets, if you tell me yours. How did you and Father become a team? What's your story? Why are you involved in all of this?"

"Before Father Timothy and I met through Brother Martin, I had read some things that primed me for what was to come. G.K. Chesterton's essay called *Eugenics and Other Evils* particularly affected me. I was unaware these things were going on in my own country. I was convinced that it was a sick and twisted movement that would bring ruin on all of society. Then they went after my daughter. And now, I think they are going after my wife. That is not something I can stand for. That is why I am involved."

Stanley looked at Mr. Malloy and saw a steel he'd never noticed. The man's jaw was set, and he puffed hard on his pipe. It just went to show you could never really know a person until it all started going south.

"I'm sorry, Mr. Malloy. Just feeling a bit rough and ragged."

Mr. Malloy nodded. "You're a fighter. I expect nothing less. That's why we're going to need you and your Knights."

Seamus shook his head. "I'm tellin' ya, it's a bad idea."

"Yeah, but as you told me before, I'm a man now, and I make my own decisions," Stanley said, sitting down. Seamus stared at him for a moment, overcome with some unknown emotion, and then he nodded.

"I guess the good Lord and all the saints are against me on this one."

Father Timothy smiled. "Not in the least, Seamus. They are, at least this time, on our side."

"So ya say, Father, forgive me."

"So, what's the skinny? How can we help?" Stanley said.

Father Timothy took a thin newspaper from his desk and lifted it up. "Have you ever heard of *The Catholic Worker*?"

Stanley nodded. "Yeah, Dorothy Day. Helping homeless people and all that. She's why I steal… eh… get food from the trash cans for others."

Mr. Malloy gave him a half smile. "You think that goes unnoticed? A few of us put out more food at night, you know."

Stanley stared at him, a bit nettled. He thought his Knights were being daring and putting it to the swells. But, come to think of it, some of the trash cans did seem a bit loaded. They'd thought it was just the swells being ungrateful swine. His head spun a little.

"Yes, Dorothy Day's group in New York. But their little newspaper is starting to gain a huge following across the country. And so that's what we are going to do. We're going to start our own little, revolutionary newspaper to get the word out."

"How? I mean, we don't have any money, or printing press, or anything like that," Stanley said.

"We do, because I just acquired everything we need. We have an editor, Father Timothy. He will use a false name, of course. But we need writers, and more importantly, we need a street network, someone who can get the papers in the hands of everyone, and I do mean everyone: colored, white, Jews, Poles, Irish, oriental, whoever can read or have someone read to them," Mr. Malloy said.

"So, what do you think, boyo, are you and the Knights up for it?"

Stanley frowned as he looked between the three men. Mr. Malloy looked out the window, as if to give Stanley his space to decide.

"So, basically, you want me and my boys to put our heads in a noose." Stanley rubbed his neck, thinking about Vinnie. "And those who love us?"

"Son, you've already done that. Once you helped Hazel and Sandy, and were in the newspapers and on the radio, you became a target. You could, of course, leave the city, get away, and hide out somewhere," Father Timothy said, giving Stanley a piercing stare. "Or, you can stay and fight the evil in the city. The choice is yours."

Stanley looked down, wondering if the priest could read his mind. He didn't say anything for a moment and wondered what to do. From what he heard, Seamus would have been more than happy to send him west with the CCC. But would he really be safe, even there? And if he ran now, he would be on the run all of his life. Besides, he'd always wanted to be a reporter and write for a paper. This could be a start.

"If I agree to do this, I'm not gonna speak for the boys; they have to decide for themselves. I'm not really the boss of them. I want to be in on all of the info, including the monk, Father Timothy. I want to know all that you know."

"Well, I suppose it's time we lay all the cards on the table." Father Timothy got up, walked over to the file cabinet, took a key out of his pocket, unlocked it, and retrieved a large shoe box.

"This is my correspondence with Brother Martin, a Benedictine monk who used to be a member of the upper class of St. Louis Society. And a member of Legion, the secret guard of The Veiled Prophet. I do believe you came across one of his letters on my desk once, Stanley."

Stanley nodded. "Yeah. I saw it. It said something about Legion."

"Yes. He used to be a part of it. You're welcome to read through any of this whenever you like."

"Okay. So how does Malloy know him? You one of the VP's goons, too?"

Mr. Malloy shook his head. "Brother Martin was a former apprentice of mine who showed a lot of promise in the world of business before he took his vows. At the time, I didn't know about his past. It was through him that I met Father Timothy, before all of this happened with you and Hazel."

"But, I mean the way you acted with me... with Hazel. Some of the things you said about the poor, she told me," Stanley said, his head spinning.

Mr. Malloy took out his cigar, contemplated the burning end for a moment, then said, "I haven't always said and done the right things in life. If someone published every careless word you ever said or every bad deed you've done in the papers— what would people think of you? The more I knew, the more my view on things changed. However, I couldn't advertise that. It shouldn't be too hard for you to figure out, Stanley, there are spies everywhere. I wanted to keep my daughter out of danger. But when they took Hazel anyway, I knew it was time to go toe to toe."

The pieces fell into place. Of course. Mr. Malloy was playing the fool and trying to keep Hazel safe. All of his anger and controlling was out of fear.

"I'm sorry, Mr. Malloy. I'm a real crumb bum for assuming I had you pegged."

Shaking out his pipe into an ashtray, he said, "Not at all, Stanley. My little ruse worked quite well."

"So, Brother Martin or whatever, he's been giving you the low down?"

Father Timothy nodded. "Yes, but we seem to be lacking key pieces of information.

We know some of the main players involved. We know some of their plans, like the clinics that are going up in all of the poor areas of St. Louis, especially in the colored areas."

"Clinics? You mean like the one Haze works in?" Stanley said, curling his fists.

"Yes. She may end up being a handy plant for us there."

"So, what information are you lacking?"

"Practicalities, boyo, practicalities. We don't know how they plan to put it all into effect."

Stanley sat back in his chair and realized that they didn't know about the diary. He and Haze had kept that part a secret. They'd agreed not to tell anyone about it, but the way she was acting, he didn't know if she was safe anymore. His stomach rolled. Everything was screwy, and he couldn't handle it all himself.

He reached into his coat and pulled out the diary. "This is the diary of Evelyn Schmidt. This may contain the missing pieces you want. She talks about The Winnowing and the whole numbers system thing. There are some code in there too—might have some answers."

Father Timothy reached out and took it from him. He opened it, and his eyes widened as he flipped through it.

"How… how did you get this?" he asked.

"Sandy had it and gave it to Hazel. We promised each other not to sing about it to anyone."

Father Timothy stood up. "This is what we need, Stanley. This will be the first edition of the paper, the murder of Evelyn Schmidt. The Post-Dispatch and the Democrat all published the official story of the Chouteau boy being crazy. We will start there."

Stanley nodded. "I'll help, but you gotta let me be a reporter and write. I don't just want to be an errand boy in all of this."

Mr. Malloy smiled. "I would not expect anything less."

Someone knocked on the door, and Father asked, "Who is it?"

"Tis Peggy, Father. Sorry I'm late."

Father Timothy gave Seamus a brief glance and said, "Come in."

Peggy walked in, and all the men got up out of their seats. She seemed startled to see Stanley there.

He couldn't figure why she was there either. "You a part of this?"

She recovered from her surprise and smiled. "I am. So, lad, you've been fighting with Miss Hazel."

Stanley looked down and shoved his hands in his pockets. "Something isn't right about her right now. She's, I dunno, like someone's messing with her head."

The maid frowned and turned to Father Timothy. "I've noticed that too. Hazel has never been rude or short with me. Lately, she's been acting like a spoiled debutante who…" She paused and put her hand over her mouth. "Ah, Mr. Malloy, sir, I'm sorry."

He chuckled. "Speak freely, Peggy. Hazel has always been a willful child. And yes, lately, there seems to have been a change."

"Okay, so, what's that about then?" Seamus asked.

Father Timothy furrowed his brow. "I do not know. Attacks come in different forms."

No one spoke for a moment. Peggy glanced at Stanley and then reached out to his eye.

"Stanley, love, what happened to your eye?"

He didn't flinch from her warm touch. Her hand was cool and comforting, and he noticed a St. Jude medal, almost exactly like the one he wore, around her neck.

"A stick poked me in the eye. It's painted black, and was put on my pillow. A little message from Legion, I guess."

"Bring that stick to me, Stanley. I want to see it," Father Timothy said.

"Okay, not much to see."

"Possibly more than meets the eye," said the priest.

"Well it met my eye, but I didn't get much out of it." Stanley smirked.

Peggy started to say something, but Seamus interrupted, "Ah, Peggy, sure, we were just discussing the newspaper. Do you think you have the house help network all square?"

She composed herself and said, "To be sure. They're all ready to do their part. I've already got my spies in place, after all. All I got to do is pull my strings, just like the old days."

Seamus frowned. "Let's hope not."

Stanley was trying to catch up with the fact that Peggy had a network of servant spies. "Uh, old days? What are you two flapping your gums about?"

Mr. Malloy stood up. "That is the past. We have to deal with the now, Stanley. You need to start working on your article about the diary for Father Timothy. It's time to get this paper up and running."

Stanley wanted to argue, but the four adults in the room seemed intent on keeping him in the dark on some of it. And he didn't feel like fighting them.

"Yeah, okay, so we need a snappy name; something that sings."

Father Timothy smiled. "Indeed. Any suggestions?"

Stanley walked over to Father Timothy's window. What name would really catch people's attention and make them read?

"How about *The Knight's Voice*? And the tagline would be, *Defending the Truth. Protecting the People*?" Stanley asked.

Everyone smiled, and Seamus said, "Gee, I wonder where that came from, Sir Stanley?"

"It's time we start doing something beyond just raiding trash cans. The boys will go for it. We got friends disappearing left and right. Nothing else to do now. The war has begun, and it's time for us to ride."

The men nodded. Father Timothy looked pleased. There was an energy in the room like a coiled snake. But this time, the good guys had fangs.

Tears streamed down Peggy's face, and she wiped them away. "You... you look so much..." But she couldn't finish her sentence.

Seamus draped an arm around her and said, "There, there, lass. Will be all right, saints preserve us." She buried her head in his shoulder, and her body shook with silent sobs.

Stanley wasn't sure what was wrong with Peggy; he was about to get nosy when Mr. Malloy said, "So we can count on you to write for us. Can you help spread it?"

"Nobody can spread news like newsies can. We'll just slip it in with the paper."

"Perfect. Then you have some things to organize," Father Timothy said.

Stanley put on his hat, nodded to everyone, and went outside into the sanctuary. He knelt at the altar rail and prayed. For St. Louis. For the forgotten people. For the pigeons disappearing. For the Knights. For himself. And for Hazel. Her eyes shone in his mind, and he gripped his hands together and pressed them into his forehead.

Please. St. Michael, protect her. Please. Let her be all right. Show us the way. Defend us in battle.

Peace and calm flooded his mind. There was no more doubt and anger. Only resolve to fight the fight. He got up, crossed himself, and walked down the aisle of the church.

It was time to gather the Knights and go to war.

CHAPTER EIGHT

Hazel took Sandy's hand and swung her arm gently as they walked down the boulevard, looking into the sparkling Christmas displays of the store windows. It seemed like forever since she was a child, and the toys on display seemed like relics of a forgotten time of innocence she could no longer connect with. Tinker Toys, dolls, little cars, tops, and toy guns would light up the eyes of kids everywhere on Christmas morning, but Hazel couldn't think of anything she wanted. Though recently she'd dreamed of kissing Stanley under the mistletoe. But that couldn't happen.

She'd needed time alone with her best friend to do something normal together like they used to do before Sandy's world was shattered. A matinee at the Fox Theater downtown was just the ticket. They had decided against a Shirley Temple movie and went instead to see *The Girl From Missouri* with Jean Harlow, the blond actress who reminded Hazel of Mumsy. During the movie, Sandy had lit up a little. She even smiled and almost laughed. Hazel's heart lifted each time.

Henri followed on a leash in Hazel's other hand. She was taking Mick's advice about taking him out more, and the young dog was behaving quite well. Sandy seemed to have a special connection with him. Sometimes Sandy would hug him and bury her face in his neck, and Hazel got the feeling that Henri knew she needed extra affection. He never squirmed away.

"Say, that's lovely. You'd look just swell in that." Hazel pointed out a red, velvet coat with white, fox cuffs displayed on a mannequin, surrounded by tinsel and greenery.

Sandy glanced through the shop window with vacant eyes. "Sure, if I want to look like Santa Claus."

"It's festive." Hazel grinned.

"A bit too snazzy to wear around our newsie hero…"

Hazel had that sinking in her stomach again. *Bananas.* Sandy was sweet on Stanley after all… and they had been pitching woo under the moon at her birthday party. Stanley chased skirts as everyone knew, and Hazel had no claim on him. Still, it felt all wrong that her two best friends would have a romance. She had never admitted to Sandy how she felt about Stanley. Mainly because it seemed to fluctuate like mad ever since her rescue from the cave. Part of her wanted to cling to him and another part wanted to run away, far from all of the memories attached to him.

Jazz music echoed out of a bar; automobiles hummed and rumbled down the street. An old Model T without a top, looking like a horseless carriage, coughed smoke into the air. Several kids about her age rode inside, whooping and hollering. Hazel recognized all but one of them. It was some of Stanley's Knights. Anino, Jakob, Shuffles, and also a girl with red hair. Crouched on the back, riding the back bumper, was Arthur, bowler hat at a slant, black suspenders over an open collar shirt.

After the automobile had passed, it screeched to a stop at the side of the street, one front tire coming up onto the sidewalk. Henri let out a bark.

"Hiya, Haze!" Jakob shouted back over his shoulder, giving her a wave.

Hazel let go of Sandy's hand to wave back. "Hey, chums. What's this?" She approached the rattling vehicle, chuckling.

"Meet my old lady. My grandpop gave me this jalopy. It's been dead in his garage since 1929. He said it died with the stock market." Jakob let out a laugh. "But I got her running. She's a honey!"

Hazel grinned and touched the hood; it shook and jumped under her hand. "Not sure this is good for St. Louis. You clowns with wheels?"

Anino threw back his head and howled. Arthur straightened to a stand on the bumper and gave Hazel a slight nod before fixing his eyes on Sandy.

Shuffles gave Hazel a wink. "It's okay, kiddo. Hop in. We'll drive you home." He wrinkled his freckled nose. "Come here, pooch!" He pushed open the door and patted the seat between him and the girl with red hair. Henri jumped in, wagged his tail, and attacked Shuffles' face with kisses.

"What do you say, Sandy?" Hazel looked over at her friend for approval. Sandy's golden-brown eyes were glued to the redhead.

"Looks crowded," she muttered.

Hazel examined the stranger who sat beside Shuffles in the back seat. The girl had long, curly, red hair that she let hang down wild to the middle of her back. It wasn't styled or set at all. Her gray sweater was form fitting, and she wore black trousers. She had a frank and direct gaze as she looked back at Hazel, chewing pink bubblegum.

"Pleased to meet you. I'm Hazel." She held out a hand, and the girl shook it with a firm grip and calloused fingers.

"Mutual." She blew a large, round bubble and let it pop. She peeled it off her mouth and nose and put it back into her mouth. "I'm Frisky." Her voice was hoarse and low, and she had a small gap between her two front teeth.

"Are you? Well… I'm feeling quite spirited myself," Hazel said.

"Nah, her name's Frisky. She's Arthur's pal." Shuffles grinned.

"Frisky Jones. And who's this?" The girl with red hair gave a side smile and raised her chin at Sandy.

"I'm Alesandra Schmidt. Always nice to meet any pal of Arthur's." Sandy and Frisky looked at each other for a moment.

"Hop on in. I can ride the back with Artie. Ain't no trouble." The redhead slid onto the sidewalk and joined Arthur on the bumper. The boy in the bowler hat remained expressionless, staring out at the street and passing cars.

"My driver was going to come for us soon. We were just window shopping until then."

"Now he won't have to. We'll get you back quicker than he can leave to get ya."

She thought a moment. "Guess it wouldn't hurt to give old Jennings a break."

Hazel climbed in, and Sandy followed. Jakob backed off of the curb, and with a jolt, they were off, swerving between cars and skidding around corners. Hazel clapped a hand down on the top of her head to keep her hat from flying off. Henri barked with glee, attracting even more attention. She hoped nobody from Lindell would recognize her. She liked the boys and all, but this would be a world of gossip for the likes of the Regina and Brigitte.

Jakob got her back to Lindell quicker than she could have imagined possible. They came to a stop in front of the Malloy mansion. Heart pounding, Hazel eagerly exited the car to get her feet on steady ground. Sandy followed, and Anino opened the back door for Henri to jump out.

"Thanks, boys," Hazel called out.

"You bet." Jakob waved.

Arthur jumped off the back bumper where he'd been hanging on who-knows-how through that ride. "Yous go on without me, fellas. Catch you around."

"You got it." Anino saluted, and the Model T pulled away with a gasp of black smoke.

The girl called Frisky clung to the back and looked back at them until the car turned a corner.

Hazel had a feeling something was weird. Aside from the goose pimples Arthur always gave her. She and Sandy waited and watched him while Henri circled them restlessly.

With his usual detachment, Arthur slowly approached them. He took out a cigarette and a match. He struck it on the heel of his shoe.

"Hear anything yet?" He took a drag on his cigarette. He squinted at Hazel and let the smoke cloud out of his mouth.

Hazel coughed. "About what?"

"Come on, Princess... you were supposed to be on the inside. Watchin' all the pretty people so you'd help us figure out who the ring master is in this circus."

"Haven't noticed anything. I think Charles was working alone. The diary..." Hazel's mind went blank, and a sharp pain went through her head. She rubbed her temples.

Arthur gave her a look of disgust. "You jerkin' my chain, swell?" He blew smoke out his nose. "Soakin' in all that fame has made you screwy. Somethin' ain't right about you. Like you've forgotten everything."

"Everyone keeps saying that. It's stale." Hazel frowned, rattled.

Sandy, who had been silent ever since they had gotten into the car, spoke up as if she had not been paying any attention to the conversation. "Who's Frisky to you?"

Arthur rolled his eyes and took another puff of his cigarette. "What's it to you, doll?"

Sandy stepped forward, and her hand shot out. The sound of the slap made Hazel jump and knocked the cigarette out of Arthur's mouth. It hit the sidewalk and threw sparks.

Arthur blinked but didn't react. Hazel was alarmed. What was going on? Henri growled, and Hazel put a hand on his head until he stopped.

"Is that her?" Sandy demanded.

"Maybe it is. Maybe it isn't."

Sandy raised her hand to slap him again, but he caught her wrist and scowled at her.

"Look, swell. You don't own me like you own that fancy bracelet and that ridiculous hat.

I ain't yours. Hit me again, and you'll wish God never gave you hands."

"Let go of her." Hazel heard her voice tremble. "How dare you threaten her? She's been through enough."

Arthur released Sandy's wrist and cut his gaze at Hazel. "Don't I know it? You two dames have bigger fish to gut. Teeth is missing. One of your famous newsies. That means none of us are safe. They aren't even being careful now about who they pick off. Just ask Stanley."

"Teeth?" Hazel's heart seemed to freeze. She pictured the young, scrappy boy, and fear prickled over her skin. "What are we going to do?"

Arthur bent down and picked up the smoldering cigarette that was on the ground. "You? Nothin', as usual." He gave her a glance as if she were a pile of useless trash, and stuck the cigarette back between his lips. He gave Sandy a look that sent a chill down Hazel's back. He rubbed his cheek where there was a red imprint of her hand. "I'll see *you* later." He turned and sauntered away.

"No you won't. You stay away from her!" Hazel shouted at him, terrified he'd turn around. He didn't.

Sandy watched him go, a small smile on her face. "It's a date," she whispered.

Hazel shook her head. "Why do I feel like I just walked into a motion picture thirty minutes late? What was all of that?"

"He wants to see me later," Sandy breathed, with a look of triumph on her face. She was breathing hard as she watched Arthur move farther away and round the corner. She rubbed her wrist where he'd gripped her.

"Did he hurt you?"

"Yeah." Sandy smirked.

"You should tell Stanley. He won't allow that."

"What does Stanley have to do with it? Arthur isn't his dog," Sandy snapped.

"No, but... you and Stanley..." Hazel swallowed, feeling awkward.

Sandy raised her brows, her eyes wide with surprise. She began to chuckle, low and mocking. "Stanley? And me? Me and the White Knight?"

"But... he rescued you in the caves, and at my party the two of you in the garden..."

"He never rescued me in the caves. He left me there in the dark with Charles. Bleeding and broken."

"You were out cold—we tied him up good and tight, and we couldn't carry you..." Realization seeped into Hazel's brain. *Arthur and Sandy.*

Sandy got a faraway look on her face. "I know," she rasped in a broken whisper. Her face scrunched up, and tears ran down her cheeks. In all this time Hazel had not seen Sandy cry about what happened, and it made her heart feel like it was tearing. "I understand all that but… I woke up, you see."

The horror of that washed over Hazel. She took Sandy by the hand and led her into the house and up to her room with Henri on their heels. Her best friend followed without resistance and lay down on Hazel's bed, weeping without a sound.

Hazel lay on her side next to Sandy and put an arm over her. "What happened down there? I've never asked before, but… my psychotherapist says that emotions we bury never die. You need to get it out." Hazel watched her best friend's profile as she stared up at the ceiling.

Sandy wiped her eyes and spoke. "Charles asked me to the VP Ball. He came to my house with a rose and asked me to go on a walk with him… I was over the moon. You know how much I wanted that."

"Yes."

"He kissed me. Hard. And he pushed something into my mouth with his tongue… Then he clamped his hand over my face so I couldn't spit it out. It hurt, and I tried to get away. He said, 'Swallow the pill, and I will let go.' So I did." Sandy stopped as a sob shook her body.

Henri whined and hopped up onto the bed, lying beside her. Sandy hid her face in the side of his furry body. Hazel watched, a lump rising in her throat. Maybe she shouldn't make Sandy relive whatever had happened to her. It was too horrible.

"You don't have to tell me anything you don't want to," she said softly.

Sandy turned toward Hazel, swallowing hard. One hand moved through Henri's fur. "I opened my eyes, and everything was blurry. I was in the caves but didn't know where I was. He wanted the diary… he wanted to hurt me. And he did. I never want to talk about what he did… It was too much…" She squeezed her eyes shut and caught her breath. "Then I told him I didn't have the diary—that I gave it to you." She turned toward Hazel, and her light brown eyes, rimmed with gold, spilled more tears. "I'm sorry, I'm sorry… I was afraid."

Hazel shook her head. "No. It's okay. Stop that." She wiped away one of her friend's tears and stroked her cheek. "He was coming after me anyway. I was there and saw him after he killed your sister. He knew Stanley and I were trying to figure out who he was."

Sandy continued, staring into nothing. "I blacked out. I heard yelling and sounds but couldn't wake up. My whole body hurt. It was dark, and my face felt funny. Sticky… tight. I reached up and touched it and realized my face was covered with drying blood. Someone was standing over me. I knew it was him… that he was back to do more things to me… He said, 'Where's the knife he done this with?' At first I thought I was seeing things or that… the devil had changed shape. But I realized it was someone else in a tilted bowler hat."

"Arthur. He went back after we left…"

Sandy nodded. "I told him there was no knife… that he carved into my face with Evelyn's ring." She twisted the ring on her finger. It glowed blood red.

Hazel gasped. "Oh, Sandy!"

"Last thing I saw before everything went black again… Arthur was bent over him, tied up on the floor, going through his pockets, and I saw the glint of the ring as he slashed it at Charles' face. Arthur did that for me."

Hazel knew Arthur had his own reasons for hating Charles, a swell who was instrumental somehow in the ruination of his family years ago. But it was clear that Sandy had fixated on the dark newsie as a hero who had evened the score for her. "Do you love him?"

"I hate him, and I need him." Sandy turned on her side, hugging Henri.

Hazel wanted to tell her that it was dangerous and twisted to need someone like Arthur. The relationship would go no place good. But she couldn't bring herself to say that to Sandy.

"Arthur isn't… our kind."

Sandy turned and looked at her, incredulous. "Hazel… how can you even talk about 'kinds' anymore? He's right, and you ought to know it. This business with the Veiled Prophet goes beyond Charles. Why are you acting like you don't know it? Why are you turning into Brigitte?"

The confusion and headache came back. Hazel shook her head. "I—I don't know. I just can't be sure." She didn't want to talk about it—had to think. "I'll get you something to eat and drink. You rest. We can talk more later if you need to. Okay?" Hazel patted her friend's back and slipped out of the room. It was hard not to feel panicked. Teeth was missing, Sandy and Arthur had some kind of scary attachment, and the facts about all that had happened seemed to slip through her fingers whenever she tried to think. And then there were the headaches.

Hazel found two Pepsi-Colas in the Frigidaire and a couple of pastries in the pantry. While she surveyed the shelves for something salty, she heard voices enter the kitchen.

"Yes, ma'am, I'll be more careful." It was Peggy. She sounded unusually somber.

"Be sure that you are. I won't have any sass. Don't forget who pays your wages."

Hazel blinked in surprise. Was that Mumsy sounding so high-hat?

"To be sure, ma'am."

"My daughter needs to find her place and can't do that while you treat her like she's your equal."

"I understand, ma'am."

Hazel had never heard her mother act this way before. Admittedly, she herself had been a little bossy and impatient with the help lately... but hearing Mumsy talk that way made her realize it sounded just awful. She waited in the pantry, the drinks cold and wet under her arm.

"I'd like that martini in my room, and make it snappy."

"Right away, ma'am."

The sound of Mumsy's heels retreating and then returning made Hazel back farther into the pantry. "And one more thing... I know how you people like to come and go. I'm letting everyone know they need to double check the locks at night. It's probably best you stay in tonight. That Sinclair maid, Maxie, was found shot to death in a heap of garbage in an alleyway today, and nobody knows who did it."

Hazel dropped one of the bottles, and it shattered on the ground, splashing her legs with cold, fizzing soda and fragments of glass.

CHAPTER NINE

When Stanley got home, Seamus was sitting on the couch, a glass of deep, amber colored whiskey on the coffee table in front of him and cigarette smoke floating around his head in a bluish haze.

"Hey, boyo, where ya been?"

"Had to go for a walk. Clear my head. A bit too full," Stanley said as he sat down in the chair next to the couch.

"Sure, ya needed it. I'd offer you one of these, but you're too young."

Stanley nodded. "I'd be tempted."

They sat in silence for a while, and Seamus reached for a paper bag beside the couch.

"I didn't know if you would still want these. But you worked hard for them. I'm guessing Vinnie wouldn't want you to throw them away."

His uncle reached into the bag and pulled out the Post-Dispatch shoes. Stanley stared at them, not sure if he wanted to touch them or burn them.

"Vinnie's family gave them to me. Wanted you to have them back. The funeral mass is in two days, boyo. They want you to serve, if you'd be willin' and able."

Stanley tried to prevent his hands from shaking. "I don't know if I can, Seamus. I don't even think I could stand the funeral."

Seamus nodded, set the shoes down on the floor, got up, and went into the kitchen. When he returned, he had another whiskey glass and the bottle. He set the glass on the coffee table, poured some more for himself, and then poured one for Stanley.

"Ya know, when my pa died, your da and I had to plan the funeral. I was a mess and drunk, per usual, I guess. But William stepped up, planned the wake, a good Irish one to be sure, and helped Father with the mass. He was the strong one, Stanley, your da. And a good man. My hero."

Stanley looked up at his uncle and understood. "Seamus, you've raised me and done the best you could. I'm not a street thug or anything."

His uncle smiled and sat back down on the couch with a grunt. "To be sure, I thought you'd go that way when you were younger. That temper of yours. Only thing I can fault you for is your skirt chasing. But the Lass of Lindell is gonna put an end to that, I'm guessing."

Stanley nodded but didn't say anything. He didn't bother correcting Seamus. He'd resolved to stop all the trouble with girls even before he met Hazel and didn't know where he stood with Hazel anyway. The last exchange with her was complicated. He couldn't figure out what to do with her. One thing at a time.

"Did ya take the stick to Father?" Seamus asked.

"I was gonna go upstairs to get it. Any leads on the Rookery?"

Seamus shook his head. "Nah, and I can't ask, at least not directly. Not my case anymore. But I'm tryin' to see what I can find out."

Stanley glanced down at where Seamus had put the shoes Vinnie had died in. "Someone has to answer for that." He stood up, and Seamus reached up to touch his arm.

"Before you go, lad, let's toast Vinnie on his journey." He slid the glass of whiskey across the table to Stanley, and they both held up their glasses.

Seamus stood, closed his eyes, and raised his glass.

"Vinnie is not lost, our dearest love.

Nor has he traveled far.

Just stepped inside home's loveliest room,

and left the door ajar.

May Vinnie see the face of Our Lord, Our Lady, and all the blessed saints," he recited, his voice husky with emotion.

Stanley and his uncle clinked glasses and drank. Seamus downed his in one gulp, grimaced, and put down the glass. Stanley took a sip and coughed and sputtered. The liquid burned his throat, and the fumes filled his nose. "Ugh. No." He opened his mouth to let the hot tingle on the roof of his mouth cool down.

His uncle laughed. "'Tis good you can't handle your liquor. May it never handle you."

Stanley made a face. "Well, I'll offer up that moment of pain for Vinnie's sake."

Seamus nodded and sat back down, lighting up another cigarette. "The VP ball is in a few days, ya know that, yeah?"

"Yeah, of course. How could I forget? I have to break out the peashooter for the parade."

"Ha, to be sure. Wouldn't mind being there myself. But I'm on duty. And for the ball. The chief wants me there."

Frowning, Stanley said, "Why would he want that? You're a detective, not a street cop."

"Dunno. But I'm doing it to keep him happy. I seem to be in himself's good graces lately, and that's good for..." Seamus paused.

"Good for what?" Stanley said.

"Never you mind, boyo," Seamus said, waving the cigarette. "Just go get that cursed branch like the good padre told ya. There's a good lad."

Stanley knew there were things that Seamus wouldn't tell him. Something was fishy about the cops in town. He went upstairs and grabbed the black stick from the top of his dresser. The feel of the wood made his skin crawl, and he decided to wrap it up in one of his old scarves.

When he got back downstairs, he heard Seamus's voice from the back porch. From the sound of it, his uncle was chatting up the widow O'Malley who lived across the alley. Stanley could never be sure, but he guessed they had a thing for each other. He never pried about his uncle's personal life. It seemed the tough cop never had much time for women. Stanley wasn't sure how Seamus could live lonely all these years. But with so much unknown in Stanley's own life, it was a mystery that could move to the bottom of the list.

He walked back to St. James and found Father Timothy still in his study.

"Ah, Stanley, excellent timing. I just finished meeting with the ladies who plant flowers around the church; a fearsome bunch." The priest grinned.

Stanley gave a light chuckle and then held up his bundle.

"I have it, Father. This is the stick."

Father nodded and motioned toward the desk. "Put it there, and let's see what secrets it holds."

He put the branch down on the desk and unwrapped the scarf. The priest inhaled and said, "That's no ordinary branch."

Grabbing for a vial of holy water on his desk, he sprinkled it over the stick, making the sign of the cross. He and Stanley crossed themselves. And then Father Timothy bent down to examine the stick, while he took out a pocket knife. He scratched at the paint, exposing the wood beneath.

"It is blackthorn wood, often used in occult ritual. It's meant as a conduit to target darkness, I guess you could say."

The hair on the back of Stanley's neck prickled. He blurted out, "How in the world do you know that?"

"I've told you before, Stanley. I have a unique set of skills that involve a series of experiences that I cannot share with you. I'm sorry."

Stanley looked down and furrowed his brow as he examined the spiny, black branch again. "Guess you won't sing."

The priest chuckled. "I know, you hate not getting an answer, inquisitive man. But I do have my vows of obedience."

"Yeah, I know, but…"

Father Timothy held up his hand. "I can tell you that I've spent years studying the occult and curses. Do you have headaches or nosebleeds? Anything unusual?"

Stanley shook his head. "No, nothing like that, but I had a terrible dream the night they put it on my pillow."

The priest nodded. "Yes. I'm not surprised. These sort of curses are designed to invade the mind, but it looks different for everyone."

Nosebleeds. Headaches.

"Father, could this sort of thing, I dunno, change someone's personality?"

"Yes, especially if they are not closing their minds, as you've seemed to do. They underestimated you." The priest smiled.

"But, Hazel, Father. I think there's one in Hazel's room. I'm almost sure of it."

He described Hazel's recent behavior. Her unusual confusion and snootiness, along with her headaches.

The priest nodded. "Yes, it sounds as if she is under a dark influence. But as she is not aware of the branch, it's seeping into her mind. Brother Martin said they use these sort of diabolical tactics."

At the mention of the monk, Stanley said, "Yeah, what's the story on him? Why is he not here, helping us?"

The priest furrowed his brow. "His Abbot fears for Brother Martin's soul, and he is afraid of putting everyone's lives in danger, but he will come if he has to."

"How can he help?"

"He knows what it is like from inside Legion and the whole history of the Veiled Prophet, why it was founded and their connections through the city. They have secret oaths and rituals that bind them together in secrecy, so that they can more easily manipulate, plunder, and murder without being caught or held accountable, gaining power with a dark brotherhood to back them. I'm sorry to say, they even extend into Holy Mother church." Father Timothy frowned.

"I don't understand."

"The Veiled Prophet's history goes way beyond the riots of 1877 and their aftermath. It goes back to the civil war, when many in this city wanted to keep blacks in slavery and wanted Missouri to join the Confederacy. So they formed secret societies to gain power. They have always terrorized those people in the city they considered unworthy. But, I suspect these groups went back even further in Missouri politics. Look what they've done in the past to Catholics, Negroes, Jews, Orientals, and Mormons. No group is safe that they have decided is inferior or insubordinate."

Stanley leaned back in his chair. "Sounds like the Klan."

The priest nodded. "They were certainly very much like them, and many of those people joined the Klan when it came into existence. You see, Stanley, people think that history is full of eras with concrete walls. When in reality, history is like an ocean with the same currents underwater, shifting to and fro. It is fluid, and when an evil disappears in one era, it reappears in another. If you look close enough, you find the connections. And in America, there has always been a group of people determined to create the perfect place full of perfect people; a city on the hill, if you will. The Veiled Prophet is just an incarnation of what has always been."

Stanley couldn't move. The enormity of this group and their power overwhelmed him, and he felt helpless. As if reading his mind, Father Timothy said, "But, you know our consolation? The Lord looks over us. Evil never wins completely, not really. Goodness always raises up people to fight. There are always those who give their lives to keep the light burning."

"So, I guess I better get writing then," Stanley said, standing up.

The priest chuckled. "As your editor, your deadline is in two days. Give me a good article on The Winnowing. Make it part one of a series."

"Yes, sir. I mean, Father."

Stanley walked outside, feeling better than he had in days. He knew how to fix Hazel. The paper would be out in a week or so. And the tide would start turning once the light started showing in the rat hole. Probably some people wouldn't believe it. But enough might.

Occupied by his thoughts, he almost ran straight into Arthur.

"Watch it, boss, I'm standing here."

"Artie, sorry, what gives?"

"Ain't gonna tell you until we get there. You smell too holy right now."

Stanley chuckled. "Whatever you say, man."

They walked in silence for a while, and Stanley glanced at Arthur. The kid was smoking like a chimney, drawing in fast and letting out smoke like a steamboat on the Mississippi. His face looked drawn, as if he hadn't eaten in a while.

"Artie, are you okay?"

"What are you, my mother?" Arthur said, lighting another cigarette.

"No, thank God. I'd kill myself if I had such an ugly mug for a baby."

Arthur didn't even crack a smile. Not that he did much anyway, but sometimes Stanley could get a laugh out of him.

"What's with you, meathead?"

Throwing away a cigarette, Arthur turned to face him. "I ain't in a laughing mood. Pigeons are going missing. My pops ain't doing so hot. And neither is my mom. And the swells are dancing in a few days, as if the whole country ain't starving."

Stanley was going to agree, but he stopped himself. Arthur didn't need gasoline thrown on the fire. The kid was on the edge. They walked until they reached Forest Park, and he realized that Artie was taking him to the boxcar. When they got there, all the Knights had assembled, and there stood Frisky Jones in all her redheaded glory.

"Well, well, look at what the cat dragged in, King Arthur his own self," she said, giving them a mock bow.

Stanley gave her a half smile. "Hey, Frisky, what's the word?"

She'd always acted tough and gave him lip. Of all the girls he'd met, only Frisky seemed immune to his charms, telling him once, "Back off, St. Stanley, I'm too much of a woman for you. I don't want you confessing me to the good Father."

But now, she played with her long, red hair, almost pulling it out of her head. The rest of the Knights looked grim. Even Shuffles' good cheer seemed to have vanished, as he fidgeted with his baseball cap.

"Teeth. My little Teeth. He's gone," Frisky blurted out.

"What? What are you talking about?" Stanley said, taking off his hat.

"It's true," Arthur said.

"He ain't been home for a few days. His mother is in fits, and that's a fact." Frisky shoved her hands into her trouser pockets and paced.

"How do you know Teeth?" Jakob asked, adjusting his yarmulke.

"What is this, a shakedown? Was just letting you know. He's gone," Frisky said, jumping off the boxcar and starting to walk away.

"Wait, Frisky, please, we need information," Stanley said, catching her by the arm.

"St. Stanley, if you don't take your masher mitts off me, I'll get you but good, got me?"

He let go of her and put up his hands. "Sorry, but we need to know information if we are going to find him."

Arthur lit a cigarette and gave it to Frisky. She took a pull and said, "You okay, Artie? You don't look so good."

He shrugged his shoulders. "I'm fine. Tell Stanny what you know."

She took a deep drag. "Well, I used to babysit Teeth. Just about everyone on the block, really. I fuss over him and make sure he doesn't do anything stupid, like join you fools. He pretends not to like it, but I can tell you, he don't run home to momma when he needs some boobs to cry on."

Anino sniggered and then covered his mouth. Shuffles turned away and pretended to cough.

"If you're done talking about your boobs, Frisky, can we get on with it?" Stanley said, pacing the ground.

"I remember a time when you wanted to do more than talk," she said, taking a slow drag.

Stanley sighed. "Frisky, please."

She nodded, looking away. "I'm sorry. You're right. He's gone. His momma doesn't know where he is, and everyone is looking for him."

"I have an idea where," Arthur said, going over to Frisky and putting his arm around her. "It's that clinic, Stanley, the one where your rich princess helps us poor folks."

"Oh, yeah, the one run by Dr. Galton. I met him at Haze's party."

"What did you think?" Jakob asked, jumping off the boxcar.

"I dunno. He was a rich snob who thought he was better than me. But what else is new? I was mostly focused on …" He stopped, and he could feel the heat rising in his face.

Frisky smirked. "Boy, he's dizzy for her, ain't he? You were spot on, Artie."

"So, what about the clinic?" Shuffles said before Stanley lost his mind.

"That's the last place anyone saw Teeth, boyo. And that maid who was found shot in the head," Arthur said.

Stanley felt like throwing up. "We need info. Fast. Everyone needs to spread out and see what they can find. I'll join you in a few hours."

"Where you goin', to do some smooching?" Frisky said, stomping her cigarette in the ground. They all looked at him for a response, and then he realized. He hadn't told them about the newspaper business.

"Look, you mugs, this thing might be bigger than we think."

Arthur shook his head. "That ain't so. I already know."

"Maybe not everything. There's a group putting together a newspaper. I'm writing for it." He told them about the meeting and what they wanted the Knights to do.

Anino smiled. "So, while we sell our papers, we pass out the rag you're writing for, is that it?"

"That's about the size of it, yeah. We know they don't print the full truth in the papers. We gotta spread the word up and down the city."

Anino nodded. "I'm in."

Shuffles put on his hat and said, "Count this Mormon in, time to go Porter Rockwell."

Jakob smiled. "And just call me Maccabee the Hammer."

Stanley could have hugged them all, but he said, "Look, once this gets out, well… You all know about the Rookery. I don't know if I can ask you to do that."

Arthur said, "We know the risks, Lord Stanley. We ain't just takin' them for you. This is for all of us."

Frisky ran a hand through her wild hair. "Yeah, pretty boy. The whole world don't revolve around your majesty."

Stanley rolled his eyes. "Good. I'll meet you all back here in a few hours after I write the article. Let's see what rats we can scare out of their holes."

All of the Knights departed except for Frisky. She was twisting her hair, tying it in small knots.

"You will find him, won't you Stanny?"

"I promise to do what I can. I love that kid, you know."

She nodded, wiping away tears. "He showed me the baseball stuff you got him. You don't even know…"

Stanley went to hug her, and Frisky said, "Whoa, there, Stanny boy, that wasn't an invitation for a free grope. Just get to work."

And then she walked away, her red hair disappearing into the dark.

Stanley stood there for a moment and then leapt into the boxcar. He found the case where he hid his typewriter and scrolled a piece of paper into place. With a deep breath, he started to type, the clacking echoing in the boxcar.

CHAPTER TEN

Days of school and worry passed. Hazel hadn't seen Stanley or heard any word about Teeth. Nothing in the papers suggested that Maxie's murderer had been captured. Hazel didn't want to think about any of it. Maybe if she ignored what was happening and stayed comfortably wrapped in her satin world, she wouldn't end up in danger again—or like Evelyn.

Peggy didn't seem to be around much either lately. Mumsy seemed to keep her busier than ever, and at night, she disappeared. Hazel longed to sit and tell her everything and let Peggy hug her and tell her everything would be all right in her soothing Irish lilt.

The Veiled Prophet Ball was only a couple of days away, and it overshadowed everything. Gabriel Sinclair had come to call after school twice. The visits consisted of small talk in the parlor with beverages and listening to music on the gramophone. He made Hazel feel shy and a little giddy now. She hated it.

After one visit as he said goodbye at her door, Gabriel leaned in as if to kiss her.

"See you soon," he whispered, coming closer.

Hazel's heart sped up and then paused when, over his shoulder out in the dimness of twilight near the front gate, she saw the shape of a person and the red spark of a cigarette. She drew back. "Yeah. See ya," she muttered and shut the door.

Was Arthur out there watching her?

Hazel watched out the window as Gabriel walked away, shaking his head, and the figure by the gate moved away down the sidewalk. She wondered how often eyes followed her when she didn't know it. What made that dirty bum think he had a right to stalk her? How would he like it? Hazel paced the gleaming, parquet floor of the foyer.

It was an hour until dinner. Hazel slipped out the front door, made her way across the lawn, and through the hedges. She wasn't sure what she was doing. On a hunch, she headed toward the Schmidt's house to see if her stalker was heading there too. Hazel and Sandy knew all of the gaps in the bushes and fences to get to one another's houses without taking to the street. She hunched down in a honeysuckle bush that climbed the fence surrounding the Schmidt's extensive garden. It always felt like reentering the summers of her childhood to push through the leaves, with a sweet aroma of the delicate flowers surrounding her. But there were no blossoms on it this time of year. Night was almost fully drawn down like a shade against the light of the descending sun. The air chilled, and Hazel shivered.

She scanned the flower-lined walkways and patios of the Schmidt estate. Her eye caught movement in the large gazebo situated in the back corner of the yard. Hazel crept quietly toward it and stopped behind a bed of orange, winter-blooming Canterbury Bells when she heard voices.

"You're early."

"I was in the neighborhood."

Hazel crouched and moved closer, careful not to scuff her shoes on the paving stones. Looking up through the bushes, into the shadowed gazebo, Hazel saw two figures facing one another, almost touching. The smell of cigarette smoke floated toward her.

"Where else you been? With Frisky?" It was Sandy, wearing a black dress and no hat. She had an angry pout on her face.

"Nah. It ain't like that with her." Arthur dropped his cigarette to the floor and stomped it out.

"Liar." Sandy took a step backward.

"Say, what's it to you?" Arthur grabbed Sandy by the shoulders and pushed her against one of the columns of the white gazebo. "Want to play in the dirt a little, swell? You liked it before."

Sandy gasped. "Ouch. I oughta slap you."

"Just you try." He pressed closer to her. "What'sa matter, swell? Afraid you'll get your hands dirty?"

"You're an animal."

"And you ain't?" he growled.

Hazel watched her friend stare down the boy in the bowler hat, Sandy's chest rising with every breath. The air seemed to crackle with electricity.

"I despise you," Sandy rasped.

Arthur snorted and wrapped his arms around Sandy. Hazel almost jumped from her hiding place to defend her friend but stopped when the two smashed together in a rough kiss that Sandy was definitely not fighting.

Hazel looked away while the couple passionately gripped one another, making sounds that made her face burn.

"Artie," Sandy gasped. "You send me." His black bowler hat fell to the floor as Sandy moved her hands into Arthur's hair.

"I'm no good," he said while he kissed her neck—more like devoured it. Hazel tried not to stare.

"I know," Sandy moaned.

They slid down the column to the floor of the gazebo. Arthur turned Sandy in his arms with a grunt, settling on top of her. She pushed the suspenders off his shoulders and started to unbutton his shirt.

"Say that you ain't better than me," Arthur breathed low. He slid one side of her dress off her shoulder and pressed his lips there.

"Yes. Yes. It's true." Sandy kissed him again, and he kissed her back. Then the intensity shifted, and Arthur pulled away and rested his head on her chest.

He let out a sigh. "You mean it, dollface?"

"Yeah." Sandy ran her hands down his back.

Arthur raised up onto his elbows and gazed down at her, his usually stony face fracturing with emotion. "You with me?"

"Yeah."

"They won't like it."

"I don't give a hang. Let them squawk and lose their tail feathers over it." She pushed up against him until he rolled over so that she rested on his chest.

"My plan for the ball? You'll help me out?" He reached up and touched her hair, a fire in his eyes.

"Anything you want." Sandy burrowed into his chest. "I don't care what happens. They deserve what they get for what they did to you … and what they did to my sister and me. I hate them."

"That's right, baby. We'll show 'em. You're like me—not them."

"Maybe that's why we hate each other."

"Yeah," Arthur said as their mouths met again.

A voice called from the back of the house. "Miss Alesandra! You out here? Dinner." It was Flora.

Sandy scrambled to her feet and straightened her clothing. "Coming, Flora." She put a finger up to her lips to hush Arthur. "Tomorrow," she whispered.

"I'm gone," Arthur said quietly. He picked up his hat and rose to his feet.

Arthur stood, looking at Sandy for several moments, and Hazel thought they would start into necking again. But he placed his bowler hat on his head, gave Sandy a slight smile, and slipped away into the shadows.

Sandy sighed to herself and wiped a hand over her mouth. She cleared her throat. The darkness seemed to hold her as she stared the direction that Arthur had gone. Hazel wondered what was going through her mind. Sandy tugged her dress back over her shoulder and stepped out of the gazebo, heading toward her house. Flora stood waiting for her. Light and soft music spilled out of the doorway to the kitchen, where servants laughed and talked while Bing Crosby crooned "Temptation."

Hazel watched her friend go, wondering what to do. Arthur and Sandy. It seemed like some kind of mess. Sandy was not the same since her kidnapping; that was for certain.

Hazel had Jennings wait in the Buick as she walked toward the clinic the morning of the Veiled Prophet Ball. She would have plenty of time to get ready. The clinic had been the last place that she'd seen Teeth and the Sinclair's maid, Maxie, and she felt drawn there.

"Lady Bananas."

Hazel turned around. Stanley. His cap gripped in his hands, hair a mess, he examined her with his blue eyes.

"Stanley. Hi. What are you doing here?" She swallowed. Something about the look on his face made her nervous.

"Looking for you." The shadow of golden stubble on his chin and the dark circles under his eyes made him seem dangerous and unhinged. Hazel had a flashback of Arthur and Sandy's heavy smooching, and for a moment, she wanted to know what it would be like with Stanley.

"Don't go there."

"Huh?" Startled out of her vision of Stanley crushing her in his arms, Hazel blushed. "What? Go where?"

"The clinic. Stay away from it."

Hazel sighed, relieved he wasn't reading her mind, which he sometimes seemed to be able to do. "Listen, Snoopy, you have your way of helping the poor, and I have mine. While the idea of raiding trash cans may be alluring, I think I'd rather keep my hands clean." She was being rude again and knew it.

His eyes darkened, and his face reddened. "I see. You think that's all I do?"

She shrugged. "I don't know what you do."

Stanley pulled a folded copy of what he'd typed up for *The Knights Voice* from his pocket and handed it to her.

Hazel's head pounded when she saw that the articles were about Evelyn and her diary. "What's this... I don't want to know."

"It's for a paper. One that will print the truth."

"This looks like trouble."

"We got trouble. We were supposed to be a team. But you're all screwy right now. Even your dad is helping. He's behind this paper we're gonna print." He stepped closer, searching her eyes, as she rubbed her forehead. "Head hurt again, huh?"

Hazel nodded. Stanley's face went from scrutiny to concern.

"They're in your head." He reached up to lightly brush her forehead with his fingertips.

She stepped away. "What's that supposed to mean?"

"Legion. They work with darkness… the occult."

"No. That's all nuts and superstition."

"It isn't." His face was grim. "I saw it around Charles the night he killed Evelyn."

"Charles is in prison. The others will steer clear of us, because people would start to suspect there was more to the story if anything happened to us now. Wouldn't that be bad for the VP?"

"They're not afraid of us or what it looks like, because they control the papers and the police. Look, we got all the info from the diary we need. There are other things I'm learning. Underground forces at play."

Hazel shook her head. "What's all this got to do with the clinic and their work for the poor?"

"The Winnowing. Eugenics. You know that word?"

"No…"

"Means they decide who lives and dies. They decide who breeds."

Hazel thought of the pamphlets she had seen, and her head hurt again. "Oh… but this is where people come for help."

"You know something isn't right here. Nobody's seen Teeth since he came to this place."

Something stopped Hazel from saying that it was also the last place she'd seen Maxie. "Doctor Galton drove him home, himself. You can ask Teeth's father, the doctor said he talked to him."

"Teeth's daddy? He's with the CCC, working out west, Bananas. The doc lied to you."

"Wait… the CCC?" Hazel shook her head.

"The Civilian Conservation Corps that Prez Roosevelt put together for men out of work."

"But the doctor said… There must be a reasonable explanation."

"For a lie? Sure. Deception is a fairly reasonable explanation. Especially when you're hiding the fact that you're evil." Stanley's voice rose and emphasized the last word.

No. It couldn't be true. "Evil! Listen to you. You think everyone is in on some plot? Some of us are just trying to help." Hazel's heart sped up, and a splitting pain made her grab her head.

"Haze…"

She shut her eyes. "Stop! Don't say anything else."

Stanley's eyes grew wide, and he stepped back with his hands up. "Okay, Bananas. Okay…" A look of fear passed over his face. He kept his eyes on her and pulled a handkerchief out of his pocket. He held it out, a white flag of surrender. "Your nose is bleeding, Haze."

Alarmed, she reached up and felt blood pouring from her nose that was now running down her chin. She took the handkerchief and pressed it to her face.

"I'm scared for you…" he breathed raggedly.

She squeezed her eyes shut. "Just a bloody nose that's all."

"Yeah… With horrible head pain, confusion, memory loss, and total personality change."

"I need to go see the doctor." She gestured toward the door to the clinic.

"Don't…" Stanley stepped forward, eyes pleading.

Hazel wanted to tell Stanley to get lost—to leave her alone, so she could go back to a happy and uncomplicated life.

"Miss? Do you need assistance?" It was Jennings. He had gotten out of the Buick and was glaring at Stanley.

"Just a nosebleed. I—I'm okay," Hazel said.

"She's aces. Just take her home." Stanley positioned himself to block her from walking toward the clinic. He lowered his voice and spoke to Hazel. "Just go on home and lay down, Haze. Okay?"

She was angry and confused, but exhausted. "Okay…" She raised her voice to her chauffeur. "All right, Jennings. I'd like to go home. Be there in a beat." Hazel mopped around her nose with the handkerchief.

The older man bowed his head and walked back to the long, black automobile, waiting by her door.

Stanley sighed with relief. "I know you're sore at me. But… I'm just trying to protect you. I don't want to lose anyone else," he said, choking up.

"Teeth will show up," Hazel said, surprised by his emotion.

Stanley rubbed his face with a bleak expression. He shook his head. "Vinnie. He's dead. They found him hanging from the rafters along with everyone else at the Rookery."

Hazel gasped and lowered the handkerchief from her face. "Stanley."

The tall, tough-looking newsie stared back at her, nodding, eyes washing over with tears. He pressed his lips together and swallowed before forcing out the words, "He's gone, Haze. Funeral done… threw a handful of dirt over him, myself, just this morning…" He stared down at his hand and flexed it, as if clutching a handful of something.

"No… I didn't know. I'm so sorry." Hazel wanted to grab Stanley and hug him tight until they both had all the answers, and the pain went away. He had helped her save her best friend and then lost one of his own without her even knowing it. It made her heart ache. "Everything is out of whack. I—I don't know what's happening."

"Then you aren't paying attention." Stanley's jaw clenched. "I need you back, Hazel. And I'm gonna figure out how to fix whatever they're doing to you."

"I'm confused—to me? Charles kidnapped me but—"

"Not just him!" Stanley's face went dark. "I'll take on the whole pack of swells on Lindell, the Veiled Prophet, and Legion, but I won't let them have you. They won't take your soul and mind while I'm around. Got it?" He punched his fist into his open palm.

"My soul and mind?" Hazel furrowed her brow and shook her head. What did he mean by that?

"Yeah. And it burns me to see them make you bleed again."

Hazel didn't know what to say to that nonsense. He was clearly not well—upset. Her nose had stopped bleeding, but her head felt as if it was in a wine press. She took a deep breath. "I need to lie down. I feel ill, and I have to be in the parade later… Sorry about the handkerchief. I'll get you a new one." She walked off-balance to the Buick, and Jennings opened the door.

Stanley watched her, his whole body tense, cap curled in his fists in front of him. For a moment, she saw him as an untamed lion. His unshaved face was aflame, strawberry blond hair scattered in a mess like it did when he fretfully ran his hands through it. His eyes burned like a hot summer sky.

Geez, but he was beautiful and fierce. Too bad he was out of his mind.

CHAPTER ELEVEN

Stanley sipped his coffee at the worn out diner with a grim smile of satisfaction. The pea shooting at the parade the night before couldn't have been more fun. He'd launched a perfect shot into Hazel's hair as she waved from the float. She'd picked it out her hair, made a comical face, and mouthed something that seemed like "Stanley." It gave him hope to see a glimpse of her old self. He knew he could free her from whatever curse was on her.

Writing that paper gave him another kind of hope. Maybe getting the truth out would pierce the darkness. If people knew, they would fight too. He needed to get to the church, pick up copies of the first edition of *The Knights Voice,* and give them to the newsies.

He slapped a nickel on the counter of the diner and walked out into the nippy, morning air. He moved briskly through the streets, whistling "Still I'm Traveling On" by the Mississippi Sheiks, his favorite blues band. Something about the blues and jazz spoke to him and his soul. The cry of sadness from the blues mixed with the wild creativity of jazz seemed to fit him somehow. He and Hazel had long talks about music and what they liked. She was into Cole Porter and all that, the popular stuff. But they both spent hours listening to each other's favorites at the Malloy mansion.

Crums, he missed her. He couldn't wait to get the old Hazel back.

He got to St. James Church and found the bundle of newspapers outside of Father Timothy's study. More would be coming as Mr. Malloy's printing press and carefully selected crew got up to speed. But it was a start.

Stanley took one of the one-sheet papers and shook it out. With grim satisfaction, he saw his article with the byline of "Arthur Roundtable," a name he came up with, thanks to Frisky and her loud mouth.

He grabbed the bundle and threw it over his shoulder. He hiked to Lindell, where he found Jakob ready and waiting.

"Hey, Cat-Lick, what's the lowdown?"

Stanley smiled. "First of the papers, you Hebrew school dropout."

Jakob pretended to be outraged. "I was held back!"

They both laughed, as Stanley dropped the papers down.

"So, just put this in with the normal papers, is that it?"

Stanley nodded. "Yeah, and the key is, don't stay in one place. That way, they'll have a tough time figuring out who sold them what. We want to be as faceless as possible."

Jakob nodded, and he picked up one of the papers. "Well, if we got a black branch, they know where we live anyway. But I'll make sure these are spread out." He read some of the headlines and gave a low whistle. "You guys aren't pulling any punches, are ya?"

"Nope. Father says we have to hit them hard. And he's probably right."

Adjusting his yarmulke, Jakob gazed up and down the road.

"Well, the morning papers should be here any moment. And the ball is tonight. What are you going to do about Hazel going with that Gabe twit?"

Stanley shrugged. "I don't know. But whatever happens, I have to help her. I think she's been cursed."

"Huh. No Foolin'?"

"Yeah, that's what Father Timothy thinks. And he seems to know all about that stuff."

"Father Timothy. Say, that reminds me. I saw him coming out of my Synagogue the other day. I think he was meeting with my Rabbi. Wonder what's shaking?"

Stanley thought for a moment. "I think he's gathering all the help he can get. The way these people think spells trouble for anyone that doesn't have piles of cash."

Jakob nodded but didn't say anything for a moment. "You know, we've got relatives in Germany. And they've been writing to us constantly about what's going on over there with that Hitler cat. Their stores are being vandalized, and Jews are getting beaten up in the streets. And afterward, everyone goes deaf and dumb. They're thinking about coming here, but I'm not so sure that's a good idea, after what I've seen."

Stanley wished he could argue with his friend, but he couldn't. The whole thing seemed connected somehow, and even the land of the free and home of the brave didn't seem all that it was cracked up to be. Never was really, for anyone who didn't fit the profile.

"Well, let's let them know they haven't won yet, shall we?"

Jakob grinned. "Sounds aces, professor. I'll be seein' ya. Go save the Princess of Lindell."

Stanley started to walk away and then turned around. "Any word on Teeth?"

"Nah. I ain't see Artie either, which is not usual. He's always prowling about. Don't you think he's been acting a bit strange?"

Stanley snorted. "You mean, more than usual?"

"Yeah, I do. I mean, he just seems unhinged lately. Usually, you can talk him down, but after the past few days, I dunno."

Shoving his hands in his pockets, Stanley frowned. "Yeah, I know. Something is up. And Teeth going missing hasn't helped. I wish we could find that kid. I kept my eyes peeled after the parade last night, but no dice. That was usually his favorite thing ever—he's a great shot."

They both stood there for a moment, and then Jakob bent down to cut the string on the paper. "Well, get going, Lord Stanley. Your damsel is waiting."

"Ah, Geez, are you fellas ever going to let that one go? Damn Frisky and her motor mouth."

Jakob burst out laughing. "She's got your number, Irish."

Stanley followed the familiar path through Forest Park to the boxcar. He needed to do some writing before he visited Hazel. She would be getting ready for the ball later, and he wanted to see her before she went.

The inside of the boxcar was chilly. He pushed the door open to let in the morning light. Stanley sat at the typewriter a moment, deep in thought. He was finally getting his words published. This was his first taste of being a reporter. Even if his name would remain unknown—his message would be heard. There were wrongs to be righted in his town, and it felt good to be a part of that. Especially since he was not doing it alone. Father Timothy, Mr. Malloy, and the others were facing it all too.

After a few hours of typing, he put away the typewriter and jumped down from the boxcar. How, he wondered, was he going to break the curse on Hazel? He assumed that if he found a branch, he could destroy it the way the priest had.

Hopefully Mr. Malloy would be home, and he could explain, because he couldn't just barge right into Hazel's room. No one would allow him even close to the upstairs. Even though the servants loved him, they considered themselves protectors of Miss Hazel's virtue. Not that he wanted to take advantage; he just wanted to help her get back into her right mind.

A picture of kissing Hazel swam into his mind. Okay, he thought, maybe he did want to take advantage a little.

Stanley grinned and made a decision. On the walk to Hazel's house, he found the nearest pretzel vendor and bought one. He remembered how they'd shared one of these the night they met after finding Evelyn dead by the statue of St. Louis. Hazel had been so upset. It helped knock down the walls between them and calm her down. Maybe it would work the same magic again.

When he reached Hazel's house, he decided he wanted to confront her alone. Stanley realized that he could just climb up the ivy trellis to her window the same way she climbed down the first time he saw her. No one seemed to be standing guard on that side of the house, so he snuck through the bushes, ran to the wall, and started up. He reached the window and pushed it open. Peering into her room, he didn't see Hazel anywhere. So he crawled through the window and walked over to her bed.

Before he searched for the black branch, Stanley gazed all around Hazel's room. Framed pictures of movie stars lined her mantle and dresser. She had a shelf full of books and a newer-looking phonograph near her bed. He wondered if she listened to records at night. Her gown for the VP Ball lay draped over the fancy, satin covered bed. Her room was posh, and how.

He took a deep breath; the room smelled like her, and it almost made him dizzy. Before he could compose himself, Hazel walked into the room, wearing only a silk slip, as she pulled the last few curlers from her hair. She caught sight of him and gave a little scream.

"Stanley, what in the world? You masher, you need to leave right now."

He put up his hands. "Easy, Lady Bananas, I'm not here for your virtue. Put your robe on. Something is cursing you, and it's in this room. I need to find it."

She grabbed a frilly, pink robe off the back of the chair at her vanity and threw it over herself, tying it in a hurry. "This is getting ridiculous."

Stanley faced her, as serious as possible, trying not to think about how she'd looked in her slip. "Haze, it's true. There are unnatural forces at work, and you know it."

She crossed her arms and let out a sigh. "Fine. Have your look around and then go. And why, Mr. Street Rat, could you not have used the door like a normal, civilized human being?"

Stanley grinned. "Because no one would've believed me and would never have let me up here."

She snorted. "For good reason. I think this is just an excuse to see me in my slip."

"As pleasant as that was, I'm not here for that."

He walked over to the bed and moved the piles of downy pillows aside. Then he pulled the billowing comforter back. Nothing. He scratched his head. If they wanted long term control of Hazel, they would put the cursed item out of sight. Stanley knelt down and looked under the bed. Reaching beneath it, he felt around until his fingers brushed something tickly and soft that sent a shock up his arm. Fighting the urge to yelp and draw back, he grasped it pulled it out. It was a large, pure white feather with what looked like dried blood on the tip. It wasn't a black stick, but this had to be it.

"C'mere, dollface."

Hazel held her robe to her chest. "Not a chance, pal."

Stanley sighed in frustration. "Look, Haze, I have other things in mind other than making woo to you." He stood and held up the feather so that she could see it. "They're cursing you and trying to control your mind. You're in serious danger, and that's facts."

She let out a laugh, but her eyes darted to the feather uneasily. "Oh come on, Stanley, that's just superstition. I seriously doubt the VP has time to go around putting feathers under people's beds."

"Okay, little Ms. Know-It-All, how did it get there?"

Hazel didn't answer for a moment. "I… I don't know. Probably… I don't know."

She grimaced and touched her head. "Ugh. Headache. You always give me a headache."

"It isn't me, at least, not this time. They're using this to control your mind."

He dug into his pocket and pulled out the small vial of holy water he had gotten from Father. Stanley glanced around and then took the feather over to the porcelain bowl on Hazel's dresser. He placed it in the bowl, relieved to put it down. He wiped his hand off on his pants. That thing had a serious bad buzz. He sprinkled it with holy water and then reached into the jacket of his coat for his lighter.

"What are you doing?" Hazel asked, pressing her hands against her temples.

Stanley flicked the lighter.

"Don't." She shook her head as if in pain. "Stop. You're gonna burn the house down." She moved toward him, hand outstretched with a frantic look on her face.

Gritting his teeth, Stanley lit the feather on fire, and to his surprise, it burst into flame on contact and burned to ashes in seconds.

Hazel bumped into his back, and he turned. Her face had drained to white, and her eyelids fluttered, her eyes rolling back. She stumbled, and Stanley caught her. Carrying her over to the bed, he laid her down and smoothed out her hair. Her body trembled and then went still.

Stanley sat there for a few minutes, staring at her face and watching her breathe. A flood of thoughts and feelings flowed through him, coming so fast he couldn't process them. He felt tired, exhausted, elated, and worried. What would she be like when she woke up? Did burning the feather help? Would it be better?

Risking a slap to the face, he kissed her softly on the forehead. "Come back to me, Lady Bananas, we have to go to war."

She stirred but didn't open her eyes. "Stanley. I've been wandering in the dark. I've been so awful."

"No, it's okay, it wasn't you. I know it wasn't you," Stanley whispered.

Hazel moaned and then lay still. He waited for a few minutes, then took her hand. It was cold and limp. "Hey, come back to me."

She slowly opened her eyes, and they looked clear, blue, and full of light again.

"Oh. Boy. You're here. I thought I was dreaming."

"Maybe I'm the man of your dreams, dollface," Stanley said, smiling.

She sat up and looked down at where he grasped her hand. "Don't get your hopes up, street rat." But she said it the way she used to, with affection and without pulling her hand away.

Stanley let out a breath of relief and squeezed her hand. "Hazel."

They stared at each other for a moment. He sat beside her on the bed and leaned toward her. She pressed her nose into his, and he could feel her breath on his lips. He breathed her in.

"You really shouldn't be here, you know. Pops would flip."

"Maybe," Stanley said, touching her cheek.

"Oh, Stanley. I feel like I've been on a long journey."

"You're home."

"Finally." She closed her eyes and kissed him with an intensity that overwhelmed him. Stanley held her tight to him and cradled her against his chest. He was kissing Hazel. His heart seemed to burn like his tattoo.

"I feel safe here, Snoopy," she whispered between kisses.

"You are safe. Always with me."

They kissed again, gentler this time. He could tell she hadn't done a lot of kissing. He'd kissed dames with experience, but this was better. Way better. More passion and less guarded, while not demanding anything else. It was honest and innocent.

This was a new experience for him. He'd been used to surviving, nothing feeling quite right. But with Hazel, everything felt right, in place, and at peace. Real.

As he held her, feeling her warmth, he knew why her recent weirdness threw him so badly. Because it had broken that safe place in half. Now, here she was again, herself. Beautiful. Unique. Different. Home. She was home.

How can I tell her all this without sounding like I'm totally full of malarkey?

Stanley remembered the pretzel. He pulled back and gazed down into her eyes.

"Stanley, what…" Hazel said, reaching toward him.

He took her by the hand and stood her up. Reaching into his pocket, he pulled out the half mashed pretzel.

"Look, Lady Bananas, the breaking of bread, well, you know, it's sacred to us Catholics. It binds us to Christ. Sharing food with someone is the second most intimate thing you can do." He winked.

Hazel acted shocked. "Stanley!"

He grinned, and then feeling shy, he held it out to her. "Share this with me, Bananas. Let's make a sacrament, you and I."

She looked at him for a moment and then nodded. Hazel broke off a piece of the soft, salty bread. She paused, placed one hand over her heart and then put the piece of pretzel up to his mouth. He ate it without a word and then did the same for her with one hand over his own pounding heart. Stanley felt his last bit of fear ebb away. Hazel was back. And she felt the same about him.

They grabbed each other and held on.

"Haze, it was awful to see what they did to you. They were controlling your heart and mind, the best parts of you. I couldn't stand it. I had to try to get you back, even if it meant you would never speak to me again."

She ran her fingers through the back of his hair. "Shhh, boy, I know. I'm back. I'm sorry."

"So am I. I know I'm not much, but I'm all yours, you know. You gonked me from the minute I first saw you."

Hazel sniffled, and she gripped him so hard that he gasped. He found her lips again and lost himself in the one girl he knew he'd never shake.

CHAPTER TWELVE

Hazel clung to Stanley, kissing him back. It was natural but exciting… like dancing to her favorite song. Tingles ran from her toes up her body and went to her head like the bubbles in a champagne glass. No… not bubbles. Sparks.

This was nothing like the cool, silver kisses on the big screen. Pressing against Stanley was like embracing summer in all of its color. With eyes closed, it felt like the hot, wet breath of a July night soaked into her skin, while fireflies flashed and rose like sparks from a campfire out of the intensely green grass that pushed up from the fertile ground.

She was floating, waving like branches in a cloudless sky, roots twining around the boy who held her so tight they seemed to fuse together in a tangle of arms, minutes, breaths, and heart-beats.

Stanley broke the kiss and buried his face in her neck. She breathed in the smell of his hair. The scent of the outdoors, ivory soap, and salty sweat.

"Gee whiz, you're swell," she sighed.

"That isn't news. Where've you been?"

She let out a quiet laugh. "Here, in my castle."

"While I've been fighting in the St. Louis crusades." He pulled her closer. "But we found each other, Haze."

His hair was long on top and unruly. She ran her fingers through it, thinking how strange it was that they were ever apart. Tears stung her eyes, and she let out a long sigh.

"How is it that anything ever seemed like a wall between us?" she whispered, pressing her cheek to his.

"Walls are taught, Lady Bananas," he said.

"I see through them now." She trailed her fingertips down his neck.

"Maybe because I took a jack hammer to them." His voice was deep and content.

Hazel snorted happily. "I like that, wisey. I remember the guy who said all swells were mosquitos living off the backside of hardworking folks."

Stanley chuckled and pulled away to look at her. His eyes were bluer than ever and shining. "Yeah. I guess we both had a kind of spell on us."

"I like whatever this spell is better." Hazel smiled up at him, and Stanley smiled back. They stared into each other's eyes for several moments, peaceful and exhilarating all at once. It was like looking into herself and into Stanley at the same time. Up on her toes, she kissed him again, her heart glowing. His arms tightened around her, and all Hazel knew was the feel and taste of his lips and the rush of her heart and breath.

"Stanley…" Hazel murmured between kisses. "What if this really is a spell?"

"I'm aces with this one." He grinned, his hand moving to her hair.

"Mumsy always said love is like witchcraft…" Hazel pulled back, realizing she'd said the word love. Flustered, she rushed on, "Mumsy is funny." Though lately, her mother wasn't very funny at all. "Say… Stanley, my mom's been acting strange."

"Hm?" The tall newsie was busy staring at her mouth.

"Snooty with Peggy and bossy with the other servants. She's been pushing me to be a debutante."

"Ah." He squinted and freed Hazel from his arms. "Check under her bed."

"Wait here, Snoopy." Hazel slipped out into the long hallway. Barefoot, she made her way to Mumsy's room without making noise.

The door was open, and nobody was inside. The maid had cleaned it and made the bed, but the vanity was scattered with cosmetics, and Mumsy's floral perfume floated in the air. She must have already gotten ready for the ball and was downstairs.

Hazel approached the raised bed, piled with satin and fur pillows. Lowering to the ground and lifting the lace skirting, she scanned the shadows under the bed. It only took a moment before she saw it. Resting in a place where Mumsy's head would be above it, was a white plume with a rusty edge that she knew was dried blood. Hazel reached out and pinched it between her fingers.

She shivered in disgust. Someone had crept into her mother's room and placed this awful thing there. Hazel wondered if her father was an intended target too. He had been helping Stanley and acting normal so it hadn't worked. Perhaps because he was gone a lot and even when he was home, she doubted he slept in Mumsy's room very often. Hazel had stumbled onto their love nest in the guest house years ago. It seemed Mumsy liked her love to be clandestine—even with her own husband. Nicholas Malloy probably had to do a lot of things to keep Mumsy from being bored. Hazel wrinkled her nose.

She returned to her room with the feather. Stanley looked up from where he sat on her bed. His face brightened. "Took you long enough, Bananas."

"I was quick." She held up her find.

"Not quick enough for me. Missed you." He hopped up and kissed her cheek then took the feather from her fingers. "Bingo."

"This explains so much. Stanley... I'm nervous. I don't want to meet the Veiled Prophet. He has powers..."

There was worry on his brow, but he said, "No problem. Just go be a snooty debutante—you're a natural." He gave her a wink.

Hazel smirked. "Thanks."

Stanley made a face at her, amused with himself. "Act like they still have you in their pocket. I'll take care of this thing." He shook the feather. "Baby, you finish getting ready."

"You sure?" She liked that he called her baby.

"Yeah." He winked and put his cap back on his head. "I'll be there lurking to make sure you're safe."

Hazel smiled despite the nervous tickle in her stomach. The Veiled Prophet Ball was a big deal and enough to make any girl nervous. But on top of everything else, Hazel knew that there was nothing good behind that veil. The ball could get dangerous for her. Then she remembered what she'd heard Arthur say to Sandy. "Arthur is planning something. I forgot all about it with this brain fog business. But I heard him ask Sandy if she'd help him do something at the ball, and she said she would. Sounded like some kind of revenge on everyone who had hurt them."

"That doesn't sound rosy." Stanley scratched his head. "Look, let me worry about that. Arthur listens to me. I'll see what's going on."

"Okay..." Hazel was unsure but determined to make up for lost time and do whatever it took to stop The Winnowing. "I'll do my part." She smiled bravely.

Stanley gazed at her as if enjoying the view. "By the way… you're beautiful. Radiant. The loveliest girl I've ever seen." He traced her cheek with his finger. "Been wanting to say that ever since I saw you that day you crawled out the window."

Hazel blushed. She could listen to that kind of thing all day long. For some reason it was different when Stanley said it than when anyone else did. "Thank you, Snoopy… Ever since the first time I noticed you selling papers, I knew you were for me. Deep down. Just took me awhile to realize what I was feeling."

Stanley grinned. "Well, she's pretty but a little slow, God bless her."

Hazel wrinkled her nose and gave his shoulder a push. "Rudest boy in St. Louis."

"As long as that's okay with you." He gave an apologetic side smile.

"You're okay with me. All of it."

He grinned and kissed her. "Just don't forget about me at your fancy dance with that frat boy of yours."

"I have an idea." Hazel went to her vanity and picked up the string with the Joan of Arc charm on it that Stanley had given her on her birthday. "I'm going to wear this with my elegant getup to remind me of who I am and to take you with me tonight. In fact… I may never take it off."

"Yeah? On the level?" A faint blush rose on his face, and he looked down at his shoes for a moment. "I know it isn't diamonds… I like you wearing it."

"I like it too." Hazel hugged him tight, pulling strength from him for the night ahead. Her mind was clear for the first time in weeks, and her heart had never been so sure.

"What a lot of nonsense all of this pomp is," Mumsy muttered. "High hats on parade. Don't let 'em infect you, Hazel."

Hazel sighed happily. Mumsy was back to being the rebel flapper. They walked arm in arm into the new Municipal Auditorium. Everyone had been talking about the new home for the VP Ball. It had just opened that year and cost millions of dollars to build. It could hold over nine thousand people, making it one of the grandest buildings in St. Louis.

Gabriel waited for her in a tuxedo at the entrance. "I'm at a loss for words, Hazel. You're the most beautiful girl here."

"Thanks, Gabe." It didn't matter what he thought. She took his arm, and he led her inside.

Upon passing the arena, Hazel was dazzled by what she saw through the doors. All of the finest people, done up like peacocks, filled a vast room, surrounded by stadium seating. There were candelabras and large vases with flowers on pedestals everywhere. On the far end of the auditorium was an elaborate stage with terraced steps and vast pleated curtains, and in front of that was the throne of the Veiled Prophet.

He sat, robed in layers of white, gold, and purple satin, wearing a lace veil over his face. A crown sat over the veil. Beside him was the empty throne, awaiting the Queen of Love and Beauty. Behind him were lined his Bengal Lancers in their cartoonish Middle Eastern costumes and false beards, holding large, ostrich feather fans on staffs. Hazel remembered how Charles had been one of those guards the year that Evelyn had been crowned.

They made their way to the back of the stadium. Gabriel leaned close to her ear. "This is where I leave you. Dazzle them." He beamed at her and brought her hand to his lips to kiss it.

Hazel gave him a smile. "See you later on the dance floor."

Hazel and the other debutantes were ushered to a roped off area behind the stage. Several men dressed as Bengal Lancers circulated, offering the girls a mint or dabbing the sweat on their brow, telling them how beautiful and special they were. It gave her the heebie-jeebies.

Hazel just wanted this part to be over with. She had been briefed on the ceremony. As one of the maids of honor, she was not in the running for Queen, but would be witness to a sort of mock wedding, where the groom is the one in the veil. While the other girls quietly whispered in excitement, Hazel filled with dread. How could she face the VP?

They waited behind the golden curtain until one by one, they were announced by name and paraded out to much applause from the crowd. When Hazel's name was announced, she passed through the curtain, overwhelmed by the size of the room and the people filling it. It felt like how she imagined the Roman Colosseum.

An orchestra played pompous music as she walked across the stage toward the Veiled Prophet, her heart banging in her chest. Hazel lowered herself in a curtsy. The Veiled Prophet raised his white-gloved hands to her.

"You are most welcome here, beautiful Hazel." His voice was low and breathy.

She bowed her head in reverence. They needed to believe she was still under their thrall. "I am honored," she whispered.

He presented her with a small, flat box tied with a gold ribbon. Hazel took it and backed away to take her place among the others. There was no chance she'd bring the little box home. It was probably another curse. Once all of the maids of honor were seated on the stage, The Keeper of the Jewels, flanked by costumed trumpeters, gestured to the orchestra to be quiet. It was time to announce the special maids.

Reading from a scroll, he heralded the next girl. "His mysterious majesty, the Veiled Prophet, summons Margaret Busch to his Court of Love and Beauty," he announced.

Margaret emerged, the long train of her gown carried by two liveried pages, and approached the Prophet. Bowing in a deep curtsy, she knelt as the faceless Mystic placed a feathered crown on her head. The entire routine was repeated for each of the twelve special maids.

Then a hush of expectation fell over the cavernous auditorium. The Keeper of the Jewels held his scroll high. "The fairest maid of his beloved city, our Queen of Love and Beauty, Jane Wells."

There was a gasp and a flutter of fans like countless moths flitting across the crowd. Hazel did not know Jane, but her reputation was stellar. She did a lot of charity work and was a state champion in track and field, as well as one who received high marks in school. She had graduated from the Mary Institute a couple of years ago.

Jane Wells glided toward the Veiled Prophet as if on a cloud. Her glossy, blond head bowed before the man in the throne. The Veiled Prophet leaned close as she knelt at his feet, and he slipped the crown with the white feather over her head and whispered into her ear. He stood and took her hand, and Jane rose, her face shining with excitement as the auditorium thundered with applause.

The orchestra began to play, and Jane was led to the dance floor by her veiled master. They danced the Royal Quadrille, turning and floating, on display for all to envy. Hazel's eyes wandered over the people crowded into the huge arena. Some were familiar to her, but most were not. Her city was full of rich and powerful people with whom she had never interacted. Which of them were part of the whole underground society and The Winnowing?

Jane's dance with the Veiled Prophet ended with more applause, and they ascended the stage again. The Keeper of the Jewels brought the Veiled Prophet a black, velvet box which he opened and reached into. He pulled out a stunning, pearl necklace. Jane covered her mouth with a gloved hand, eyes wide. As the necklace was put around her neck, like a noose, Hazel thought, the crowd clapped and murmured with approval. It was not that long ago that Evelyn Schmidt stood in Jane's place. On top of the world. Most admired and beautiful in all of St. Louis. The VP had placed a ruby ring on her finger and sealed her doom.

Jane took her place of honor on the plush throne next to the robed man in the lace veil. The Bengal Lancers did a semi-comical marching routine for the entertainment of the assembly. Hazel scanned the auditorium again and saw Sandy with her escort, watching the proceedings with a dark look on her face. It was hours until the ball ended, and following it would a special midnight dinner for the maids of honor and the special maids, as well as some honored guests. Hazel had no intentions to remain for that.

Music began again, and the ballroom floor filled with couples. The maids were all dismissed from the stage to find their escorts who waited at the bottom of the stage steps for them. The next hour or so was fuzzy and strange in Hazel's mind. She felt detached and outside of her body.

Hazel danced with Gabriel and several of the boys of her set. She made mindless chit chat befitting a debutante and smiled when appropriate. It wasn't like other parties and dances. There was a solemn air of propriety and decorum. She flirted with Gabriel just the proper amount and nodded to all of the important people. But she was distracted by the veiled figure who seemed to loom over the entire auditorium and the thought that Arthur and Sandy were up to no good.

"Next dance, Hazel Malloy?" Gabriel grinned down at her, straightening his spectacles. His hair was slicked in place, and his tuxedo made him look like a leading man in a motion picture.

"Gabriel, I need to rest my feet for a minute. Do you mind?"

"Not a bit. Let me get you a drink. You're as beautiful as a bouquet of flowers, and we don't want you to wilt."

"You're a pip." Hazel smiled. Gabriel gave a slight bow and moved away, disappearing into the crowd.

Hazel searched the auditorium for Sandy. So far, nothing bad had happened, and although she trusted Stanley to intervene with Arthur, she was concerned about her friend. Everyone seemed to be having a good time, or rather, were succeeding at seeming to have a good time. She eyed Mr. Slayback with a circle of important men around them. They were the power in the city. Possibly in with the VP. She should probably try to wiggle her way into the Slayback's graces. It made her sick to think of, but it had to be done.

Brigitte Slayback glided by on the arm of her escort. She nodded at Hazel when their eyes met. It was time to get in with her. But how?

Hazel pictured her favorite actresses. Who could she be to approach Brigitte? Being Greta Garbo, Hazel would only come across superior or aloof and just anger her. Brigitte liked to be the tops. Hazel could be like Myrna Loy… no, too confident and smart. Jean Harlow… too saucy and perhaps cheap. Joan Crawford… yikes. No. She didn't want to scare her.

Carole Lombard it was then… a little dizzy, not intimidating, but classy.

"Oh, Brigitte. You look simply divine!" Hazel gushed as sincerely as possible, a bright smile on her face.

Brigitte did a slight double take and narrowed her eyes. She came to a stop and turned toward Hazel. It was impossible to ignore her, now that Hazel had been chosen as a maid of honor. "Hello. Where is Gabriel?" She glanced around the crowd as another song started up.

"Oh, he's getting me something to drink. Isn't it hot in here? I have no idea how you pull off looking so cool and so-phisticated all the time." Hazel fanned her face. "I'm always a mess even under the best of conditions." She giggled. "Your lip-stick is perfection. How do you get it to look so smooth?"

Ah, the power of flattery and self-deprecation. Brigitte's eyes lit up, and she smiled at Hazel. She turned to the young man beside her and gave him an irritated look. "Get me some-thing to drink too. This is girl talk."

The tall boy with slicked back hair nodded and drifted off with a look of relief on his face.

Hazel hooked her arm through Brigitte's. "Please tell me all your secrets. I'm hopeless, as you know." They walked to the edges of the crowd, while the dancers took the floor again.

The snooty blonde scanned her from head to toe and pursed her lips. "Well... not everyone has *sens de la mode*. That's no crime. Neither is that gown, by the way. Much nicer than I im-agined, considering who the designer was." She dropped this stale crumb with a look of benevolence and generosity.

Hazel forced a smile. "Truly? Thank you. That means so much. I haven't admitted this before, but I look up to you. I real-ized that the things you said about that newsie and everything else was true. You were just trying to help. I value good friends who are willing to say things I don't like."

Brigitte glowed. "Well, I do my best. We Lindell girls need to stick together. Say... I have an idea. Why don't you let me make you over?" Her eyes widened with her grin. It was almost frightening.

"That would be swell." Hazel nodded eagerly.

Regina Peck danced by with her date and glanced at the other two girls talking. Her face scrunched with confusion to see them smiling together.

Brigitte waved at her dark-haired friend and then turned to Hazel to snicker. "Regina thinks she is so posh. I tried to tell her that gown was a mistake, but she didn't listen. Her hips look as wide as the Mississippi in it."

Just like that, the social dynamics had flipped, and Hazel was giggling at being mean with the worst girl she knew. It was working. It reminded Hazel of how Henri laid down to show subservience to Mick to get his belly scratched.

After several minutes of Brigitte chatting about makeup and the right perfume to attract rich, frat boys, Hazel glanced around to see where the Veiled Prophet sat up on the stage, in his jeweled robes and lace-covered face, flanked by two Bengal Lancers. Even though the room was filled with hundreds of people and his face was covered, Hazel felt a chill, as if he watched her alone.

"Your family is one of the highest in St. Louis… do you ever wonder who the VP is?"

Brigitte gave a knowing smile and tugged the wrinkles out of her elbow-length, white gloves. She liked to seem important and be in the know. "Well… I'm pretty sure I heard my daddy talking to him once," she said in a low voice.

Hazel gasped. "On the level?"

"Yes. It was late at night, but I had sneaked downstairs for some warm milk. I heard him in his study on the telephone. So naturally, I pressed my ear to the door. He was saying things about who might be the chosen debutante and said something about donating to the 'great cause' or something. It all seemed very secretive."

"I'm so curious. You're the only person I could think of who is smart and connected enough to help me guess it."

Brigitte smirked. "There are theories flying about, of course. Anna Busch swears it's got to be the Governor. Some say it's one of the Lemps. Regina says her daddy comes and goes at odd times at night. She thinks he's having secret meetings with important people. But if you ask me, he's meeting with a burlesque dancer." Brigitte snorted. "Personally, I think it could be someone in law enforcement. It's been nothing short of a miracle the way the streets have been cleaned up lately."

"Like maybe the chief of police?" Hazel asked, her brain whirring. "Or the Chouteaus?"

Brigitte pursed her lips. "Well, that family has been disgraced by Charles, so I doubt they would have the privilege. Besides they've been living abroad for years now."

"Have they?"

"Yes, Germany, I believe… which is why Charles had been left to his own devices. His older brother lives in Boston or something… and the pressure of carrying the family business here must have cracked him," she rattled on, her eyes gleaming at having so much information to offer.

"I see…"

Gabriel appeared at Hazel's side with a crystal mug of red punch. "What are you girls gossiping about?"

"Oh, just speculating about the Veiled Prophet. Who do you think it is?" Brigitte simpered, fluttering her lashes at Gabriel.

"Ah. Well, that's the question isn't it? Not that it matters. It's only honorary. It changes constantly. Could be either of your dads at any given time." Gabriel straightened his bow tie and scanned the room. "Hm… who important is missing?"

It would be impossible to tell in a crowd so large, but it occurred to Hazel that he was basically right. Anyone and everyone of importance was invited. As she searched the familiar and recognizable faces around her, she spied Sandy slipping out of the auditorium.

Hazel handed her untouched drink to Gabriel. "I need to powder my nose. Brigitte, do you mind dancing with Gabriel and keeping him company?"

"Glad to," Brigitte purred.

Hazel hurried away before Gabriel could respond, weaving around the elegantly clad people who danced and talked in clusters. The smell of cologne and sweat mingled with the scent of champagne and wine. Sandy was wandering the halls of the building, her gown trailing behind her.

"Sandy!" Hazel called out over the sound of the live music and festive crowd.

Sandy whirled around with a funny look on her face, like she might burst into tears.

"Was looking for you," Sandy said, fidgeting with the emerald necklace around her neck.

Hazel let out a sigh. "This night is dragging. Having that creepy, veiled guy in the same room is unnerving. But I guess I expected something dramatic to happen."

Sandy bit her lip and looked up at the ceiling. "I'm not staying past ten. You shouldn't either."

Hazel studied her friend's face. There was a film of sweat on Sandy's brow, and she glanced around as if something might jump out at her. Whatever she and Arthur had cooked up was making her nervous.

"Sandy. I know you and Arthur are up to something."

"What? How? See here, I was going to tell you. This place is not going to be safe after ten o'clock. At least… not for some of these people. Promise me you're leaving before then."

Hazel's stomach dropped. "What's going to happen?"

"We're getting rid of the problem. Avenging my sister and what happened to us." Her response was flat and emotionless.

"How can you decide who needs to pay for it? Charles isn't even here."

"You sure about that?"

A tickle went down Hazel's arms. There were men in those ridiculous Bengal costumes all over the place. With those false beards and large turbans on, it was difficult to tell who they were.

"In my sister's diary, Charles was one of the guards, and he was serving the Prophet. What do you suppose all those fellas in there do after hours?" Sandy scowled, pointing to where the music was coming from.

"Whatever you're thinking about doing… don't."

"All I'm doing is opening a door." Sandy turned away, heading toward the back of the building with Hazel close behind. A couple guards walked the halls, but the exit doors were not blocked off.

"Sandy. Stop." Hazel hurried to catch up.

Her golden-haired friend stopped with her hands on the door and gave Hazel a serious look. "Find Mumsy and leave."

CHAPTER THIRTEEN

S tanley adjusted his bowtie in the bathroom mirror. He'd nicked the monkey suit from a row of them in the bowels of the Municipal Auditorium. He hoped that some poor server wouldn't get in trouble for losing the suit. But, from the looks of it, they were the spares.

In either case, he had no choice. Since Hazel told him about Artie, the back of his neck tingled, that curious sensation he got when something bad was about to happen. And the fact he had not seen his friend for a few days, with Teeth missing and everything else going on, worried him.

He still couldn't help feeling a twinge of jealousy when he thought of her dancing with that idiot Gabriel. She was so beautiful in her gown, and he hated that Gabriel would be ogling her body, which Stanley had so recently held tight to his own. Hazel was not just another hot tomato, and any mug who looked at her that way needed a poke in the nose.

But mostly he was worried for her. She had been so nervous about tonight, and it was hard to know what would happen with

Arthur on a possible rampage. Everyone would probably be watching, including Legion and the VP himself, to see if she was still in line. Stanley needed to watch Hazel without anyone noticing him, something a bit harder to do now that he was semi-famous.

Sighing, he gripped on to the sink, and his stomach rolled. Stanley closed his eyes, and pictures of the Rocky Mountains from the Civilian Conservation Corps brochure illuminated in his thoughts. Everything there looked so peaceful and uncomplicated. Just hard work, three squares, and beautiful hikes. No need to worry about any of this.

No. He would not run. He would not leave Hazel. He would never be able to live with himself… or without her.

Stanley stood up, adjusted his coat, and gave himself a smile. "You handsome devil. Go get 'em, killer."

He left the bathroom and found his way through the maze of tunnels to the server station. Grabbing a tray of waters, he went through the door and into the main auditorium. Stanley couldn't believe his eyes. The whole place looked like a cross between an Egyptian temple, a throne room, and an elegant ball, at least, as far as he imagined them. Everyone was dressed to the nines, and the debutantes wore long, colorful gowns that must have cost a fortune. Even though he knew there were okay swells out there, he felt like punching the whole room. The money spent on this event could have fed the entire neighborhood of Dogtown for a month, at least.

He took a deep breath and forced himself to focus and observe. Stanley zeroed in on the Veiled Prophet himself, draped in an outfit that looked vaguely like a bishop's robe: white, purple, and lined with gold. His face was covered in lace so that no one could see. Hazel hadn't been able to find the identity of the VP, but he doubted she would be able to. He was pretty sure that was a closely guarded secret.

The prophet looked back and forth over the ballroom. One of the weird lancers with a fake beard came up to the throne and prostrated himself. Stanley scoffed out loud and then lowered his head when it drew looks.

The whole scene unnerved him. The swells tried to pass this off as a huge game and fun, like the Mardi Gras parades of New Orleans. But this didn't even seem to come close. There was no fun, laughing, or joy anywhere. Instead, everything seemed rigid, controlled, and designed to demand obedience. Even the dancing seemed forced.

In fact, Stanley thought, *that was exactly what it was.*

He scanned the crowd for Hazel, and he finally saw her. She looked beautiful in her gown, talking with her mother. His heart did a little flip, and he thought of how they had kissed and shared a pretzel. She was his girl now.

Then he noticed the look on her face. Hazel was bending over Mrs. Malloy, gesturing toward the door, her face lined with worry. Hazel seemed to be trying to get Mrs. Malloy to go with her. But why? She was too far away to wave at, and if he didn't want to attract attention, he could whistle for her.

Maybe she didn't want to go to the bathroom by herself, he thought. But there was a tickling at the back of his neck.

The Bengal guard who had knelt at the VP's feet got up from the floor and said in a loud voice, "My lord, allow me to present, from the swamps of deepest Louisiana, and to show their complete submission to you as their lord and master, a group of Negroes who wish to play some of their quaint and backward music for you as an offering."

Stanley couldn't believe it. He didn't like how degrading that sounded. Would they really allow black people in here?

He watched as the musicians emerged from the crowd and saw shades of white peeking out from what he thought was black skin. Then he realized they were white people wearing black shoe polish. He'd seen this kind of performance before and used to think there was no harm in it. But one Sunday, Father Timothy preached a blistering sermon on dehumanizing people and used the so-called "black-face entertainment" as an example.

And now, Stanley saw why. The white musicians walked with exaggerated strides, with arms swinging, and they started dancing like fools. The whole thing was designed to make black people look almost ape-like and not human.

He scowled. The whole thing was more disgusting than he had ever realized. The crowd tittered with amusement.

Just as he was about to turn away, one of the musicians caught his eye. The kid carried a guitar case and didn't seem as in to it as the others. When they all took their place right near the throne, the guy with the guitar just stood there. And then Stanley noticed the black bowler on top of his head.

No. Holy Jesus, no.

Stanley moved fast through the crowd, shoving indignant swells aside. He burst onto the open ballroom floor. As he did, Arthur bent down, opened the case, and took out a tommy gun. He cocked it, the loud metal echoing through the silent ballroom. The crowd gasped but seemed unsure if this was part of the show or not.

Arthur yelled at the top of his voice, "For all the people you've killed, and the lives you've destroyed. For my dad. For my mom. For the Rookery. For Teeth and my pigeons. Death. Death and judgment."

Stanley ran toward his crazed friend, as the Bengal guards leaped in front of the Veiled Prophet and Jane Wells fell out of her throne, screaming.

As Arthur raised the gun to fire, Stanley launched himself at his back, hitting him hard. They fell to the ground in a tangle, and the gun clattered to the floor and slid a few feet away. The auditorium erupted in shouts. Arthur grunted and flailed angrily.

"What the hell are you doing, Artie? What the hell are you doing?" Stanley screamed, gripping his friend's wrists.

"What you can't, Lord Stanley. They deserve this. Let me do it. Get off me," Arthur raged, trying to scramble toward the gun. But Stanley was bigger and pinned him to the ground. A lancer clamored down from the stage and seized the gun.

The whole assembly had erupted in chaos, women screaming, and men shouting, fleeing from the auditorium. Someone grabbed Stanley from behind.

"You're under arrest, both of you. Get on your knees," a voice growled.

"But I didn't do anything, you bastard. I was trying to stop it."

The cop smacked him on the back of the head. "Enough. We saw you. You rushed the stage."

"You idiot flatfoot. Get your mitts off me," Stanley roared.

Another blow to the back of the head, and the cop wrenched Stanley's hands behind his back.

Stanley tried to get up, but a voice whispered in his ear, "Cut it out, boyo. I'm here to get you and this idiot outta here before someone kills you both."

He pushed Stanley through the commotion toward the door, while a uniformed cop dragged Arthur.

"Make way, folks, I'm taking these street rats downtown. Don't worry, they ain't getting out anytime soon, to be sure," Seamus said, pushing Stanley through the door.

When they got to the hall, Stanley said, "Seamus, I..."

"Shut your trap, boyo. This ain't the time to bump gums. Move your stupid, Irish ass."

Stanley bit back a reply and let his uncle lead him outside past staring and outraged swells to a squad car. The uniformed cop practically threw Arthur into the back, tossing his bowler hat into his lap, and then got in the front with Seamus.

Arthur settled his hat back onto his head with cuffed hands and turned away from Stanley to stare out the window.

"What the hell were you two thinking? You've blown it all up now." Seamus slammed his hands on the dashboard.

Before Stanley could respond, Arthur said, "This ain't on Stanley. He knocked me down before I could shoot." His face was covered in black shoe polish, and his eyes glinted with hatred.

"Well, now we're all in the fire," Seamus spat.

The squad car pulled away from the building as more cops arrived. The streetlights flicked rectangles of light across the floor of the squad car, like God dealing glowing cards that Stanley was afraid to pick up. They were in for it now.

"Why, Artie?" was all Stanley could manage.

Arthur shook his head. "That's a hell of a question for you to ask me, Stanley. You know why."

"Okay, fine, then how? How did you even get in?"

"I could ask the same of you, Lord Stanley." He gestured toward him with cuffed wrists.

Stanley shrugged. "It was easy. Found an open bathroom window and crawled in."

"Well, I had help," Arthur said with a thin smile.

"Help. You mean Sandy. What is it with you two?"

Arthur didn't say anything for a moment. His face twitched, as if he was fighting some sort of inner battle. Slumping his shoulders a bit, he said, "We've got a thing, that's all."

"So, you two planned this together? For what? Revenge?" Stanley said.

Chuckling, Arthur said, "Nah, not a bit. I've been planning this for a long time. I used my pigeons to gather all the info I needed, the ball, the program, the so-called 'Negro band.' But I needed a way in, and Sandy was more than happy to provide an open door."

"So, that's why you were making woo to her, to get an open door."

Arthur turned toward him and scowled. "She offered. I didn't ask."

"And the gun?"

"A parting gift from the Raven. Before they strung him up."

Stanley didn't know what to say. He always knew Artie walked the line between good and hate, but now he realized how serious it was. The kid had been ready to tommy gun a room of people. He just couldn't take in it.

On the other hand, a part of Stanley—that he hated—wished he'd never tackled Arthur. Let him finish the job.

"How many people have to pay for what Charles did?"

"Just the ones on the stage. For now." He raised his cuffed hands and wiped his arm across his face, leaving a smeared section of white.

Seamus piped in, "It was stupid, Arthur. Whatever revenge you may have gotten, you had to know what this will do to the entire city. It's going to tear it apart."

"We're already at war, don't you know that? Black people live on the margins in our city. Jews suffer persecutions. You Catholics should get that real well, as none of the Lindell set can stand you, 'papist trash,'" Arthur said, trying to mimic an upper class voice. "They have been at war for years, but it's been lop-sided, see? Nobody fighting back."

The cop next to him turned his broad face to them and said, "That is where you're wrong. Good people have been fighting them. Just behind the scenes."

Arthur sneered. "Yeah, and they're doing such a bang up job of it."

The car stopped. Stanley looked out of the window and saw the huge, green dome of the St. Louis Cathedral rising up above them.

"Why are we here?"

"A meeting," Seamus said, getting out of the car to open the back door.

Stanley stepped out onto the sidewalk, and the other cop pulled Arthur from the car.

"Can I get these off, please?" Stanley said, raising his cuffed hands.

Seamus unlocked both his cuffs and motioned toward the Cathedral. "Get inside. We're going to the crypt. And not a word."

"What about me?" Arthur shook his cuffed hands.

Seamus ignored him. The boys were lead into the Cathedral, and Stanley looked up. He couldn't help it. The mosaics on the spacious, arched ceiling always amazed him. Father Timothy told him that this church rivaled anything that he'd seen in his travels to Europe. And Stanley, while he preferred the cozy holiness of St. James, never got tired of coming here. But now the shadowed space felt ominous and condemning, as if the dark void above would swallow him up.

They approached the high altar, and Seamus and the cop bowed and crossed themselves. Stanley did the same, a stab of guilt in his chest. He felt to blame for what Arthur had done and how it put them all in danger now.

Arthur scowled over at Stanley and at everything around him and shrugged his shoulders. But he didn't run or try to get away as they went around the altar to the back of the cathedral.

Finally, they found themselves descending into the crypt. The small stone and marble space was full of people, including Father Timothy, Mr. Malloy, and Peggy again.

"Seamus, why are you here? Why did you bring them? They are not a part of the Order," a bearded man asked.

What Order? Stanley searched the faces of the people in the dim light of the crypt.

"This boy," Seamus said, gesturing at Arthur. "Tried to tommy gun the entire VP ball. The only reason he didn't kill someone is that Stanley knocked him down." His words echoed off the stone walls. With shocked faces, everyone stared at Arthur.

Arthur's cuffed hands twitched. He wanted a smoke. "See, I ain't gonna be part of another group. I'm tired of 'em. All you do is get in my way." He looked at Stanley. "Thanks for being my pal. But I ain't a Knight no more. I'm on my own. You can use my pigeons for info if you want, but I'm out."

"Artie, please. You swore your allegiance to the Knights." Stanley ran his hands through his hair. He never thought Arthur would welsh on him.

"Sorry, Stanny. I'm loyal to me. Time to make tracks."

The cop who had walked him into the crypt put a hand on his arm. "You stay put."

"I'm sorry to hear this, Arthur. I can't save you from the law if you go rogue." Seamus rubbed his face. "Isn't safe to have you wild."

In an instant, Arthur stomped on the cop's foot and then jerked his elbow back into his face. The man hit his knees with a groan, and Arthur darted from the room, his feet slapping a beat on the stone steps ascending from the crypt.

"Get after him!" Seamus shouted.

The cop jumped back up, hand to his face, blood running through his fingers. He turned and chased the sound of Arthur's retreat.

Seamus shook his head. "He won't get far. And if he does, he won't go anyplace without a tail. I have a few guys watching the place."

"He's slippery. Even in those cuffs, he might get away," Stanley worried aloud.

Seamus made a fist and cursed under his breath. "We have bigger fish to fry. Got enough to worry about without havin' to put on a manhunt for that fool."

Father Timothy raised his hand in a peaceful gesture. "Seamus, the boy has already set things in motion. Now we need to focus on what comes next."

Stanley wanted to go after Arthur, make him see reason. But something told him that he needed to stay. "Why was I brought in here? What is the Order?"

Father Timothy sighed. "You know Peggy … Perhaps she can tell you better than I can who we are, Stanley, and why Seamus brought you here, even if it was a bit premature."

Stanley scoffed. "Forgive me, Father, but I think Seamus did the right thing. I'm tired of being in the dark. I like writing for you and all, but I want to know who I'm working with."

Peggy played with her hands. "Stanley, there is so much to tell you. I don't know where to start."

"Try the beginning." He removed the jacket he'd worn as a disguise at the ball and leaned against the stone wall.

She sighed. "Well, we are an order, as you've been told. The Order of St. Michael the Protector… it started not long after the Veiled Prophet parade began."

Stanley nodded. "Okay."

"After the labor strike was shut down and broken and scattered, a group of men and women came together in the old cathedral, near the river, vowing to keep up the fight. That was long before my time, of course. Since then, we've had many members, including…" She paused a moment, as she looked at everyone in the chapel. Stanley could see that most of them were her age or older. He was the youngest in the room by far.

"Including who?" Stanley had that weird tickle on his neck again as Peggy walked toward him.

Peggy stood before him, her eyes connecting with his. "Including me and your father."

Stanley stared at her. "That's how you knew my dad?"

"It's how we met…" Peggy pulled out the St. Jude necklace that she wore around her neck. "He gave me this."

Stanley realized her necklace matched the one he wore. He hooked a finger on his own and held it up. "I got this from my…"

"Mother," she whispered with emotion.

He looked into Peggy's bright eyes and realization hit him. Why she seemed so familiar. How could he have not seen it before? His knees buckled, and he sank to the floor, overwhelmed. Stanley's mind turned inside out, and his heart felt as if it had burst open. He wasn't an orphan after all. He looked up at Hazel's Irish maid. "Are you really… my…"

Peggy knelt down and put her hands on his shoulders. She nodded, her eyes shining with tears, and a sad smile on her face. "I'm so proud of you. Your da would be so proud of you. All of us are. You gave us hope to gather again."

Stanley let her wrap her arms around him. "I didn't know…" A mix of emotions surged through him. He had so many questions… but there was a room full of people watching, and he felt tears coming. So he cleared his throat and pulled away a bit. "What happened? Why did the order end?"

Peggy frowned and stood, pulling him to his feet. "We were betrayed. And the VP hunted us down one by one. They murdered your father on that ship when he went to Ireland to ask for help. And they committed me to an asylum for 'hysterics.'"

"And that's when Seamus took me in." Stanley glanced over at his uncle who looked a bit teary himself.

She nodded. "He hid you for a while, so they wouldn't take you to an orphanage. He tried to visit me, but they wouldn't allow it. And then they took my baby…"

"Baby?" Stanley asked, not sure he wanted to hear the answer.

"Yes. You probably had a brother or sister. I'll never know. They took the baby from inside me and then made sure I could never give birth again. Then I was cast into the street. I told Seamus not to come near me, so they wouldn't suspect who you were. I met a wealthy woman on a streetcar one day, and she offered me a job, said she had a child, and needed all the help she could get. I was so bereft over losing my own children, and Mrs. Malloy was a wild young woman and didn't know what to do with a baby girl."

"Hazel," Stanley said, the connections of his life all falling into place. He looked over at a small icon of St. John, who supposedly wrote the book of Revelation. The poor guy had his whole view of the world changed in an instant. Stanley could relate.

He looked at Mr. Malloy with new understanding. "I can see why you didn't want Hazel hanging around with me…"

Mr. Malloy gave a mild smile. "Yes, imagine my surprise, Stanley, when Hazel mentioned your name for the first time. I had only learned of Peggy's past since becoming involved with the Order. I felt it was my duty to protect her secrets and you."

"That makes sense… does your wife know?"

"Gertrude is unaware that you are Peggy's son."

Son. The word hit Stanley with fresh meaning. His mother was alive.

Stanley dared to look at Peggy. The mother he never knew he had. She stared back at him and held out her arms. He stepped into them and let her hold him. Stanley didn't know what else to say, his brain locked, frozen, or had just fled the building. He didn't know whether to feel angry, happy, sad, or what. He felt numb in Peggy's warm arms. That seemed to be the safest emotion for the moment.

He pulled back and said, "I got your smile, don't I?"

Peggy grinned with tears. "Indeed you do, my boy."

Seamus coughed and rubbed his face. Trying to control his voice he said, "You've got William's eyes, lad. And his sass."

Peggy let out a chuckle. "Also true."

Father Timothy spoke up gently, "Not to interrupt this tender, family moment, but tonight changes everything. The war is on now, everyone. What happened to Peggy is happening to women all over the city."

"There are hundreds of cases we know of, most hard hit in the slums," said the man with the beard. A few others in the room nodded.

Father Timothy wrung his hands together. "It has been confirmed by my sources that the Sinclair maid, Maxie, was not shot like the papers reported. Rather she bled out after they took her ovaries, but the coroner filed a false report."

Stanley took that in. Anger sparked inside of him at the injustice and the deception.

"Thanks to Stanley, we have Evelyn's diary, and we better understand the master plan now. Sterilization is just one of the tools they are using to cleanse the city. But The Winnowing is much worse. The Vatican has authorized me to do what must be done to help the people of St. Louis."

Mr. Malloy chimed in, "What does that mean?"

"It means that I'm no longer required to obey the civil authorities, and I'm bound only by God's law. So we must carefully choose what is to be done. This isn't just about publishing a newspaper anymore. Arthur's open attack has put us all at risk and escalated our plan of action."

"He needs help, Father. Can you?" Stanley said.

Father looked at him for a moment and then slowly nodded. "I shall do my best, Stanley. I promise." Then he looked around the room. "I need all of your input in the next few days. We cannot decide anything tonight. Go home. Pray. Stanley, no more running things on your own. The Knights are to bring us information only and distribute the newspapers. As for you, lay low for the next few days and hide out. It's not safe for you after tonight."

Stanley frowned. He wanted to talk back about how he'd been doing just fine without anyone else's help. But, he realized, that was not entirely true. He'd been stumbling along in the dark without anyone to guide him in this mess. He just didn't want to admit that out loud.

"Okay, everyone, get home to your families. Be ready for when I call. Peggy, Mr. Malloy, and I will discuss the next meeting time. Go in peace." He blessed them, and they headed out, all except Peggy, Stanley, and Seamus.

"Thank the saints, you know everything, Stanley. I hated keeping it from ya, but it was for your own good," Seamus said, putting his arm on his shoulder.

Stanley nodded, but stared at his mother. His mother ... that seemed so strange to say. "I know you were tryin' to save me. But I needed you."

She nodded, tears spilling down her cheeks. "I know, Stanny. After they took the baby, I went crazy. When I got healthy, you were just five years old and still in danger. Seamus and I agreed it was for the best."

"The best." Stanley just didn't know what else to say.

"Yes, the best. Seamus might be a knob of the first order, but he did what he could, to be sure," Peggy said, giving him a half smile.

Seamus gave a sigh. "I didn't always have William's patience... and maybe I used the fist a bit much. But I wanted to make a man of you, while trying to be one myself and not always knowing how."

Stanley patted his uncle's back. He could be angry at Seamus, or he could accept that his best was all he had to give. "You did all right. You gave me a home."

"And I thank you again, Seamus, for looking after my boy all these years," Peggy said, sniffing back tears.

He was someone's boy. Tears rolled down Stanley's cheek as he looked at the woman who was his mother. She stepped toward him, and he met her in a hug. Stanley reached for Seamus. They clustered together and wept, with the only witnesses being the dead princes of the church.

Later, they ascended the steps out of the crypt, and it occurred to Stanley that this was a new life for him. One that had a family and a deeper purpose than ever before. He was a part of something that was bigger than anything he had done on his own. Stanley said, "I gotta get back to the boxcar and finish my article. I need to let my Knights know about the changes." A pang of regret went through him. Arthur would not be gathering with the Knights anymore.

"And I have to get back to the house and find Hazel," Peggy said. "I'll watch her for you." She winked.

"And I have to go explain to the Chief how you two got away," Seamus said, grinning a bit. "We need to find Arthur and lock him up, I'm afraid."

Stanley nodded. "That's the way it needs to be now."

"May St. Michael guide you both," Peggy said, right palm raised in a blessing.

CHAPTER FOURTEEN

The grass was cold through her gown. Hazel sat on the lawn outside of the lit-up building where the elite of St. Louis had been carefree and secure only minutes before. Dancing, talking, breathing, with no clue that death could swoop past their privilege and finery to snatch at them.

Now, they streamed out of the building, afraid, suddenly aware of their mortality. These people who survived the stock market crash. The indestructible ones. It didn't occur to those kinds of people that life was fleeting and could end suddenly and without notice, regardless of money or status.

That was a terrifying thought. But worse by far was to look at her best friend and not know her. How could she have thought such a horrific act of violence could be justified? Sandy stared up at the starry sky with a blank face, as tears streamed down her cheeks. Maybe she realized how insane this all was. Hope rose inside Hazel. It was just a strange moment of madness. Sandy was okay. She just needed to see a doctor and talk things out.

She looked up at her friend who paced a few feet away. "Sandy. You need help."

"I had help. They just took him."

"Not Arthur. This whole Bonnie and Clyde act isn't helping either of you. Can't you see how serious it is that you were about to allow him to kill people?"

"People? Parasites."

Hazel stood and faced Sandy. "Human beings. People with families and feelings."

"I have a family. I had a sister!" Sandy's voice came out fractured like broken glass, as if the words cut her throat to say.

"I know." Hazel's eyes stung as tears filled them. "You of all people know how much it hurts when someone takes away someone you love."

"He was going to aim for the stage. We just wanted the VP and some of his minions."

"So, eradicate them, not knowing who is truly responsible and then maybe some others in the process?"

"They're all the same."

"Just like all newsies are the same? All debutantes? All humans?"

Sandy scowled. "You know the oppression our class is responsible for."

"Some. Yes... most of them are guilty of being unaware more than anything. Why, I feel like I didn't know anything about life outside of my house until I met Stanley. I never meant to hurt anyone. Did you?"

"Sometimes," her friend admitted. "I liked making Flora and the rest cower and take orders. I sometimes went out of my way to give dirty looks to bums on the street."

"Oh..." Hazel thought about that. "Did they ever look back at you with hatred?"

"Sure. Some. I've had my share of harassers."

"Sounds like people need to learn how to treat each other better. It's easy to find fault wherever you look for it. And sometimes..." She thought of Stanley and how different they were. "It's easy to find the good too. If you don't make assumptions, and you give people a chance."

Sandy snorted. "The scales are not balanced, Hazel."

"No. They aren't. But if you do the same thing to other people that you hate them for—that makes no sense."

"People need to get what they deserve," she growled, the jagged scar down the side of her face wrinkling as she frowned.

"What would that look like... if we all got what we deserved? Does someone without work deserve a house and food? Do you deserve to be in prison for the stunt you pulled tonight? Think hard about that."

"You've got this all wrong. Someone has to make it right."

"Who's qualified to decide how? You? You can somehow make everything fair for everyone by killing off a handful of people who might be guilty of being unfair themselves?"

Sandy's eyes burned with rage. "Unfair? Unfair! They aren't just unfair. They're killers."

"Like you and Arthur just tried to be." The words fell heavy between them.

Sandy shook her head. "You don't get it."

"What I get... is that people are not groups. They're people. Anyone who says everyone in a group is the same, is plain wrong."

Sandy pointed at her, a sneer on her face. "You don't know what it's like to lose someone you love. You don't know how painful it is every day." Her voice shook, and fresh tears ran down her face. "Come back and judge me when you've lost someone."

Hazel hated to see her friend in so much agony. Tears slid down her own cheeks now. She realized that Sandy's pain needed something to blame and punish. Logic was not going to do anything. "I love *you*. I don't want to lose you… and it feels like I am. I'm scared."

Sandy's face relaxed, and she dropped her accusing finger. "Hazel," she whispered. "God help me…"

Mumsy's voice sliced through the chugging of the automobiles and people leaving. "Girls! I've been losing my mind. You're safe." She scurried over in a swirl of satin and feathers, throwing her arms around Hazel and Sandy. "Let's get out of here."

Hazel's parents sat and comforted her and talked out what had happened that night for over an hour. They were not sure what to do about Arthur and Stanley, but one thing was for sure, Hazel had to avoid any public association with them until they knew how the papers would spin it. There might not be a way to convince the Veiled Prophet that Hazel and Stanley's connection ended with all of the publicity after the kidnapping, but they had to try.

It was past midnight, and the house had settled down. Under the bed covers, Hazel was fully dressed. She was determined to somehow make sure that Stanley was okay. Her father had said he'd seen him safe, but that Arthur was loose. Hazel thought about Sandy and wondered how to help her friend. It was a good thing that Stanley had shown up when he had to stop what Arthur was planning to do. In Hazel's heart, she believed that Sandy would have been destroyed by guilt and regret.

She heard Peggy come into her room, so she closed her eyes and pretended sleep. The Irish maid approached the bed and laid a gentle hand on Hazel's head.

"Father, protect this one," she whispered. "Thank you for givin' me a child to love all these years while my heart missed my own. Shield them both from evil… and please let us all be a family someday. Amen."

Peggy stood there a few moments more before letting out a sigh and leaving the room. Hazel lay still, wondering about what she'd just heard. After a few minutes of waiting and listening to make sure that it was safe, Hazel slipped out of bed and pulled on her warmest coat.

Nobody noticed as she slipped out of the back of the house with Henri on a leash. He wagged his tail with excitement but obeyed her no-barking command.

The temperature had dropped, and there was frost on the lawn. The eerie silence that happens after a shock is the quietest kind of quiet. Hazel's neighborhood was still, and many families left their yards lit up. As if they didn't want to be taken by surprise by anything that may be hiding in the shadows of night. It felt as if everyone had vanished in the middle of an evening garden party.

She wrapped her fur coat tightly around her shoulders and held her chin high. Henri helped her feel brave, as she made her way down the sidewalk. A deep need to find Stanley had roused her from the safety of her bedroom. He'd been a hero again that night in front of everyone. But heroes were irrelevant. All some of them would remember about that night was that two ruffians trespassed into one of the most important and exclusive nights of the year.

Arthur had made it all worse. The Knights would become a target for Legion for certain. A line in the sand had been drawn, and all of St. Louis would have to choose a side. The problem was that the enemy was the one defining what the sides were. They had established the "us against them" rules without regard to personal choice or individuals. The divide was merely one of class and status. But in real life … the truth was never that simple.

The now familiar walk through Forest Park seemed longer in the dark, but Hazel charged forward, ignoring the night voices and the shadows that moved and, at times, followed her. Henri growled and barked at times as they went. Nobody approached her. Though her heart raced, Hazel didn't feel afraid. She felt determined and eager to find her newsie safe and sound. Hazel's gut told her Stanley was at the red boxcar. If not, it was a shortcut across Forest Park to Dogtown where he lived anyway.

The moon lit up the bare trees and filtered light onto the ground in gauzy patches. The hideout was close. Suddenly, Henri stopped and let out a whine. His ears perked up, and a low growl sounded in his throat.

"Anhalten," Hazel commanded.

Henri obeyed with silence but continued to stare into the darkness in front of them. The hair on Hazel's arms prickled. "What is it, boy?" she said in a low voice. She strained to hear footsteps or breathing, but there was only the faraway sounds of the people who huddled around fires for warmth. Hazel's own breath came out in white clouds. She rubbed her hands together to warm them.

Tugging on the leash, Hazel continued forward in the direction of what the newsies called The Castle. In the thick of the trees, she saw the rectangular, leaning shape of the abandoned boxcar. Then she heard it: the soft tappity-tap-tap, like a distant tommy gun starting and stopping, starting and stopping.

It was coming from inside the hideout where a soft, yellow glow leaked from under the crooked sliding door. The closer she got, the more Hazel began to question the wisdom of coming here alone. She swallowed. "Stanley?"

The tapping stopped.

"Hello. Stanley are you in there?" She stood poised, ready to run.

"Haze?"

She sighed in relief to hear his familiar, deep voice.

The door slid open with a rusty scraping sound, and Stanley's tall body was outlined by the soft candlelight coming from inside the boxcar. "How did you know I was here?" His voice shook.

She wanted to tell him that she felt it in her gut—like a homing beacon. But instead, she gave the logical answer. "I figured after your uncle let you go, you'd end up here," Hazel said as Henri bounced and barked happily to see Stanley.

"You shouldn't have put yourself in danger and come here." Stanley sounded angry, then his firm tone cracked. "But thank God you did. You're a sight for sore eyes." His shoulders slumped, and he covered his face with his hands.

Was he crying? Hazel's insides flipped. "Oh, Stanley. Baby." She held up her hands for him.

He reached down and pulled her up inside the boxcar. Stanley clung to her tightly with strong arms, breathing hard with emotion into her shoulder. She rubbed his back in a small circle as they pressed together that way until a warm peace encircled them.

"Heh. Sorry, Bananas. So much has happened."

"I know." She didn't want him to be embarrassed about crying. Behind him, she saw a small, black typewriter on the table and several lit candles.

She pulled back. "So that's what I was hearing. Thought maybe you had Fred and Ginger in here, tap dancing."

Stanley smiled, grateful for the comic relief. He wiped his eyes and then ran a hand through his hair. "Sure. They just left."

Hazel wrinkled her nose at him. "Thought so."

Just looking at him this way made her heart squishy. He'd removed the jacket and bowtie from earlier that evening, his collar was open, and he wore suspenders. He'd finally shaved, from the looks of it.

Stanley was hers. No mistake about that.

Henri jumped up inside the boxcar and wound around Stanley's legs until he bent to scratch the dog's head. Stanley grinned, but his face was tired when he looked at Hazel. "I'm writing an article about the missing kids in town. I want people to start to notice and talk about the tattoos—tell them what it all means."

"Well. There's a war on now. Your articles, along with what happened tonight, are going to start a big stir."

"I already have a target on my back, Hazel."

"I don't want anything to happen to you, Snoopy." She shivered and briskly rubbed her arms.

"I know." He reached out, held both of her hands, and led her to the old, sunken sofa at the back of the boxcar. They sat, holding hands without speaking. She could see that Stanley had his brain full of things he was thinking about.

Hazel watched how candlelight flickered on the angles of his face. His hands were strong and warm on hers. Unlike everything else in her world, he was so real and solid. Losing him was unimaginable. It made her heart squeeze to think of everything he'd been through lately, and that maybe this was only the beginning. How could she shield him while he was taking on the powers of darkness?

Stanley stared across the boxcar, lost in his mind. "When they got Vinnie, I knew none of us were safe. So I figured... if I'm going down, I gotta get the last word in. I know you don't like it, but that's why I'm writing."

Hazel nodded. "I understand that. I just wish someone else would do it instead. Maybe the Veiled Prophet is grateful you saved him tonight… but this paper business won't be ignored."

She picked up one of his hands and pressed it to her cheek. "I am so sorry about Vinnie."

"Thank you. I loved that mug." Stanley blinked away tears.

"It hurts to lose someone … I think it destroyed Sandy to lose her sister. I feel like I've lost my best friend in a way too—she's not who she was. But…" Hazel stifled a sudden sob. "If I lose you, I won't be able to bear it."

Stanley turned toward her, his face soft and vulnerable. "You'd miss me that much, Lady Bananas?"

She nodded, unable to speak.

He caressed her cheek, his blue eyes catching the candlelight as they searched her face.

"How'd I get so lucky? Sometimes I'm not sure if anyone really gives a crumb about what happens to me."

"I do."

"I won't let them take me from you. I found you in the cave, didn't I? Then I took your soul back from them. They can't separate us. Ever."

Hazel wrapped her arms around him, breathing in his scent. "But what if Charles is out? He could be loose, and we wouldn't know. The police are dirty… Sandy and Arthur have lost their minds, nobody is who they seem to be."

Stanley patted her back. "Slow down there. One thing at a time. If Charles is out, he won't hide forever, and we'll deal with it again. The police may be dirty, but not all of them. But who needs them? Father Timothy and the others have formed their own squad."

"Still. The odds are overwhelming."

"David against Goliath. I know."

"What do we do about Bonnie and Clyde? I still can't believe what they did tonight. I can't make sense of it."

"I'm not sure what to do." Stanley frowned. "I thought I knew Artie better. Those two will have to be muzzled. Father Timothy and Seamus will deal with Artie—once they find him. But we have bigger things to face right now. There's more…"

"More?" Hazel sat forward, eyes wide. "More than being up against all of the powerful elite in St. Louis?"

"The maid found in the trash heap. The papers said she was shot. But it turns out that wasn't true. We have an informer who saw the original coroner's report. She had internal bleeding… her baby maker was removed. Something went wrong, and she bled to death."

"What?"

"We think she was forcibly sterilized. Seems there have been a lot of cases lately across the United States. Women claiming they were tricked into it or forced."

"Controlled breeding," Hazel said in disgust.

"They call it racial hygiene."

"A pretty phrase for such an ugly thing."

"The aggressive colonization of ideas always comes with a code language to sugarcoat things. It's going on over in Germany too. 'Life unworthy of life' is being dealt with."

"Stanley, that must be terrifying for poor folk."

"Hazel … it's terrifying for everyone. It means at any time somebody can decide your group is next. See? Now, it might be the poor, feeble, or a certain race. But one day it might be … people with blue eyes and curly hair." He touched one of her curls. "Then it's people who go to church, or don't go to church. People who like their eggs sunny side up, people who own dogs, and people who like Cole Porter… Get what I'm saying?"

"Yes. I do, and you're right. I tried to tell Sandy a similar thing. She sees all rich people as a group who are the same—

even while being a rich person who is quite different. It makes no true sense."

"It's madness."

"Oh, Stanley. Everyone is whacky. Who is there even left to trust?"

"Me. You. Your dad and Father Timothy… A handful of ratty Knights. I'm sure there's more. The trustworthy ones are usually silent. They do things, not just spew rhetoric meant to control thoughts."

Hazel nodded in agreement. One of the things that she loved about Stanley was that he was a thinker, and his life hadn't stopped him from searching for truth and learning. The other Knights joked and called him professor sometimes, but they admired him too.

"You can trust Peggy, Haze. She's fighting in this too… maybe that's why it's in my blood."

Hazel made a face. "Fighting Irish?"

"More personal than that… You're right, it's hard to trust when everyone is lying or crazy. Seamus has been lying to me for years about my parents…" He gave her a long look, as if waiting for her to catch up.

"In your blood…" Then she saw it. The hair, something about the shape of the eyes, and the quickness of the smile. "Peggy…"

Stanley nodded with a look as if he barely believed it himself. "Yeah. Turns out, I'm not an orphan. Peggy is my mom."

Hazel let out a gasp, her heart beating with surprise and joy. "Stanley."

"She and my dad belonged to an order that has fought Legion all along. The Veiled Prophet is just another manifestation of Legion's dark work. They killed my dad, and Peggy—my mom—was locked up in the loony bin for years. After she got out, it was safer for both of us to let Seamus raise me." He reached into his shirt and pulled out his St. Jude necklace. "She has one just like it," he said.

Hazel was speechless as her mind raced through outrage that Stanley had lost out on a lifetime of having a mother, to elation because Peggy and Stanley were her two favorite people in the world. It was so clear now how alike they were.

"Stanley... this is amazing. I thought maybe she had a child who died. But you... you're her son." Hazel could not decide what to say or think of it all.

"Yeah." Stanley nodded and quickly wiped his eyes. "I've got some mixed feelings, that's sure. I understand why she did it, but she was right there all along, and I grew up without her." His voice sounded strained.

"And I was practically raised by the mother you never got to have."

They sat together in their own thoughts. It was strange how their lives had been woven together long before they had ever met. Before ever knowing Stanley, she'd see him sometimes on the sidewalk selling papers as she drove by. There was a connection there even then. It seemed to Hazel that fate had led her to the Hi-Point movie theater to see that baseball picture last fall. Because Stanley and she were always destined to meet... and then what? Fight darkness together? He from the outside and her from the inside? Or was this about love?

"This doesn't make you my sister, by the way," Stanley joked, breaking the silence.

Hazel laughed. Everything was so heavy, she'd take any excuse. "Then kiss me, and let's forget all of this for a minute."

"Gladly." Stanley's smile sent a thrill through her. He pulled her into his arms, and they kissed on the sunken sofa in the abandoned boxcar as if it was Paris in the rain.

Some minutes later, Hazel leaned against Stanley on the couch, wrapped in his arms. "Stanley," Hazel whispered. "How can I help? I mean… trying to find out who the Veiled Prophet is isn't simple. Especially if he keeps changing. I think knowing who he is, is less valuable than knowing how they are organizing The Winnowing and how to stop it."

"Do you think you could find proof that the papers lied about Maxie's death?"

Hazel thought, tracing her fingers down Stanley's arms. "I sometimes file things for the doctor. There might be something in there about her last visit. She'd come in complaining about her stomach."

"That might be something. Other than that… lie low, okay? Be a debutante, and avoid me and the Knights for a while. I want them to think we're through. Don't want them to think you're mixed up in what Artie did. It might be the only way to keep you safe."

"I don't care about that. I want to help. And I don't want to stay away from you."

Stanley sighed and released Hazel from his arms. "Look at me. C'mon… I want to see those blue peepers."

Hazel locked eyes with Stanley. "What?"

"You got your bracelet to remind you of me and take me with you wherever you go. Joan of Arc is a protector. She was a tough dame… like you. And you've got Henri." He gestured to where the dog lay on the floor, sleeping at their feet.

Hazel felt like crying. "What about you? What will protect you?"

Stanley slipped one side of his suspenders off and unbuttoned his shirt. He opened it so she could see the tattoo on the left side of his chest: a heart pierced by a crown of thorns, surrounded by blue flames. "See? This is the Sacred Heart of Jesus. It represents his love for everyone. That's what protects me. Although Henri would probably do a great job too." He grinned.

His religion felt foreign to her, but she knew what it meant to him. "I'll try to trust your faith." Hazel kissed the tattoo and then looked up at Stanley. "Now it represents my love too."

Stanley placed his hands on either side of her face and kissed her forehead and then her lips. "Thank you," he said.

Hazel smiled.

Henri yawned and looked up at Hazel on the couch. Hazel bent to scratch his head. "Braver Hund. Look at you, keeping me all safe."

Stanley laughed. He stood and stretched. "I'm sorry, baby. I gotta finish typing up this article. Things are going to get dicey after what Artie did. We have to be ready."

"Okay. Think you could walk me home?"

"Sure thing, doll."

CHAPTER FIFTEEN

"Wake up, Lord Stanley." A husky, feminine voice worked its way through his unconscious.

He opened his eyes and groaned. Sleeping on the boxcar floor hadn't done him any favors, but his legs were too long for the sofa. Stanley stretched, and his back crackled. Rubbing his eyes, he saw Frisky and the rest of the Knights standing over him. All of them looked scared.

"Frisky. Guys. Good morning." He pushed the old, plaid blanket off and yawned.

"More like, good afternoon, lazy pants," Shuffles said, offering Stanley his hand. He took it and pulled himself up.

"Where is Arthur?" he asked, putting his suspenders over his shoulders.

"That's what we wanted to ask you," Jakob said.

"I don't know. He disappeared last night, telling me he was done with the Knights."

"What happened at the Veiled Prophet Ball? It's all over the newspapers this morning," Shuffles asked.

Stanley sighed and then told them what Arthur did and what happened at the crypt afterward.

Anino whistled. "I always knew Arthur was cracked like an egg, but I never thought he would try to kill anyone."

"I did," Stanley said, hanging his head. "But I always thought that's because he lost his mind for a moment."

Furrowing his brow, Jakob said, "What's that about?"

Sighing, Stanley rubbed his muscles and walked to the boxcar opening. "It's when we first met. You know how we always talked and joked about him stabbing me? Well, he actually did, but he wasn't aiming for me."

Frisky put a hand on his arm. "What's the story?"

"I was walking home from, well, a date, and I took a shortcut through an alley in Gaslight Square. Artie was there, confronting a group of swells; college boys. They were all mocking him. He attacked them, and they started to beat the crap out of him. I stepped in, knocked a few heads, until there was one guy left. Artie took out a knife and started swinging at the frat boy. I tried to stop him from killing the guy. But he turned on me and got me in the shoulder. But I'd scattered the mob and saved him from the meat wagon. So after that, Artie felt some kind of loyalty. Not that I asked for it," Stanley said, rubbing his face.

That night swam into Stanley's memory. Artie had looked wild, uncontrollable, and capable of killing. But he'd always dismissed it as a reaction in the moment. And in the few years since then, Artie had calmed down, didn't mutter about revenge, and seemed to take to the Knights mission to help those who needed it. He'd developed the pigeons, trained them, and even ended up recruiting Shuffles into the Knights. Now he realized that Arthur had been using the pigeons for his own purposes. He had revenge on his mind the whole time.

"Was Charles there?"

"No, not that I remember. But Artie was looking for him. Or something. He never told me the details about what happened between their families."

Frisky raised her chin. "I know, Stanley. He never told anyone but me."

Anino said, "Yeah, I always figured it had to be bad, to make him the way he was."

"It was bad. Worse than you can even imagine," Frisky said, tears filling her eyes. Stanley had never seen her like this.

"Okay, so Frisky sounds like she has all the skinny. So, what happened?" Jakob asked.

She shook her head. "I can't say. I ain't gonna squeal on Artie."

Stanley sighed. "We need to help him, Frisky. And the only way we can do that is to get the low down."

She didn't say anything for a moment. "Artie was a sweet kid, you know. Gentle, kind. Innocent even."

Shuffles snorted, and everyone looked at him. "Sorry. Just hard to buy that one."

"Well, we grew up together, played together, and even shared our first kiss." She wiped a tear away and cleared her throat.

Stanley raised an eyebrow, but Frisky said, "Don't get the wrong idea, King of the Lips. It was a kiss between two kids, nothing more. He's more like my brother and always has been."

She sighed. "But then, the Chouteau family started hanging around. They were such a fancy family, and the Stewarts were in awe to have such important friends. They got to hang out in their mansion and have picnics and such. But they wanted something… Artie's dad was a smart mathematician and developed some sort of numbers thing."

A chill ran up Stanley's spine. "For what?"

"I dunno, a way to catalogue people, I guess. Artie explained it once, but I couldn't make heads or tails of it. It was meant to help the military in some way. But the Chouteaus wanted it for some private purpose."

Jakob's face went pale. "The Winnowing. They wanted it for The Winnowing."

Frisky scrunched up her face. "What's that?"

Stanley shook his head. "Later. Finish your story."

She nodded, sitting on the sofa, hands in her lap. "Well, they wanted to buy it from him and IBM. But I think Artie's father got a bad vibe or something. And he refused to give up his research. IBM tried to force his hand and then fired him. But still, he wouldn't budge. So I guess they went one step further." Frisky paused, twisting her curly, red hair like mad. "Sorry, it's all so nutty. Sometimes I doubt the story, to be honest."

Anino sat by her and said, "It ain't so nutty. We've seen some pretty crazy things lately."

She nodded. "Artie told me some of it. Including about that Sandy dame. She's no good for him. I think she's gone crazy after what happened to her sister. She's kinda pushed him over the edge too."

Stanley always thought Arthur dragged Sandy into her darkness. But maybe it was mutual. Hard to pull that knot of anger apart. Probably one fueled the other.

"Well, anyway, one night, they kidnapped Artie and his mom. And Charles was one of them; the leader I think. Artie never gave many details. But they tortured them in front of Artie's dad, who finally broke, gave his ideas to them and IBM. His dad went into the bottle and never came out. And his mom went insane from whatever happened that night. They locked her away. It broke little Artie, made him dark and want to kill the world." Her voice was raspy with emotion. She dragged a hand through her tangle of red hair.

Silence filled the boxcar, broken only by the sound of Frisky's sniffing back tears. The other Knights seemed lost in their own thoughts. Stanley sat on the edge of the boxcar and stared out into the trees. So that's what happened. If that had happened to him, he might have done worse things than Artie had. Then he realized, it did happen to him. They tortured Peggy, stole her baby, and turned her loose on the streets. And made it impossible for her to be his mother.

Anger welled up in Stanley, and he wanted them to pay. Maybe he shouldn't have stopped Artie last night. But then, he realized, he didn't do it for the swells, he did it for his friend, to keep him from destroying himself by becoming a killer.

Stanley couldn't give up on Arthur, especially now, when the VP and Legion world would be hunting him and probably Stanley too. They were in this together, and he couldn't just leave his friend to a possibly brutal death. He was a brother, just like Vinnie had been. And you don't leave family, no matter what.

"We have to find him, boyos, that's facts," Stanley said. "We can't just leave him out there by himself."

Much to his surprise, Frisky stood and grabbed Stanley in a huge bear hug, breaking down and weeping. Looking up at the other Knights, they all just stared at her. No one had ever seen her like this. So Stanley wrapped her up in his arms and patted her on the head.

"This is all you get, Ladies' Man," she said, mouth muffled in his chest.

He sighed and shook his head, amused. "Where would Arthur go after all this?"

She sat back down on the sofa and wiped her eyes. "Well, his mom just got moved to this swanky asylum down in south city. It's high class."

"Oh? How could they afford that?" Jakob wondered.

Frisky shrugged. "Don't know, but it's where all the crazy richies go, I think."

Stanley said, "Yeah … loony swells like Charles Chouteau…" Stanley scratched his head. "Okay, you mugs, we need to keep getting *The Knights Voice* out there. I have a new edition all typed up. Make sure it happens. Frisky, can you get me into the asylum?"

She nodded. "I'm on the visitor list. All the nurses like me. I go there once a week to read to her. I don't think you're gonna get the skinny from her, Stanny."

He shrugged. "Maybe not, but maybe we'll run into Artie there." Stanley looked at all of them and said, "I probably don't need to say this, but things just got a hell of a lot worse last night."

Shuffles nodded. "Seen the papers. They're calling for the streets to be swept clean from the vermin and rabble."

Jakob snorted in disgust. "Yeah. They're even calling for the roundup of 'undesirables' to be shipped to work camps so they can be 'reeducated.'"

"Funny how it's all the swells and eggheads calling for this. They make evil sound reasonable and sensible, that only a nut would disagree with," Anino said.

"Yeah, well, other than passing out papers, I want you mugs to lay low. No more trips to Lindell for a bit. Don't go far from home," Stanley said, smoothing out his hair and grabbing his hat.

Anino frowned as he grabbed him by the arm. "What about the families who need us? And need the food."

"Won't be more food if we end up in the cooler or the meat wagon. Or worse," Stanley said. "I can't make you all obey me, but I'm asking you to."

They all nodded, and Anino said, "All right, Lord Stanley. To hear is to obey."

Stanley snorted. "Just get out of here, you mugs."

After they all left, Frisky recovered herself and said, "Well, your plan to get us alone has finally worked."

Stanley hopped down and then held out his hand. "Sorry, Frisky, I'm a one woman fella now. You might as well tattoo Hazel's name on my chest."

She chuckled. "I know, Catlicker. I just like giving you stuff. I like this fancy girl. She's tamed the beast and all that."

They took the trolley into the city and then walked ten blocks to the insane asylum that was surrounded by a tall, wrought iron fence. Stanley marveled at the well-manicured lawns and trees surrounding the entire grounds. There was a large fountain and statuary out front. It looked more like an English manor than a nut house.

"Guess it pays to be rich and insane," Stanley said as they passed through the high, arched gate and walked up the stone stairs to the entrance.

"And how. This place is like a country club."

Stanley frowned. "Then how did Artie's mom get here?"

Frisky shrugged. "Dunno, exactly. The nurses think it's some richie swell footing the bill, a Good Samaritan and all that."

They went inside, and Stanley could hear Brahms playing from a loud gramophone somewhere down the spacious hall. Frisky approached the large, wooden visitor desk and gave the nurse there her best smile.

"Hiya, Frieda, I'm here to see Mrs. Stewart."

The young nurse, not much older than Stanley and Frisky, smiled. "She's in the recreation room today. It seems to be a good day. No fits."

"Was Artie hear to see her?"

The nurse shook her head. "I've not seen him, but then, I just got on duty about half an hour ago. I'll tell him you were looking for him next time I see him."

Frisky nodded and then said, "This is Artie's best pal, Stanley. We were supposed to meet here."

The nurse looked Stanley up and down, giving him a wide smile. "Well, aren't you a grand friend."

"Easy there, Frieda, Stanny boy is taken up with a swell." Frisky raised a pinky as if drinking from a teacup.

"Shame." Frieda winked. "Well, here are your passes."

Stanley took his and pinned it to his shirt. Frisky led him down the hallway and said, "Whew, you didn't need me. All you had to do was look at Frieda, and she would've done whatever you asked."

He coughed. "I doubt it."

Frisky grinned. "Whatever you say, Casanova."

They got to the recreation room, and Stanley looked around. It had tall windows that let in plenty of sunlight but were blocked by thin, metal bars. There were tables and chairs and shelves of books and games. Some people played checkers or cards and looked pretty normal. But one lady with long, thin, black hair walked around in circles, muttering, "I'm a victim. I'm a victim. I'm a victim." And a man with a big, bushy, black beard looked around, head cocking like a bird and then said, "Whoop. Whoop. Whoop."

"One thing I can't figure out about this nut house," Frisky said, as she scanned the room.

"What's that?" Stanley said, brows furrowed.

"Well, they give everyone a tattoo here."

Stanley's heart jumped and skipped into his throat. "What did you say?"

"Yeah, numbers. I think that's how they keep track of everyone," she said.

He looked at all the patients' arms, and he could make out the faint ink stains, very similar to Evelyn's and Vinnie's tattoos.

"Christ have mercy," he said. "They are marked by The Winnowing. Artie's dad's system."

Frisky gripped his arm. "My God. Why didn't I connect the dots before?"

Stanley didn't say anything, because he noticed the tall blond-haired doctor striding through the room. It was Dr. Galton, the guy Hazel worked for. His skin prickled. Of course that mug would be tangled up in all of this.

"Frisky, find Artie's mom. I gotta do something. I'll meet you back here."

"You got it."

Stanley took off his hat and slipped back into the hallway. He cracked open a few doors until he found one with something useful. He grabbed a white coat that someone had left at a desk. He picked up a notebook and pretended to read it as he hurried down the hall he'd seen Dr. Galton following. As Stanley rounded a corner, he saw the doctor trotting down a flight of stairs. Stanley waited for a few moments and then snuck down the stairs after him.

He peered around the corner and saw a brick hallway. The doctor had disappeared into one of the doors at the end of the hallway. Stanley crept down the hall and pressed his ear against one door. He could hear the murmur of voices but couldn't quite make out what they were saying.

Looking around, he opened the door next to that one and found himself in a dark room with a large conference table and no windows. Stanley thought he could listen in on the next room through the wall, when suddenly a door opened up between the rooms, and the voices became louder.

They were coming in.

Stanley dropped to the floor and slid under the table just as a light clicked on in the room. Several people shuffled in, talking, with drinks and folders in hand. Stanley watched in horror as they began to seat themselves at the table. A few dresses and several suit pants later, he was surrounded where he hunkered beneath the table. The sound of glasses being set down and papers being rustled mixed with bits of conversation. They were talking about the VP Ball.

"The young boy's rash actions were actually a good thing, and no one died, thanks to the newsie hero," Dr. Galton's voice rose above the others.

"Indeed, the Mystical Seer is most pleased. The papers are, with our prompting, practically screaming for a public version of The Winnowing. The people are afraid, so they are cooperating. This has accelerated his plans. The great sweep will begin," another man's voice said.

"What about the camps? Are they ready?" a woman asked.

"They are. And the train cars are ready to be filled. We've been keeping candidates in the Lemp caves for some time. Fortunately, they were not discovered when that incident with Legion and those girls occurred. The police on the scene were helpful. Now that batch is ready to be moved for reeducation," Dr. Galton answered.

"The mayor is going to sign the order sometime today to get rid of the Hoovervilles in Forest Park and round up any women deemed unfit, subnormal, or genetically defective, along with any sort of street riff raff. Soon our streets will be safer than ever. Our city will be an example to other chapters," a quiet, male voice announced.

There were sounds of relief and murmured approval, and Stanley wanted to punch them all. He tried to keep his breathing quiet and stay balled up as small as possible to avoid any legs that might stretch out.

"We will be a model to the world. I can tell you that Germany is watching what we do with eagerness. Thanks to the U.S. Supreme Court, we can now do what we need to do without impediment." The doctor sounded so reassuring. He truly believed what they were doing was good.

One man with a deep voice said, "You mean the Buck case." Cigar smoke billowed down from where he sat and drifted under the table. Stanley felt a tickle in his throat and fought the desire to cough.

"Of course. But the weak minded and shortsighted are fighting us every step of the way. Like the Catholic Church here in Missouri. Thanks to that young man with the gun, they are losing any sympathy they might have manufactured."

There was a response of approval around the table again.

"Legion will go out again tonight for gathering. We are seeing progress but must be ready for the new influx of patients. Process them, tattoo them, and then get them ready for the trains."

They all applauded politely. Stanley felt like throwing up. He did not understand how people could reach this point, convinced that imprisoning or eliminating people wasn't just an evil necessity, but a good they all desired, something to dedicate your life and money to make happen.

After several minutes of discussion, chairs scraped away from the table. The people stood up to shake hands or whatever, and Stanley waited until they had left the room and the light had been turned off. Slipping out from under the table, he hurried to the door and peeked out. The hallway was empty.

Running hard, he followed the hall and bounded up the stairs. Taking deep breaths, he tried to look calm and cool while finding his way back to the recreation room. He found Frisky sitting next to a woman with Artie's nose and eyes, but her hair was completely white.

"Ah, Lord Stanley, this is Artie's mom, Mabel. Say hi to Artie's friend."

The woman raised a trembling hand to him. "Nice to meet you, Lord. Where is my Artie? They tortured him, you know."

Stanley removed the white coat he'd put on and knelt at her feet and held her hand. "I know, ma'am. I'm sorry."

Tears welled up in her eyes. "Can you keep him safe, Lord?"

He looked up at Frisky, but for once, she didn't say anything. And he felt the weight of everyone's expectation. It seemed like everyone was convinced that he could pull a rabbit out of the hat and make it all aces. The Rocky Mountains appeared in his thoughts again. That's what he wanted to do: run and hide.

Gripping the older woman's hand, he said, "I'll do my best, I promise."

She nodded and then put her hand to her head. "The knives, they hurt. They hurt."

Frisky stood up and said, "I'll be back soon, Mabel. God be with you."

When they passed the desk on the way out, Stanley leaned against the counter and caught Frieda's eye. "Say, I hear you have that Charles Chouteau locked up here."

The young nurse narrowed her eyes. "Wait a minute... you're that Stanley. Of course! The newsie who saved those two rich girls with Arthur?"

He grinned. "Yeah... that's me."

Her eyes went wide, and she leaned forward. "I don't share information about patients... but..."

Stanley bent forward across the desk. "Yeah?"

"He hasn't been on the residence list for weeks. Word is he's been moved," she said in a low voice and then shrugged.

Moved? Or released? This was probably not a good thing.

Stanley gave her a wink. "You're a peach. Thanks!"

Frisky didn't say anything until they got outside. It was a bright morning, and it lit up her red hair. "Well, that bit of information gave me hives."

Stanley said, "Frisky, you need to get home and not go out. Tonight and the next few days is going to be bad. Really bad."

He told her about Dr. Galton and what he overheard in the conference room. Frisky twisted her hair harder and harder as she listened. "I guess I better get the kids out of the streets."

Stanley nodded. "Yeah, I think so. I'll let the Knights and pigeons know too."

CHAPTER SIXTEEN

Peggy seemed more cheerful than she had in a while. She hummed as she brought a breakfast tray into Hazel's room. Hazel yawned, pushed herself to a sitting position, and propped her pillows behind her. It was late morning, but she felt as if she had hardly slept. "Morning, Peggy."

"Good morning to you, angel face. I know you had a big night last night, so I thought you might like a bite to eat in the comfort of your bed. Besides, your folks have already eaten and gone out for the day."

"Mumsy too?" It seemed unusual for her mother to be up so soon following a bash like last night.

"Up and stone sober. Said she had some Christmas shopping to do. I'm to watch over you." Peggy set down the tray across her lap, laid out a linen serviette, and poured the coffee. Then she glided across the room and pulled back the drapes to let the morning sun into the room. "There now."

Hazel's eyes teared up. Peggy was such a good mother. "Thank you ever so much."

"Happy to serve." Peggy smiled until she noticed Hazel's eyes. "Oh, now, now. Last night was a terrible night, to be sure." She sat on the edge of Hazel's bed.

Hazel nodded, reaching for a piece of toast. She was bursting to talk about Stanley but didn't know how to start. "I hear you had quite a night yourself."

Peggy furrowed her brow. "Well, Arthur sure made a right bag of things last night. There will be hell to pay, to be sure. But this has been a long time in coming. Perhaps things needed to come to light this way."

"Arthur is a menace. Between his mess and the things that Stanley writes, I'm sure there'll be retaliation. Stanley says things that will make him a target." She waited to see Peggy's reaction at the mention of his name.

"Many a time a man's mouth broke his nose. Stanley is no stranger to speaking his mind and paying for it. But this time he speaks for everyone, and he doesn't stand alone. He is a good lad, and I'm fond of him."

Hazel smiled at the glow on her maid's face. "You're proud of him… he's grown up to be like his father."

"That he has," Peggy answered, and then realization lit her face. "So he told you then?"

Hazel set down the toast she had been holding, her lip trembling. "He did, and I think it's just about the duckiest thing I've ever heard."

Peggy let out a laugh and hugged Hazel. "It is, darlin' girl. It is. I've waited for this day for so long. There, there, are you cryin'?"

"I'm happy crying, Peggy. You've been such a swell mother to me. I'm so happy for him to have you now too."

"Now you've done it." Peggy wiped a tear from her own eye.

"I love you so much and… I love Stanley too."

Peggy patted her cheek. "I know, dear. I saw it from the start."

"Did you?"

"Oh, yes. I saw it on you and all over him as well. He always knew… he has a gift for feelin' things, I'm guessin'. The two of you have a special connection that goes beyond just me."

Hazel's cheeks heated. "I feel like myself with him. I feel like I found my true home."

Peggy nodded. "Anam Cara."

"What's that mean?" Hazel took a sip of coffee. It felt so good to be sitting and talking about Stanley this way with Peggy. She wanted to pretend that the rest of the world was not falling apart for just a little while.

"Oh, it's old Irish, meaning soul mate. One with whom no divides or walls have power. You could be as different as the sun from the moon and still share the same sky forever."

Hazel sighed. "That sounds heavenly. But… he sure makes me mad sometimes. It isn't all rainbows."

Peggy chuckled. "Love is a fiery thing, lass. And to be sure… he is a man after all. Bless their souls."

Hazel's heart swelled, picturing Stanley in all of his moods. Remembering his kisses filled her with unspeakable joy. All at once, she thought of how she had to stay away from him, and her insides sank. "I don't know when all of this madness will end, and I can see him again."

"He told you to stay away then?"

"It's better if they all think we're through."

"Be patient. I have a feeling things are on the brink of change."

"But… what if they come after all of us?"

"Under the shelter of each other, people survive." Her Irish sure came out when she was happy.

Peggy's dimple showed, and she smoothed Hazel's curls. It was something she'd done for as long as Hazel could recall. The simple gesture that often started her day. As a child, if Hazel was scared of the dark or sad, Peggy would smooth her curls and hum her to sleep.

In another life, Peggy would have done the same for Stanley. But instead, he'd been a lonely, little boy with no one to tell him that everything would be okay. Hazel wanted to be the one to smooth his hair and comfort him. It was only fair.

"Now, eat your breakfast before the eggs get cold."

Hazel took a forkful and gave Peggy a wink. "You got it, mom."

The Irish maid grinned. "I like the sound of that."

Stanley wanted evidence about Maxie's visits to the clinic. Hazel had easier access to what they needed than anyone else. After explaining why she needed to go to the clinic, Peggy said she could as long as she brought Henri along, and that it was right and natural for Hazel to do her part… as long as she was careful.

Hazel had spent an hour that afternoon at the clinic doing the usual tasks of cleaning and assisting Doctor Galton with patients. So far, there had been a little girl who needed stitches on her chin, an old man with a bad cough, and a Chinese woman with a rash.

The doctor was efficient and friendly, as usual. Hazel had to keep reminding herself that there was something sinister going on. It was strange that he had not mentioned what had happened at the ball. In fact, he had barely spoken to her at all.

After the woman with the rash had gone, Doctor Galton washed his hands thoroughly, and Hazel handed him a towel.

"Thank you, Hazel. I'll be in my office for a while doing paperwork. You can go home early today if you would like. Marie will be here any minute to do anything else that I may need here." He adjusted his glasses.

"Are you sure?" Hazel hesitated. She needed time to search his files. "Do you have anything new for me to organize? Or maybe ..."

He smiled at her. "If you call Jennings now, you'll get home before dark. Days are short this time of year. Go have some fun—school is out for the holidays."

"I think I will... Henri is waiting patiently outside. I'm sure he'll be happy to go. Let me finish cleaning the exam room first." She gave him one of her sunniest smiles.

"Good!" He turned and went into his office and shut the door.

Hazel took a deep breath. She'd recently filed a lot of the new patient files for the doctor in a room across from his office. It was lined with filing cabinets, some of them locked. It occurred to her that it was an awful lot of paperwork for a new clinic. It couldn't all be patient files... She walked softly and shut herself in, flipping on the light. Pulling open a drawer, she found a stack of empty file folders where there used to be patient charts.

A couple of empty drawers later, she opened one that had forms written in German. There were people's names at the top, and it looked like information about their height, weight, where they lived, and their jobs. At the bottom, each form had a serial number in bold.

The numbers. The tattoos.

Hazel lost her breath for a moment and flipped through the forms as fast as she could. Name after name and serial numbers.

In the next drawer, as she paddled through the files, a name lit up from the page. "Robert Guido." It took Hazel a few moments. That was Teeth's last name.

Then, voices came through the wall. Marie was talking to the doctor in German. Hazel's hands went still as she strained to hear what was being said. Whatever they were talking about, it got intense. She crept to the door and opened it a crack. From across the hall, the harsh tones of their voices peaked and fell in sharp staccato. She wished for the second time in her life that she spoke German. Then one word stood out to Hazel … an attack word that Mick used with Henri.

"Vernichten." Destroy. Kill. Exterminate.

Hazel's skin crawled. The cold fingers of evil seemed to rake down her back. She didn't want to be there—had to get out. In her hurry, she shut the cabinet drawer too hard, and the half-full cabinet rocked just enough for the empty coffee mug sitting on its top edge to tumble to the floor.

The sound of it smashing on the tiles stopped Hazel's heart, and the voices across the hall quieted. In a panic, Hazel searched the room for a place to hide. No dice. There was a push broom leaned against the wall behind the door. She snatched it just as the door to the office across the hall opened. Hazel held the broom tight in both hands in case she'd need her Escrima skills.

Marie entered the room first, a scowl on her face. "*Was ist los?*"

Hazel lowered the broom, struggling for words.

Doctor Galton came in behind the nurse. "You all right in here, Hazel? I thought you'd gone by now."

She swallowed, summoning her inner actress. "I'm so sorry. I'm such a klutz. I was looking everywhere for the broom—it wasn't in the closet. Then I knocked the mug down with the broom handle when I walked by. It was stupid." Her voice shook from nerves, but it sounded like tears were coming.

The doctor eyed her carefully and then nodded. "It's only a mug. And I apologize, I was the one who left the broom in here."

Whew.

Marie said something under her breath, and the doctor shot her a look. There was tension between the two of them. "Things are in hand here, Marie," he said in a firm voice.

The nurse briskly left the room.

Doctor Galton sighed and removed his eyeglasses. "It seems everyone is on edge right now. Marie will sweep up. Go take your holiday, I insist."

"Okay. I am a bit distracted lately. I didn't sleep well last night." She leaned the broom against the wall.

"Sorry to hear that." He paused and put his spectacles back on. "Perhaps you could make plans with your newsie?"

Hazel's heart paused. It felt like a test. She made a face. "He's a swell kid. But not really my type… and he seems to find trouble wherever he goes." The morning paper had not mentioned Stanley by name, and she didn't know what the doctor knew. It probably didn't help the Veiled Prophet to mention the "newsie hero" being a hero again. They needed a scapegoat. The focus had to be on the ruffian attack. "Anyway." She smiled shyly. "Don't tell anyone…" She lowered her voice as if she was about to tell a secret.

The doctor leaned forward, brows raised. "Yes?"

"I think Gabriel Sinclair is a dream." She sighed and patted her heart.

He grinned at her. "He is a handsome boy. And from an excellent family. I wouldn't have this clinic if it weren't for them. I guess not everything that happened at the ball was a disaster then?" He'd breached the subject. She had to be very careful now.

She shook her head. "Were you there?"

"Oh, no. As a simple neighborhood doctor, I would not be invited to such a prestigious event."

Hazel wondered if that was true. He had all of the right connections. "Well… it was spectacular at first. Simply heavenly until that nutty street rat tried to wipe us all out." Tears stung her eyes. "Oh, it was so awful."

His expression was sympathetic. "It must have been frightening. I read about it in the papers. A close call."

"It was. I saw my whole world threatened."

The doctor nodded. "Yes. It was indeed threatened. As long as unfortunate souls like that are allowed to roam free, we are all in danger. The poor boy is a product of bad breeding and mentality. His suffering becomes everyone else's."

Hazel shivered. "I see what you mean. I wish there was something I could do about all of this."

Doctor Galton's smile seemed forced. "You are doing something. You're helping me to help all of them. We do what we can to eliminate and relieve suffering. For the good of all."

"Creating a safer place for everyone," Hazel said.

"That's right. In the meantime, don't worry too much. Things will work out. There are good people working on the problem."

"Thank you." Hazel's adrenaline had dissipated, and she was suddenly tired and wanted to be home.

"Take a few days off. I'll see you after Christmas?" His smile was encouraging.

"Yes… I'll be here. Have a merry Christmas."

"Thank you. You do the same."

Hazel smiled and walked away. She realized she hadn't called Jennings, but she didn't want to ask to use the doctor's office telephone. Henri could walk with her to the trolley to catch a ride. She went to her locker, hung up the apron, and grabbed her coat and handbag. There were a few people waiting in the reception area as she left, and Marie was talking with one of them, holding a clipboard.

Hazel stood out in front of the clinic with Henri hopping around her legs for several minutes, staring out at the street. It was nearly evening. She buttoned her coat against the chill. A few people walked by, some automobiles passed. Up the street, there was the sound of Christmas music coming from a tavern. The world went on fairly peacefully despite all the talk of danger and destruction.

A loud scraping echoed from the shadowed alleyway beside the clinic. Hazel tugged on Henri's leash. "Fuss." He quickly followed her to the side of the building.

Light from the low sun did not reach the cluttered alleyway. In the shadows, Hazel saw a man with his hands against the large trash container. It had been pushed against the clinic under the window of one of the storage rooms stacked with a disarray of tables, chairs, and boxes.

It was just a trash man. Maybe there to salvage something. Hazel was about to turn back to the street when the man adjusted his bowler hat with a familiar gesture.

Arthur. Why was he still loose?

Hazel flattened herself against the brick wall of the alley and slid down to crouch behind some empty wooden crates stacked there. "Ruhig," she whispered to her dog. He went still and quiet.

The renegade newsie climbed on top of the metal box and forced the window open a crack with a crowbar he produced from his baggy trousers. Then he sat and lit a cigarette. He puffed on it a few times before reaching into the inside pocket of his oversized coat. He pulled out a bottle that sloshed with liquid and removed the cork.

He took a handkerchief and stuffed it into the bottle of liquid, leaving a tail of it hanging out of the top. Pinching his cigarette between two fingers, he contemplated the tip, while smoke trailed out of his nose.

Henri sniffed the air, and his ears perked. Before Hazel could stop the young dog, he jumped and let out a bark.

Arthur sprung to his feet, turning in Hazel's direction.

Bananas. She squeezed her eyes shut, hoping he wouldn't see her where she crouched.

"Peek-a-boo," Arthur said, slow and deliberate. "I see you, Princess."

Knees shaking, Hazel slowly stood to face him. She gripped Henri's leash. He was her only defense.

"C'mere."

Hazel shook her head. *Not a chance, buster.*

"Not here to stop me then? Wanna watch?"

"What are you doing?" Hazel demanded.

"First, I wanna show you something." With the cigarette between his fingers, he cupped his hand around his mouth. "Help me!" he squealed in a high pitched voice.

Hazel glanced around in confusion. Behind her was the outlet to the mostly empty street. The alley echoed as he screamed again. "Help!"

Nothing happened. Nobody came running. He looked down at her with a piercing glare. "This is Dogtown, bright eyes. Not the good ship lollipop."

She got the message. "Sandy would never forgive you if something happened to me. I'm the next best thing to a sister that she's got left."

"And she may never forgive me if I don't finish what we started…" He gestured at the open window with the hand that held the bottle. "See my problem?" He stuck the cigarette between his lips and breathed in.

"She wants you to sneak into the clinic and have a party?" Hazel smirked, getting some of her sass back. He was no Al Capone, just a crazy kid with a grudge, but he had a couple of weak spots. She sensed it. Sandy and Stanley.

He squinted at her like she was an idiot. "This ain't to drink. It's gasoline, dollface."

"I see… and you light it up and…"

"Now she's got it. I know this kind of stuff only exists in the movies for you."

Hazel bristled. "Don't do it…" She tried to think of what would convince him to stop.

"Why? Because your hero doc is still inside? I'm counting on it." He sneered.

"There are others in there besides. People from your own neighborhood. Henri and I will run out to the street and get help."

He set the bottle on the windowsill and pushed the window open wider. "I'll be done and long gone by then."

Desperate, Hazel pointed at Arthur. "Fass!"

Henri burst from her side and galloped toward Arthur. He leaped up on the side of the trash bin, scratching and barking. Arthur slipped and scrambled backward, away from the snarling dog. Hazel's heart thumped. Henri was truly intimidating. Mick had been working hard to turn him into a killer, and it was working.

Arthur's sudden fear turned to anger. He picked up the crowbar and clutched it in both hands. Cigarette dangling from his mouth, he grated, "Get this pooch away from me, or you'll be scooping up his brains with those manicured hands of yours."

Hazel didn't doubt him. There was a look on his face that terrified her. She approached the trash bin. "Anhalten," she commanded.

Henri backed away, a deep growl in his throat. Then he turned and trotted back to Hazel, his tongue hanging out and tail wagging. "Braver Hund," she said, patting the dog's head, her eyes not leaving the boy in the bowler hat. Her mind skipped to a new tactic. "Listen… Stanley wants me to find evidence in there about the murdered maid. I haven't found it yet. Burn it down, and we lose the chance."

Arthur lowered the crowbar. "I have all the evidence I need about this place."

"This isn't just about eliminating the people you see as problems. It's about the truth getting out to the public to stop the whole thing. For that we need proof."

Arthur removed his hat, anger still simmering on his face. "They've been taking my boys," he said.

"I know… I saw the files. Names and serial numbers. There might be more about where they are now and what's happened, but I can't read German."

Arthur's eyes lit with interest. "You on the level, swell?"

She could see she had him. The anger was draining from his body. "Yes. I saw one with the name Robert Guido on it. Thought maybe he was a relation to Teeth?"

Arthur blinked. "That ain't nobody but Bobby 'Teeth' Guido himself."

"They have him, then. The question is where?"

"Why don't I just go in there, smash in the doc's skull, take his papers, and find out?"

"His nurse is in there too and some patients. Just give me a couple of days. I'll get what you need and what Stanley needs."

It looked as if he might argue, when a police siren split the air. Arthur grabbed the bottle and his crowbar and jumped down from the top of the large, metal bin.

"You better make good on that." He pointed the crowbar at her and then turned away and ran down the darkening alleyway, away from the street.

Hazel wandered out to the street in a daze. The sunlight had drained from the sky, and the neighborhood was in the shadow of the buildings now. Shaking and on the brink of tears, she watched as a police car passed the clinic and stopped at the tavern up the street. There was a small crowd of men on the sidewalk, walloping each other and shouting. The siren turned off and two officers exited the patrol car; one had his gun drawn.

She sadly shook her head and turned her back on the violence. If the Veiled Prophet didn't kill everyone off, they might just do the job themselves.

CHAPTER SEVENTEEN

"We still haven't found Arthur anywhere," Anino said, sipping on a cup of coffee that Stanley had just made.

All of the Knights had come to Stanley's house at various times in the past day or so to report on what we as going on. Pigeons were missing in droves now, and no one could find Teeth either. Stanley sipped his coffee and swallowed hard.

"Yeah. He shook the tail that Seamus and Mr. Malloy put on him. So, there's that. Should have known. Artie knows this city better than anyone, he's got the whole place wired."

"And either the pigeons that are left don't actually know, or Arthur has scared them into not singing like canaries," Anino said, rubbing his head. "What was it like at the ball, by the way?"

Stanley stared at the inky blackness of coffee for a moment, as if trying to conjure images of the swell's party of the year. "Well, it ain't America, that's for sure, at least, not the part of America I believe in."

Anino furrowed his brow. "How so?"

"No one seemed interested in the fact that 'all men are created equal.' They have stacked the deck, and they intend to keep it that way," Stanley said. "And now, Artie has given them a blank check. They had to hide a bit before, speak in code, start clinics that're claiming to help poor people. But in reality, it's all smoke and mirrors."

"I've been thinking. Why does the Veiled Prophet hide his face then? What would be the point if they have all this power and all that?"

Stanley snorted. "This ain't like The Shadow, pal. No mustache twirling villain of the week to defeat. They want to be faceless, because if you can name your fear, you can beat it. So, their power is in taking a symbol rather than a face. Evil never wants to see the light of day. It likes the dark. Only light shows its true face."

Anino grinned. "Well, it's a good thing all of this hasn't changed Lord Stanley The Philosopher's way of doing things."

Sighing, Stanley tilted back in his chair. Frisky had gotten them all to start calling him that. "Anyway, point is, I don't see us finding the bad guy, tying him up and waiting for the authorities to cart him off to jail."

They both sipped their coffee in silence for a moment, and then Anino said, "I'd better get to the morning papers. What's Seamus doing these days?"

Stanley shrugged. "No clue. He's off investigating something, but he's not saying what. I only get a grunt or a 'doin' fine, boyo' when he comes home. I think he's rattled that Artie is still out there."

Stanley put his coffee cup into the sink. "I have to see Father Timothy and give him an update. So I'll walk with you to the corner."

They walked down the street toward Anino's corner. Stanley breathed in the cold air, relishing the smell of oncoming winter. He wondered when it would snow and remembered last winter when the Knights led an epic, two day, snow battle in the neighborhood. Everyone had gotten into the act; adults, kids, and even the cops came to play. For a while, there was no depression, no hungry bellies, and no lost jobs. Just everyone throwing around a bunch of snow, laughing, and counting their bruises from snow that had been packed a bit too hard.

Stanley sighed and shoved his hands deeper into his coat pockets. Everything was changing. In the past few days, a lot of questions about his life had been answered. The mystery of his parents was now solved. He and Hazel were all aces now. If all this had happened a few months ago, he would have finally felt like his life made some sort of sense. But maybe that was the way of things; when one part of your life gets figured out, other parts go nutty.

"Stanley, look at this," Anino said, bending down to his papers.

A black branch stuck out from the stack of papers, and the tip was coated with blood.

"They know how *The Knight's Voice* is getting into the world," Anino said, taking off his hat and running his hand through his black hair.

"Yeah, it was only a matter of time," Stanley said.

"But did everyone get one of these? How could they know who was doing what?" Anino glanced around, nervous.

Stanley walked across the street to the nearest newsie, who was busy selling papers.

"Hey, Frankie, see anything unusual in your papers this morning?"

"What, like your mother?" Frankie said, smoking his pipe hard.

"Nah, like a painted stick or something," Stanley said, grinning.

Frankie shook his head. "You're crackers. Only thing I got was pay, such as it was. Now maybe I can get a can of soup or somethin'."

Stanley walked down a few blocks and checked with a few other newsies. No one else had gotten black branches. So they were targeting Anino and maybe the other Knights. Somehow, they figured it all out. He walked back to Anino in a hurry.

"No one else got a branch."

Anino nodded. "Kinda figured. They've got us pegged, Stanley. I gotta say, that scares the piss out of me. I don't want my family hurt or nothin'."

Stanley sat on the curb with his head in his hands. "Yeah, me either. I don't want anyone to have any trouble. But we got it anyways."

"I guess, Stanny, but I didn't sign up for all this when I joined the Knights."

Standing up, Stanley said, "You think I did, you mug? I just wanted to nick some food for some hungry people."

"Yeah, but you got dizzy with some rich dame and had to walk her home. Now, here we are."

Stanley hissed, "Don't blame Haze for all this. This is way bigger than any of us. They've been doing this a long time. Planning and putting things into place. Kids disappearing. All of that was gonna happen anyway. But at least now we know why."

Crossing his arms, Anino stood his ground. "Maybe. But seems like you and Artie added gasoline to the engine, stepped on the gas, and took us along for the ride."

He wanted to argue, but a part of him thought that maybe Anino was right. Maybe Stanley wasn't any better than Arthur.

Maybe he should have just left it all alone and not gotten involved, because now people he cared about were in trouble.

"Look, pal, I didn't ask for any of this. A few months ago, I was a kid with a gang who helped people. Now, everything is screwy, and I'm in love with a dame I probably won't ever be able to marry."

Anino stared at him for a moment. "You just said 'in love,' palsy."

Stanley's hand went to his chest, and the tension went out of him. "Yeah. Yeah, I did."

"First time I've ever heard you say that about any dame."

He was right. With all the girls he'd been with, Stanley could say he never loved any of them. Sure, he liked most of them. But love? No way. But he did love Hazel, and that was facts. No point even trying to deny it.

"Well, it's because I mean it. I love that dame, and I'm dizzy for her. But what good will that do me? I've got no money or connections."

Anino grinned. "One step at a time, there, ace. You gotta survive all of this first."

Taking off his hat, Stanley rubbed his head and said, "You said it, wheat, and how."

They stood there for a moment, watching the cars go buy, belching out exhaust, and honking, as if that would make the morning traffic go by any faster.

"So, what are you going to do?" Anino said.

"Make good so I can buy a life worthy of her." Stanley curled his fist, determined.

Anino laughed. "Not about the dame, about the stick and the Veiled Prophet."

Stanley blushed and then shrugged his shoulders. "Oh... I have no idea. Guess I should go see Father Timothy and sound things out. Maybe he's got some answers."

"Yeah, maybe. Listen, Stanny, I'm sorry I lost it before. You know you can count on me. I got your back."

Grabbing him in a bear hug, Stanley pounded on Anino's back. "Thank you, my brother, thank you."

"Easy there, Papa Bear, you almost crushed me."

Stanley let him go and grinned. "All right, you gangster, I'm off."

He walked fast to St. James and found Father Timothy in the sacristy, taking off his robes from the morning mass.

"Ah, Stanley, missed you this morning."

"Sorry, Father, Anino and I got to talking. He had a black branch in his stack of papers this morning."

Father Timothy pressed his lips together. "That's a tidy, little threat. Any news on Arthur or Teeth?"

"No, but there are others missing too. Way more than before."

The priest didn't say anything for a moment. He took off his stole, kissed it, and put it on a wooden hook. Then he took the alb off his head, and as he did, his hair stood on end from the static electricity. Stanley laughed, in spite of himself.

The priest grinned. "That's one thing they didn't teach me in seminary; how to deal with the hair-raising experience of wearing the sacred robes." He smoothed down his hair. "Follow me to the rectory. I have someone I think you should meet."

Intrigued, Stanley followed the priest into the short cloister that led to the priest's living quarters. He always felt this made St. James seem like a mini monastery, and when he was younger, before he discovered girls, he dreamed of being a priest. The whole life appealed to a side of him that needed order and simplicity. Another part of him realized he would never be satisfied with that sort of structure. Still, he breathed in the peace of the sacred space all around him.

Father Timothy led him into the rectory and then the kitchen. There, sitting at a table, was a black-robed monk, drinking tea and reading the Post-Dispatch. The whole scene jarred him a bit, as he imagined monks living a life of austerity and prayer. He looked up and smiled.

"Ah, this must be the lad himself. Stanley, I'm Brother Martin."

Brother Martin. The guy who had been in the ranks of the Veiled Prophet and got himself out. He looked younger than Stanley expected, but laugh lines had already started to appear around his eyes and mouth.

"It's great to meet you. Heard so much about you."

The monk grinned. "Hope that's a good thing." He motioned to the table. "Please, join me."

"So what brings you to St. Louis at last?" Stanley said, taking a seat at the table.

The priest looked at Stanley. "I contacted Brother Martin after I received your message about what you overheard in the asylum the other day." He filled the tea kettle back up and put it on the stove.

The monk eyed Stanley. "It seems The Winnowing has truly begun, so here I am." His face was grim, but then a small smile crossed his lips. "And I must say, I was curious to meet the guy who stole the boss's girl's heart."

"The boss? Who's that?" Stanley asked, furrowing his brow. "I mean, if I kissed her and all that, I'm not like that anymore. I hope I didn't hurt her or cause trouble."

The monk and the priest exchanged amused looks. Stanley frowned. "Am I missing something?"

The monk said, "The boss is Nicholas Malloy. He used to be my boss and mentor in business before I took my vows."

The pieces started to fall into place in Stanley's head.

As if reading his mind, Father Timothy said, "Yes. Brother Martin is how Mr. Malloy and I met. But perhaps I should let him tell the story."

Brother Martin shifted in his seat. "It's not a pretty one, Stanley, and I'm not proud of most of it."

Stanley shrugged. "I'm not your judge. I'm not proud of a few things myself."

The monk chuckled. He seemed like a fellow who was quick to smile and have a good laugh. Stanley liked that.

"Ah, you're just like Nicholas and the good Father described you. Excellent." He beamed before switching into story mode. "My melodrama starts near Dogtown, actually. My father built up a hugely successful ice business. He did so well that he was able to buy a house over on Lindell, not too long before I was born. I was the youngest, you see, so I never knew the struggles that my parents went through early in life."

The tea kettle began to sing, and Father Timothy retrieved it from the stove. He freshened Brother Martin's cup, and filled two mugs of Irish breakfast tea for him and Stanley.

"Thank you, Father." The monk took a sip. "So, I grew up with a lot of money and opportunity. I was a spoiled child." He peered into his cup before continuing, more serious now. "The hooded men first came for me when I was twelve. The ritual was frightening to me. I was sure … there were other beings present. There was a darkness that I later explained away as the kind of fear and hysteria that a child experiences around a campfire when scary stories are shared. I realized later, that as a child, I was actually right."

"Other beings…" Stanley thought of the times he knew he saw dark figures swirling in the shadows. Like when he and Hazel had found Evelyn's body.

Brother Martin gave him an understanding look. "You've seen them."

"I think so." Stanley shivered and took a drink of his tea.

"However, these visits were a mere initiation compared to what would come later in my life. As a child, my role in the secret society of Legion was to pledge loyalty and participate in a kind of hazing when a new initiate would enter. Harmless mostly. But I was bound by my word to serve the Veiled Prophet and indoctrinated to believe that we were special. Above other people."

Stanley listened, the tea warming his hands as he gripped the cup. He wondered if it had seemed to a young kid like joining a club like the Knights. Brother Martin probably had no idea what he was getting into.

"As a young man, I ended up attending Princeton. I excelled there and began working as an intern for Nicholas Malloy. He was a good mentor, had high hopes for me. While there, I met August Chouteau; he was older than I and had also been initiated into Legion as a youth. He's the older brother of Charles, whom I know you've met."

Stanley snorted. "That's the understatement of the year."

Brother Martin nodded. "Yes. In case you're wondering, the whole family is like Charles, civil when you first meet them, but underneath is a strain of cruelty and sadism like I've never seen."

He crossed himself and sipped his tea. "August said it was time for me to ascend. He told me that serving the Veiled Prophet was more than a club for kids. He hooked me up with the Bengal Guards, and my family was invited to the Veiled Prophet Ball. Everyone was thrilled and honored. My parents bought into the whole thing, hook, line, and sinker. They still went to mass on Sunday, but their real faith was the Veiled Prophet and his teachings." Sighing, he went on, "We don't speak anymore.

"And so the Bengals began to train me and initiate me into the different levels. At first, the initiations were more college hazing type things, no different than the fraternity I joined at Princeton. But the more I progressed, the more disturbing it became. And I regret to say, I did not stop it right away."

"How disturbing?" Stanley wondered.

Father Timothy frowned. "That's a personal question, Stanley, and under the seal of the confessional."

"No. He must know, Father. They want blind obedience and submission, Stanley. So they make you do things that are shameful or criminal, so they can use it against you if you betray them. I found myself..." He paused, staring into his cup again. "...doing and saying things I never dared to consider. Dishonest things, immoral things. Then, beating people, especially colored people, as they could easily be taken off the streets, and no one would ask any questions. But the worst of all, were the rituals and elaborate ceremonies. Each one progressed to something darker until..." Brother Martin raised his eyes to look at Stanley.

Stanley shifted in his seat. This is not what he expected at all. He wasn't sure if he wanted to hear anymore. "What happened to make you wanna get out?"

The monk stirred his tea for a moment, as if to gather his thoughts. "I'm not sure all the penance in the world will cover it."

Putting his hand on Brother Martin's shoulder, Father Timothy said, "Peace, brother. You know that's not how it works. You have forgiveness. Always."

"I know, Father, or at least I hope I do. Stanley, you're going to find, the older you get, the harder it is to forgive yourself." Sighing, he continued, "But the Abbot has given this to me as my penance, and I pray that will be enough."

Brother Martin closed his eyes. "One night, they took me to an island somewhere. I'm not sure where, to be honest. But when they took off my hood, I was surrounded by thirteen men in Veiled Prophet outfits, the whole regalia. And somehow, I don't know if they drugged me or what, but they spoke together in one voice."

Silence filled the kitchen. Stanley had expected there to be just one Veiled Prophet, commanding and giving orders. "Why? Why thirteen? I don't get it."

Father Timothy rubbed his unshaven face. "Groups of the occult tend to mock and distort for their own purpose. In this case, thirteen is the number of Jesus and his apostles."

Stanley nodded. "I see. Like a dark mirror."

Father Timothy folded his hands on the table. "Evil often reflects good in a distorted way. Brother Martin's story told us that the soul of St. Louis was rotten to the core and had turned itself over to the dark powers. That is why the Vatican sent me."

Stanley always sensed the darkness, but it was something deeper and more sinister than he ever thought until the day they found Evelyn's murdered body. It wasn't just the poor suffering and the rich ignoring it. "Tell me more. What happened after they took you to the island?"

The monk sighed. "They spoke to me in one voice, telling me this was the initiation into my final test."

"Test for what?"

Brother Martin hung his head. "There was a family. They had to be taught a lesson… and there was something the Veiled Prophet wanted from them."

Realization clicked on in Stanley's head. "Artie's family. The Stewarts."

"Yes. Charles Chouteau was a newer initiate. It was his task to do the worst of it, but I was there to help. It went too far… I didn't expect it. Their young boy witnessed his father and mother being tortured in horrible ways, waiting for his own turn. He was the… motivation for his parents to cooperate."

"That kid… that was my best friend, you bastard." Stanley slammed his fists on the table. "Do you have any idea how that destroyed him?"

The monk squeezed his eyes shut, nodding his head. "It was the look in his eyes… innocence shattered, fear … then the begging. Something in me snapped. I attacked Charles and allowed the boy to escape." His voice was strained and rough. "Then I went into hiding. I reached out to Nicholas with my story; I needed someone to help me get out."

Stanley swallowed more tea, trying to calm down. This man was one of the reasons why Artie was the way he was. "How did you know Mr. Malloy wasn't in on it?"

"Well, I did not know for sure. But he was always good to me, and I knew there was defiance in him. And… I'm guessing that nobody in league with the Veiled Prophet would have married someone like Mrs. Malloy."

Furrowing his brow, Stanley said, "I guess that's true." He thought of Mumsy and how different she was from the high society dolls. She was more like the kind of woman who hung out in Dogtown speakeasies back in the day and danced on tables. It sometimes amazed him that Hazel was her daughter.

Brother Martin shrugged. "I couldn't trust my own parents. Nicholas had been like an older brother, almost a father really. And somehow, he believed me. He told me he'd been hearing rumors for years about an island and strange rituals. Mr. Malloy trusted me at my word. I think he must have had some other reasons for believing me that I don't know about. In any case, I pleaded for help to leave the city, that I wanted my Catholic faith back, anything to protect me and my soul."

Stanley nodded. He could understand what Brother Martin was feeling.

"He went to a trusted, Jesuit priest with my story who contacted his Provincial General, who, I think, contacted Rome.

They flew in Father Timothy who met with Mr. Malloy here. And they arranged for me to go to St. Meinrad in the middle of the night. Later, I wrote my parents, telling them I had run off to Germany." Sighing he said, "And that's how I became Brother Martin and how Father Timothy came to be in St. Louis. He and Nicholas have been working together to figure out what we are up against. My stories, and those I have collected from other VP defectors I have found, were only the beginning. Nicholas Malloy has been invaluable to the cause. People with money and power are good allies in a war like this one."

Stanley stared into his tea, as if trying to read the leaves. Overwhelmed, worry rose inside of him. This was all so much bigger than he could fathom. He knew the monk and the priest were watching him for some sort of reaction. And then he looked up. "Do you know how much you've both piled on me? I have Knights to worry about, and the paper, and Hazel, my sweet Hazel. And now, you just put one more thing on to me? It's like you want me to lead like my father did. I'm just a kid. Why bother telling me any of this? Three months ago, I was worrying about what girl to kiss. Now, I'm worried the girl I love might die, I just found out my mom is alive, and all my friends are disappearing," Stanley said, running his hands through his hair.

Father Timothy and Brother Martin stared at him for a moment. They didn't say anything, and finally the monk said, "I was young when I started with the Veiled Prophet. Younger than you are now. You've already faced more than most people and beat it all. Now because of you and Hazel, we know about The Winnowing."

Stanley slumped back in the chair. "I've just tried to do my part. That's all."

Father Timothy patted Stanley's hand. "That's all any of us can do. But while I'm not a soothsayer by any means, I feel like you have more of a part to play in these events. You have a good grasp on what's happening in the streets. We aren't asking you to do this alone. It may be tempting to think we're the only ones fighting evil, but we're not. We can each only do our bit. And you have always done yours."

Brother Martin said, "We've all been brought here. I'm staying with Father Timothy for a while. It's time we put an end to this. And maybe, just maybe, The Lord will bless it."

Stanley sighed. "Okay. Well, now what? Do we find this island?"

"I'm going to try. And I'm going to help with the newspaper. We're getting some ... unique help from Rome soon. But finding the right island might take some time," the monk said.

Stanley asked, "What do you want me to do?"

"Keep up with The Winnowing articles. Help us find Arthur, and keep us informed if anything new happens. We are working things on this end, and I'm trying to find the right people in power who will help us. That may take some time." Father Timothy stood and opened a window. A breeze swept in, ruffling his hair.

"Well, let's get to work then," Brother Martin said. "My first stop is the city library."

CHAPTER EIGHTEEN

The next morning, Hazel's father sat at the breakfast table, reading the paper. When she joined him, he smiled. "Good morning, Hazel. Been reading this latest article written by the anonymous newsie." He pulled out the loose page that had been slid between the pages of his morning paper. "It's brilliant work. He's a talented boy."

Hazel glanced at it, anxiety rising in her chest. "Yes. He's sharp as a tack."

"I know the two of you don't have any secrets from one another, so you will have heard of some of our efforts. In the past, you've censured me for being an unfeeling 'swell.'" He smiled at his daughter.

Hazel opened her mouth to argue, but Mr. Malloy raised a hand. "No, I am proud of you for challenging me. I hid things to protect you, and because what I do is not for recognition. But now that the cat's out of the bag, I want you to know that I've always helped in the ways I can. I'm honored to see my money put to good use. And if I'm honest, your opinion of me matters. I want to be a father you can look up to."

Hazel swallowed the lump in her throat. "Gee, Pops… I think you're grand. Honest."

Her father smiled at the nickname now. It was a rare sight on his face that made him look younger and more dashing.

"I've always wanted to make you proud. Be the perfect debutante daughter for you—just never could."

"I'm proud of you as you are, my little flower." He had not called her that since she was very young. "And as long as I'm being honest, other than the reputational advantages… I find debutantes dull in the extreme. Why do you think I married your mother?"

Laughing, Hazel got up from her chair and hugged her father, scrunching the newspaper he held. "Oh, Daddy. You're aces."

He squeezed back and then cleared his throat. "Indeed. Now have some breakfast."

Hazel plopped back into her seat, feeling light and cheery. She gave her dad a wink. "I always suspected you were a bit of a rogue."

Nicholas Malloy's cheeks reddened slightly. "Gertie wouldn't have me any other way." He almost smiled again, she could tell by the way his moustache twitched. "As I was saying," he said, laying the paper down. "This paper is starting the kind of talk that we had hoped. The mayor is being bombarded with questions. It was time both sides of the story were told. Let the people decide the truth."

Hazel nudged her bacon across the plate with her fork, and it slid onto the table. "I'm going to search the clinic for a file that proves Maxie didn't die the way the papers are saying." She pushed the bacon onto the floor and heard the thump of Henri's tail wagging from under the table.

"They are not focused on you right now. Find what you can but only if you can do so without risk."

"Doctor Galton is convinced I'm in love with Gabriel Sinclair, and that this latest outrage with the newsies has me against them."

"He might not think much about you 'organizing' his files, unlike if anyone else did. Just be discreet and smart."

"You got it. I plan on trying to go in tomorrow… I gotta invent an excuse for being there if I'm caught."

"I'll write you a check. You can say you are delivering a donation." Her father raised his dark brows. "Most people are deeply distracted by money."

"That's awfully clever." Hazel liked that her father was treating her like one of the resistance. She wanted to do her part and not wait in the ivory tower while other people rescued her. "No wonder Gabriel and the other boys worship you."

"I've got a mind for business." Her father took a bite of his eggs benedict and then wiped his lips with a serviette. "Speaking of Gabriel, he was here earlier. I believe he left you a note with Roberts."

"Oh? I can't imagine…"

"Can't you? You're a beautiful girl, Hazel."

"Dads have to say that." She pursed her lips and tucked a curl behind her ear.

"Nonsense."

"But his father paid to start the clinic… makes me uneasy."

"Proceed with caution." Mr. Malloy picked up his coffee and took a sip then rang the little silver bell beside his plate.

A few moments later, Roberts strode in, his gray head held high. "Yes, sir?"

"Say, bring that note young Sinclair left for Hazel, won't you?"

"Of course." Roberts exited swiftly to obey.

Hazel took a bite of her breakfast. This was already turning out to be an interesting day. If only she could tell Stanley all about it. She missed that mug.

The delicate, gold Rolex on Hazel's wrist told her it was after five o'clock, and the December sun had already set. She drummed her fingers on the marble counter of the soda fountain uptown. This was where and when Gabriel wanted to meet to have a serious talk. She hoped it was not a relationship talk or something. He may have been her first kiss, but kissing someone didn't make you love them. To kiss someone you already loved... that changed the game.

Several other teenagers sat on the round stools at the long counter. Some drank Coca-Cola or colored phosphates, others dug into tall, fluted glasses full of ice cream, heaped with toppings with long, silver spoons. She watched the freckle-faced boy behind the counter making an ice cream soda. The sweet smell of syrups, along with the savory smell of sizzling hamburgers and french fried potatoes, made Hazel's mouth water.

A jumpy, jazzy version of "Jingle Bells" played on the large, wooden radio on one end of the space that was crammed with small, round tables and wrought iron chairs. Silver tinsel and paper bells were strung along the walls. It was a lively place. Again, it flipped Hazel's mind that this was the world that was at war. It seemed so carefree. Where was all of the hate? Most folks could come and go on the street, work a job and eat at diners without harm. She wondered if people living in Dogtown and places like that felt the same... perhaps not.

"Hazel."

There was Gabriel, peering down at her through his black spectacles, hair slicked back, in a snug-fitting, white polo shirt, sports coat, and college scarf.

She stood up and let him give her the customary peck on the cheek. "Hiya."

"I called a few times after the ball to see if you were okay," he said, slipping his scarf off. "Did Roberts tell you?"

"Sure. I appreciate it."

"I see…" He nodded. "Hey, soda jerk. Two vanilla ice cream sodas," Gabriel called to the kid behind the counter.

"You got it, mister."

Hazel would have chosen chocolate, but it didn't surprise her that Gabriel hadn't bothered to ask. "What's on your mind, Sinclair?"

Gabriel folded his hands together on his lap and cocked his head at Hazel. "I saw what Fields did the night of the ball, and I find myself in a psychological dilemma. You see… I had my mind made up about things not so long ago. I knew my place in this world. And I knew the place of people like your newsie."

Hazel didn't bother objecting to Stanley being called her newsie. "Snug in your views, were you?"

"Well, yes. Until… you." He looked at her with admiration. "What I mean by that is… you showed me something different. Hazel, you are who you are. You don't follow the pack. You've always been a bit odd…"

Hazel scrunched her nose. "Says you."

He chuckled. "I'm starting this badly."

Ice cream sodas were placed in front of them, and Gabriel stared at his while Hazel played with the straw in her own.

"So, I'm odd, and you know your place?" Hazel took a sip of her drink, wondering what Gabriel was thinking.

He flashed a smile, put his elbow on the counter, and leaned his face on one of his fists. "The way you stood by Fields and his little band of riff-raff through everything. You defied the rules."

"Well, sure. They're good people and bad rules." She was not expecting a conversation like this with Gabriel Sinclair.

"You see? They're just people to you. Not street rats…"

"I didn't always think that way, Gabe. I didn't know anyone outside our circles. It was new to me."

"You gave them a chance."

Hazel stirred her drink. "I suppose so. But I stumbled into the middle of some stark truths that blew the top off of the world I knew," she said.

He nodded slowly and took a sip of his soda. "And then when Fields threw himself on the kid with the gun … to save a room full of swells who never regarded him as anything more than scum or a novelty…" He stroked his chin as if searching for words. "I realized that he saw us as people too." He chuckled at himself. "Is this all making sense? People seeing people as people?"

Hazel smiled. "Yes. It does."

He let out a sigh. "Most of my life I have seen things cock-eyed. Through a warped lens."

"That's true for everyone."

"Some people won't learn. Like my father," he said, his face darkening. "He acts the saint… building clinics for the poor and all of that. But he wants to look good. He wants to be mayor someday."

Hazel wondered if Gabriel knew anything about what else went on at the Family Care Clinic. She watched him, and he seemed to be struggling with something.

He put his hands over his face and took a deep breath. "After Evelyn was killed, I began to notice other things. Politics. Secret meetings. Men who had been best friends and business associates for years turning against one another. The mass murder of the St. Louis gangs. Servants whispering about disappearing neighbors…"

Hazel held her breath. Gabriel was coming awake before her eyes. "What else?"

"Then Maxie was killed…" The handsome, society boy gave a frown. "I'm ashamed to admit that she served my family for years, and I barely knew her … I have more to say about all of that, but…" He turned in his seat and faced Hazel. He pulled a paper out of his pocket. "A couple of days before the VP Ball, I found this between the pages of a newspaper I bought."

Hazel knew what it was before she looked at it. She took the copy of *The Knight's Voice* and looked at the headline. *The Winnowing Is Stealing Our Freedom and Our Future.*

"Do you believe any of this business?" Hazel asked, searching his eyes.

He swallowed. "I—I don't know what to think… After the ball blew up, I noticed how the papers described what happened. It was like Evelyn's murder all over again. The truth was clouded."

Hazel waited as she saw him trying to control his feelings.

"Hazel. I just don't know what's real. Charles was a close chum for years." His voice broke. "I had no notion he was capable of such brutality. They say he was crazy, but… I think there is something else."

"He's working for the Veiled Prophet," Hazel blurted.

Gabriel removed his spectacles and rubbed his eyes. "So this paper is true then." He groaned. "Hazel."

She leaned forward and put a hand on his shoulder. "What is it?"

"My father… I think…"

A familiar voice broke in. "What's the big idea?" Stanley stood behind them, his hands held up in question, a look of confusion on his face. "What's this all about, Haze?"

"Stanley!" Hazel was so excited to see him, the look on his face didn't soak in. She stood and hugged him.

He was stiff in her arms. "When I said we had to avoid each other for a while, I didn't mean you should make googly eyes with this chump."

"Cool your heels, Fields." Gabriel sipped his drink.

"Why you…" Stanley grumbled.

"You following me, Snoopy?" she murmured into his coat.

"We were tailing this goon. His whole family, actually. So what's the skinny here?" Stanley gently grasped Hazel by the shoulders and pushed her back so he could look into her eyes. He raised a brow.

She stuck out her tongue, and he cracked a smile, catching on that this was not what it seemed. "Listen and find out, silly," she said.

"Hello, Fields," Gabriel said, pulling himself together. "Actually I'm glad you came. I'm just getting to the part that may interest you and your renegades."

"Huh? What are you gumming about?"

"I was just about to tell Hazel about Ruth," Gabriel said, replacing his spectacles.

Stanley kept one arm around Hazel and plopped down on her stool so that she sat on his knee. "Go on."

"Ruth. The girl I met a year ago between semesters. She's beautiful, clever, graceful… a real pip at tennis. I thought I would just have a lark with her. But then, I fell in love, you see."

Hazel grinned and clapped her hands. "Casanova caught by Cupid."

He rolled his eyes. "Yes. I was caught. I knew I wanted her in my life, so I started to think about the practicals of that. Her family was moderately wealthy. Her father ran a successful winery before Prohibition, and then bootlegged until that came to an end, and started back up with wine. He's legitimate. Even knowing her family wasn't up to my family's standards... I hoped." He crumpled the paper he held in his hands.

Stanley glanced down and seemed to recognize the paper. He turned his face to Hazel and raised his brows. She nodded and then leaned back against his chest. "What happened?" Hazel asked.

"My father couldn't get past that she was a Jew, and that her family was not the right kind. He forbade me to see her again. Of course, there were the clichéd threats of losing his financial support etcetera, etcetera. Common behavior, even for him." He shook his head in disgust. "But, ever the dutiful son, I obeyed. I let her go in my never ending effort to please that man."

Hazel felt sorry for Gabriel. "That breaks my heart," she said.

"But giving her up ... has proved impossible. I can't seem to move on no matter how I try." Gabriel shook his head.

"And nobody has tried as hard as you," Hazel said.

He gave Hazel an apologetic look. "My father said to date someone more appropriate."

She laughed. "My dad used to sing that tune. He was keen on me dating you too."

Stanley's voice was unexpectedly kind. "Gabe, every boy wants a proud father. No shame in that."

"Every son wants a father to be proud of too. I can barely look at mine ... he's a hypocrite and maybe worse." He picked up his soda and took a swig without the straw as if it were beer.

"Need something harder than that for this next part?" Stanley said.

The conflicted frat boy wiped his mouth. "Brother, you have no idea."

Hazel and Stanley waited while Gabriel summoned the courage to speak. "My father... had a thing for Maxie. I saw them together once in the kitchen late at night. And they weren't making *dinner* on the table."

Stanley shifted uncomfortably. "That so?"

"Oh." Hazel's face burned when she understood.

Gabriel nodded. "I don't know if she felt the same back… Didn't get the impression she was as… enthusiastic about their liaison."

"Oh. No…" Hazel frowned, thinking of Maxie being trapped in a situation where she had no power.

Gabriel stared at his hands. "I heard the rumors. I put two and two together. Maxie was pregnant. Then the next thing I knew, she was murdered."

Hazel let out a deep breath. It was even worse than he knew.

"He objected to me loving Ruth because she was a Jew. While he took a Negro servant as a lover whether she liked it or not. Maybe my dad had her shot when he learned she was pregnant? I don't know. I sound coo coo." By now, Gabriel's voice shook with rage. "Hypocrite," he spat.

Hazel slipped off of Stanley's lap and hugged Gabriel. It was all she could think of to do.

"Thank you…" He patted her back.

"Why did you want Hazel to know all of this?" Stanley had his detective face on, as if he wasn't sure he could trust Gabriel.

"Because after everything with Evelyn and Charles and all the rumors, I just felt like I was raised in a nest of snakes. I don't know who to trust. Hazel's always been different. And then, seeing the two of you standing against the crowd … I don't know. I just wanted to tell someone all this who wouldn't judge me. Then I read this." He held up the crinkled article Stanley had written. "Whoever wrote this knows things, and I always thought that somehow Hazel did too."

Stanley stood. "Let's go for a walk, pal. I have more to tell you, and that radio may not be loud enough to cover what we say. Especially if you feel like yelling."

Confused, Gabriel stood too. "Yelling?"

"Yeah. It's about the clinic… and Maxie's supposed shooting."

Gabriel's brow wrinkled in alarm. He placed a couple of dimes on the counter and followed Stanley and Hazel outside to hear the rest.

Gabriel Sinclair was ready to hear the truth. He reacted angrily when he learned that Maxie did not die of a gunshot the way the papers said. It was like his whole world had been dumped upside down. Hazel knew the feeling.

She was surprised at how well he and Stanley got on as they talked. At one point, Gabriel even said to Stanley, "I'm sorry about socking you before. I was full of resentment that night and missing Ruth. And… it angered me that you and Hazel had each other."

In response, Stanley had said, "No worries. I didn't realize you'd socked me. Felt more like a breeze went by."

Which then led to a ridiculous amount of back and forth insults and chuckling. Hazel didn't understand boys.

By the time they'd finished talking, Gabriel had sworn to use all of his knowledge, influence, and money to help stop what was happening. Stanley didn't mention that he was the anonymous writer for *The Knight's Voice* or the identities of others in the Order of St. Michael. Hazel figured that in time, trust would come.

After the frat boy had gone, wiser and galvanized to action, Stanley and Hazel walked hand in hand down a quiet, middle class, residential street. She told him about her encounter with Arthur outside the clinic.

"That idiot is in hot water. We're still trying to find him. Good to know he might be haunting the clinic," Stanley said. "Proud of you stopping him that way."

"Well, Henri helped."

"He's a swell pooch."

Hazel saw that Stanley was tired. He seemed to carry the deaths of Evelyn, Vinnie, and Maxie, the vanishing of countless boys, and the grief of too many women who would never be mothers.

"It isn't all up to you, you know. The whole world is responsible for all of this," Hazel said.

"Yeah. I know. But do they know that?" He gave a small smile then raised their clasped hands and kissed the back of hers.

The moon was bright in the sky, casting shadows of the trees that lined the sidewalk. The deep indigo sky was sprinkled with stars like a shattered tiara over a world that had forgotten who it was. Frost glowed on the grass and fences. It was cold, but holding Stanley's hand made Hazel feel warm all over.

"I know we aren't supposed to be seen together, Snoopy. But I liked being with you at a soda fountain like a normal girl sitting on her boyfriend's knee."

"Boyfriend?" Stanley grinned. "I liked that too, baby."

Hazel let out a sigh. She and Stanley had been an influence on Gabriel and perhaps countless others. Maybe the class divide would shrink if more people crossed it.

"I guess we go back to me playing the fool and avoiding one another for a while?"

"I don't want that," Stanley said. "But maybe we should." He squeezed her hand.

"Just don't forget about me," she said.

"I'm putting all my eggs in one basket, Haze. You're the only girl I love."

Hazel's heart pounded. "I love you too."

They stopped walking and faced one another. "Then we've unlocked the biggest secret of the universe," Stanley whispered. "Everything else is just an afterthought."

Hazel lost track of how long they stared into one another's eyes. It didn't matter how many minutes went by, how cold it was, or what might be in the shadows. They were together.

Hazel rose up on her toes, and they held one another, kissing slow and forever. Home. Soul mates. It was like Peggy said, they could be as different as the sun and moon but would always share the same sky. No matter how terrible and whacky the world was, as long as Stanley was in it, there was no other place Hazel wanted to be.

CHAPTER NINETEEN

Stanley walked along the river with a small smile on his face. His cold breath came out in regular bursts of steam, but he didn't mind. Thoughts of Hazel sitting on his knee in front of Gabriel and smooching on him made him feel aces and kept him warm.

Gabriel. It just went to show there was no way you could judge someone too quickly. Sure, the guy could be a first class swell, but love had changed him, made him see the truth. Father Timothy talked about love being the burning heart of the world, and that it could transform everything. Stanley had been skeptical of all that, even as he tried to embrace it. But Gabriel's about-face was a strong argument. And really, Hazel's love for him was changing him too. In a way, it was love for others that made the Order of St. Michael fight a long, losing battle for all these years.

He stopped to watch the driftwood floating by and thought about Arthur. That's what Artie never got. Hate was not enough. It could destroy and even the score, Stanley guessed. But in reality, it didn't make things better. It didn't take away the hurt or the pain. Not even close.

Sighing, he took a rock and threw it into the river. He needed to get back to the city. But he just wanted to stay here for a few more moments. Stanley leaned against his favorite tree and looked up and down the river, letting nature do its healing work.

"Stanley."

His name brought him up short, and he turned around. Walking toward him was Lincoln Thompson, a black newsie who acted as a go-between for the Knights and the black community. They funneled food through to him, and he distributed it in his neighborhood. They'd met last year when Stanley got tangled in a newsie strike in the wrong neighborhood and was accused of being a scab. Some palookas thought he needed a hammering, until Lincoln had intervened. Good thing, too, because he'd been outnumbered but good.

"Link, what's the skinny?" Stanley said, reaching out his hand.

"Looking for you, white boy. And here you are." Lincoln smiled, shaking his hand.

"Seems like the whole city is looking for me lately," Stanley grunted.

"Well, that's what happens when you piss off white folks in power. They don't like people a-meddling in their business."

"And how," Stanley said. "So how did you find me?"

Lincoln shrugged. "Somehow, I figured you'd be here. We talked about this place, remember? It's where you come to feel calm. And with everything that's been going on, brother, you need it. If you weren't here, I would have gone all the way to Dogtown."

Frowning, Stanley said, "That would have been risky for you. Something wrong?"

"You could say that. Last night, a little, lost white boy came stumbling into the neighborhood, half drowned. He had bruises all over his body and his eye swole shut. Old Mama Jefferson brought him home and put him to bed. I went over to see him, and he was raving about trains, a camp, guards, and other such nonsense. But he kept asking for you over and over."

Stanley shivered, and it wasn't from the cold. "What did this kid look like?"

"Come see for yourself."

They walked up the river bank and made their way to Lincoln's neighborhood. Stanley rarely went up to the north side of the city, so he relied on Lincoln's guidance as they chatted away about the Cardinals and talked about the St. Louis Stars and the defunct Negro baseball league. He found himself wishing he'd paid more attention to the team when they existed. The way Lincoln talked, Cool Papa Bell was the best ball player in history.

"So then, Papa started to dive and…" Lincoln tensed and grabbed Stanley by the arm.

"What? What gives?" Stanley asked.

"In the alley. Go, boy. Now." Lincoln shoved him off the street and into a small alleyway between two brick buildings. They moved until they found two trash cans, and Lincoln motioned for him to get down.

Stanley furrowed his brow and raised his hands in confusion. Lincoln shook his head, and motioned toward the road. They watched as a gang of ten white guys with closely clipped hair and dark trench coats walked past the alleyway. Lincoln waited for a moment then leaned over to Stanley.

"Some weird new gang, man. They're bad news, from what Mama Jefferson is hearing. Rumors are they're snatching kids from our neighborhood, but I think that's just bull."

Stanley shook his head. "It's not, or at least, it's not about to be. I think I know who they are."

"Okay, who?" Lincoln asked.

"Just take me to the kid. I'll tell you later."

Lincoln stared at him for a moment and then said, "All right. But I need to know who is invading my neighborhood, and you owe me."

Finally, they reached a small, wooden, shotgun house, and three old women sat on the front porch, rocking.

"Who's your friend there, Link? He's awful white," one asked, and they all cackled.

Lincoln took off his hat. "Ma'am, he might be, but he's a saint, I can promise you."

Stanley nudged him and then said, "I'm here to see the kid. He's been asking for me."

The three ladies looked each other. "So, you're Stanley? The kid who fought that crazy boy from Lindell?" one with white hair said.

Nodding, Stanley bowed. "At your service, ma'am."

One of the ladies stood up. She was full-figured and had a kerchief wrapped around her head. "Look at you, ain't you pert? Well, well, Stanley the Knight, I'm Mama Jefferson. You're welcome in my house. You a good, young man, I can tell. Come on in, and I'll get you some coffee."

Lincoln nodded toward the house. "Go on in, I'll stay out here with the other ladies and entertain them. Sort of paying the gatekeeper, you know."

Stanley went inside, the floorboards squeaking beneath his feet. Old Mama Jefferson's house was neat, but sparse. She obviously insisted on keeping her little house neat and tidy. And it smelled of freshly baked bread. Stanley found himself wishing he could just stay here and hide from the madness that was engulfing the city.

Mama Jefferson swept into the kitchen and poured him a steaming cup of coffee. "Now, sit yourself down, and let's gab a spell. Then you can go see that boy. He's laying down in my bed. I've been payin' attention to all the news, and I've seen the little newspapers that are going out. You have somethin' to do with that?" She sat down in her rocking chair and gave him a pointed stare.

"Well, not sure I can answer that question, ma'am," Stanley said, sipping his coffee.

"Ah, you think ole Mama Jefferson is gonna turn you in? Chile, you don't know me at all." She chuckled. "But I see your mind and respect it. You keep your secrets. But just know, all of us here are behind you. You just tell us what you need, and you have it."

He'd never met Mama Jefferson in his life. Yet here she was, asking him to name whatever help he needed. Stanley swallowed hard and felt the tears welling up in his eyes. Embarrassed, he looked away. He was more overwhelmed than he'd thought.

She reached over and patted him on the arm. "Yes, yes. I know. You've suffered. Our precious Jesus knows. He suffered himself, you see." She pointed to a huge picture of Jesus that hung on her wall. "He wants us all to rest in him and fight for good. That much I know. Lord knows, you have fought, chile, you have fought the good fight, as the preacher says."

"Thank you." It was all he could manage and sipped his coffee some more. Taking a few deep breaths, he said, "So, tell me about the kid."

She nodded. "Someone beat him up good. His eye is swollen shut, and I can't see how bad it is inside. Not even sure if he's gonna be able to see out of it. He's covered in bruises head to toe."

"Stanley… they're coming… Stanley." The shout from the back bedroom made Stanley's skin crawl. There was a tone of desperation and pain that he'd never heard before.

"Maybe you should go see for yourself, chile," Mama Jefferson said gently. "I'll be along directly. Bedroom is on the right side, opposite of the kitchen."

Stanley didn't have far to walk, and he opened the door. A small, frail form lay encased in a mountain of mismatched Afghans and quilts. He approached the bed and held back a gasp.

Teeth. Or whatever was left of him.

Sitting on the bed, Stanley touched Teeth's slight form, and the boy stirred. Mama Jefferson had been right about the eye. Teeth opened his good eye, which widened when he saw who was on the bed.

"Stanley. I got away. Aren't you proud of me? I got away," he rasped. Stanley poured a glass a water from the pitcher on the nightstand and gave it to Teeth, who drank deep.

"What do you mean, you got away, Teeth? What happened?"

The kid shook his head. "Legion got me and gave me this."

He held up his arm and showed Stanley the tattoo of numbers, the mark of the Veiled Prophet.

"Spin the story, kid."

Teeth laid back down and closed his good eye. "Sorry, Stanny, my head hurts."

"It's okay, kid. But I need you to tell me, and then you can rest."

Teeth frowned. "Don't remember much. I was at the clinic, and the doctor gave me a shot. I started feeling sleepy, and next thing I knew, I was in this weird train station with a bunch of other kids."

Stanley nodded. "Where is this station, Teeth?"

The kid scrunched up his face. "Well, couldn't see much. They gave us a bunch of shots and herded us into a boxcar."

"Just one?"

"Nah. Three of them. But ..." He paused, and his face lit up. "I do remember something!" Teeth said, trying to sit up.

Stanley placed a hand on his shoulder. "Don't get up. Just tell me."

"Well, when we pulled out of the weird, little station or whatever it was, I saw the Eads Bridge."

Eads Bridge. Not far from here. But Stanley couldn't remember ever seeing a train station anywhere near there.

"Are you sure? There's no station there."

Teeth sat up. "You calling me a liar?"

Stanley pressed him back down. "Easy, killer, I'm just saying, I can't think of where…"

He stopped. That was not entirely true. Just on the other side, was a collection of warehouses, and a new train line had gone up there a few years ago. Everyone said it was just to ship goods from the tugboats up north. But he wondered now.

"Okay, kid, I'll go check it out. What else?"

Teeth lay there for a moment, breathing heavily. "Well, I can't remember how long the train ride was, seemed like hours, but maybe not. It was all hazy. They got us out and put us on a boat. It was dark, but I saw an island with trees, with lights glimmering there. And just as they tried to put me in a boat, I kicked one of the guards, and they beat me something fierce. But then, other kids tried to escape, and it all got nutty. Somehow, I crawled out of there and hid in a fallen tree. They never found me, motherless bastards," Teeth spit.

"Watch your language, kid. You did good. And you just followed the river?"

"Yeah, I remember you tellin' me the river flowed south, and I thought we'd gone north. So I walked. Dunno how long, Stanny, I kept fainting, and I couldn't see."

Poor kid.

So Brother Martin was right. They did have an island someplace, and they were taking kids there. At least they had a direction where they could start: north. He'd have to take the Knights on a walk and see if they could find it. Maybe as a Christmas outing, Stanley thought with irony.

"You did aces, Teeth. You did real good." And then he kissed the kid on the forehead.

"Aw, Stanny, kissin' is for girls."

"Nah, it's for friends too. Brave friends," Stanley said. "And I'm gonna send Frisky down here, would you like that?"

"And ole Haze too? I'd prefer their kisses," Teeth said, looking eager.

"Easy, tiger, one of those dames is mine."

Teeth closed his eyes and smiled. "I'll fight you for her."

"Maybe someday. Rest," Stanley said and left the room.

Mama Jefferson sat on her rocker, and he heard Lincoln singing on the porch, strumming a guitar that one of the ladies must have gotten for him. He wailed "Dark was the Night and Cold was the Ground" by Blind Willie Johnson.

Dark was the night, and cold the ground
on which the Lord was laid;
his sweat like drops of blood ran down;
in agony he prayed,
Father, remove this bitter cup
if such Thy sacred will;
if not, content to drink it up
thy pleasure I fulfill.

The lyrics reached into Stanley's ribcage. He trembled, feeling as though something huge was coming. Something he would have to give up. Stanley had lost too much already, and the thought of more sacrifice terrified him.

The old lady fixed him with another glance and said, "What about you, boy? You ready to drink the cup the Lord has for you?"

Stanley twisted his hat in his hands. "I don't know. I think about runnin' sometimes, off to the mountains and forget all this."

She nodded. "Sure. All of us do. Some of us don't have no choice. And you don't either. You gotta go and do what you can do." Mama Jefferson got up out of her rocking chair with a groan and then said, "Come over here and give me a hug now. Let Mama Jefferson bear you up."

She hugged him with strength that surprised him. And she said, "Lord bless you, boy, you got a road before you."

Stanley nodded and said, "I hope I have enough strength to travel it."

"Sure you do. We all will bear you up. You ain't gotta worry. You ain't alone, not by a long shot."

She let him go and then spanked his bottom. "Go on now, and get to it."

He forced a grin, put on his hat, and tipped it to her. "Yes ma'am."

When he emerged from the house, Lincoln stopped playing the guitar and looked up. "What's shaking? You know the kid?"

Stanley nodded. "You know those warehouses just above Eads Bridge?"

"Yeah, sure. We don't go near there much. Some gang has the charge over that area."

"Wanna go poke around with me a bit?" Stanley said.

Lincoln grinned and put down the guitar. "Sure enough, boy. Let's go."

They walked back to the river and cut down through the city to Eads Bridge. They stole down through the pillars and into the warehouse complex. It didn't take long for them to find the train tracks.

"Here, look, Stanley, they go between the buildings and then…" Lincoln pointed to a large, brick building hidden among the rest of the warehouses.

"How in St. Peter's name did neither of us ever seen that before?"

Lincoln frowned. "Dunno. It's like it's designed to be hidden or something. Or maybe we just weren't looking with the right peepers. Besides, we don't spend time on this side … heard rumors the gangs here are rough."

They watched the building for a moment, but no one seemed to be stirring. Walking up to a door, they tried to open it, but it wouldn't budge.

Lincoln pointed up to a window. "Looky there. An open window. Think you can climb it?"

Stanley looked up to see a wide, open window about twenty feet up. He looked at the jagged bricks and picked out a few toe and hand holds. "Yeah, but the last, little bit will be hairy. I'll have to jump."

"Well, you's tall enough. Use that."

Furrowing his brow, Stanley said, "Thanks a lot, Lincoln."

"I aim to please," he said, grinning.

Stanley gripped onto the first hold and climbed up. He still had a good three feet, when he ran out of places to grip. The window sill was just out of his reach. With a deep breath, he jumped, and his fingers caught the edge of the wood. Grunting, he scrambled up, trying not to think of the drop below him. He pulled himself in and dropped onto a catwalk.

Looking below, he saw the train tracks dip down to meet a platform about forty feet below him. He noticed rows of crates on the platform. No… not crates; they looked more like cages, designed to hold hundreds of people, he guessed.

A huge banner covering the wall at the opposite wall from where he stood, depicted a tree with gnarled roots, just like in Evelyn's diary. It read: *Eugenics is the self direction of human evolution.*

"See anything?" Lincoln called out in a stage whisper.

"More than I ever wanted to…" Stanley shook his head. "I'll be right there."

He walked down the catwalk to a set of stairs down to the platform. Walking around, he saw dark spots on the floor. Bending down, he saw they were red, probably dried blood. Other than that, everything looked wiped clean.

Stanley shook with fear. This was the place. Or maybe one of them. He didn't know. Maybe there were places like this all over the city, hiding in plain sight. There had to be. And how had he missed them? Stanley took pride in knowing the ins and outs of his city. But this place made him realize secrets could still be kept, especially if you didn't bother hiding them. He suddenly had that prickling at the back of his neck. He was being watched.

He spun around and didn't see anyone. Stanley hurried to the door, unlocked it, and went outside. Lincoln stood there with his hands in his pockets.

"You okay? You look like you saw a ghost."

Stanley nodded. "You said it, pal, you said it. Let's make tracks and blow this place. I gotta get to Father Timothy and fast."

They ran back to the bridge and followed the road into the city.

"I gotta get back, Stanny. My momma and Pops are waiting for me." Lincoln reached out his hand, and Stanley shook it. "If you need anything, white boy, you just tell me."

Stanley smiled. "Thanks, pal. I'm gonna send you a crazy redhead by the name of Frisky. She's kinda like Teeth's mom. Let her help Mama Jefferson, if you don't mind." He paused for a moment and then said, "If something happens to me, get to Father Timothy, over at St. James parish. Tell him what we found."

Lincoln nodded, smile gone. "May the angels watch over you, Stanley Fields."

"Hope so, Lincoln, and thanks."

They parted ways, and Stanley hurried to catch the trolley back to Forest Park.

CHAPTER TWENTY

Mumsy opened the cardboard box, and what Hazel could only describe as the Christmas ornament smell, rose from inside of it. Her mother smiled, and a wistful look passed over her face. "Remember this one, Hazie?" She pulled out a red, felt Santa that Hazel had made in school when she was little. It was crooked, and one of the button eyes was missing.

"Yeah." She peeked into the box at the assortment of colorful glass and crystal ornaments mixed with homemade ones from her childhood.

Mr. Malloy stood in the arched doorway of the living room, holding his pipe and watching them with a content look on his face. He crossed the room and surveyed the tall pine tree that Roberts and Willy had brought in and secured. "That's a fine tree," he said, taking a puff on his pipe.

Hazel breathed in the spice of the pine tree, tinsel, and sweet tobacco; it was like breathing in her childhood. Mumsy stood and went to the phonograph to put on her favorite Christmas record. There was a plate of fudge and sugar cookies on the coffee table. Hazel's parents were not somewhere else.

It felt like the proverbial calm before a terrible storm. Hazel wanted to stay cocooned in this moment.

Mr. Malloy hung the lights on the tree, and she and Mumsy had fun hanging the ornaments and reliving old memories. When they had finished, her father crowned the tree with a large, gold star. Then the three of them sat, gazing at the tree. Her parents held hands.

Growing up, Christmas was about presents, family, and good food. It was the time of year when Mumsy's drinking was festive rather than embarrassing, and Mr. Malloy was home more because business took a break. Mrs. Flannigan always made sure there were plenty of delicious things to eat, and Peggy always had little surprises for her. It was the time of year when Hazel felt the safest and most loved.

It was a little less shiny this year. Probably because it was the first Christmas since Evelyn died, the kidnapping, and everything else that frayed Hazel's sense of security and peace. Maybe this was how adults experienced Christmas every year. The realities of life pressed down on them all the while. She thought of how many people suffered and went without year round. She wondered if that made Christmas a more painful time or a happy distraction.

Stanley had once told her about the Christmas when he was ten years old. His uncle got drunk and almost burned the house down because he thought he could make a flaming pudding his ma used to make back in Ireland. They beat the fire out of the curtains together. Stanley was ready for his uncle to explode in rage over it. But Seamus laughed, slapping his knee and hooting to the roof. Then he made them hot chocolate, and they decorated a wreath to hang on the mantle. That was the Christmas that his uncle handed him a package wrapped in newspaper and said,

"Open it, boyo. You're big enough now." Inside was the faded, flat cap that Stanley still wore. It had been his father's. Stanley said it was one of the happiest days of his life, even though they had nothing but each other. It was too bad it couldn't always be that way.

Hazel arrived at the clinic that afternoon with a check from her father in her coat pocket in case she needed an excuse for being there. She hoped to slip back into the file room without being seen. If the doctor knew she was there, there would be no way to excuse herself to go rummage. She had Jennings pull up to the back of the building by the alleyway. Her father had instructed the old chauffeur to wait to bring Hazel home.

Henri hopped out of the car behind Hazel, and they walked down the alley to where they confronted Arthur. The large trash bin had not been moved, and Hazel could see that the window was still open. She could hardly believe her luck. That supply room was usually locked, and nobody went inside, and the cluttered alleyway was no place the doctor and Marie would stroll, so the open window had not been discovered.

Hazel climbed up onto the smelly trash bin, and Henri whined and stood up on his hind legs, front paws on it.

"Bleib," she said to make him stay.

The window was old, and the wood was swollen. With effort, Hazel was able to tug it open enough that she could duck through. She slipped to the floor and landed behind a stack of chairs and several toppled boxes. She plugged her nose to stop a sneeze. Dust swirled in the shaft of light coming in through the window.

Stepping around the obstacles in the room, she made it to the door. She pressed her ear to it and listened. It was quiet. Hazel wondered if the clinic was even open. Perhaps the doctor was on holiday too. She closed her eyes and held her breath. A voice.

Bananas.

The low murmur of Doctor Galton's voice came through the door. It sounded like he was in his office down the hall, perhaps on the phone. Hazel unlocked the door, opened it a crack, and peeked out. To the left, was the empty reception room, and down the hall, one of the exam room doors was ajar. She thought she saw Marie's white uniform flash by.

As the doctor's voice continued on the telephone, Hazel slipped into the hall, quietly moving toward the file room across the hall from his office, keeping her eyes on the open exam room.

A few steps from the door, she could make out words.

"…leave the station as agreed… yes. I'm doing my best. There have been some snags. No, sir. This neighborhood is in order."

Hazel slowly turned the knob on the door and stepped into the dim room just as the click of the telephone hanging up sounded.

Easing the door shut, she stood and waited. After a minute, footsteps moved from the doctor's office and out into the hall. "Marie, come in here please."

More footsteps, the office door closed, and then the low sound of conversation.

Hazel tiptoed to the cabinets, and drawer by drawer, she carefully searched for anything on Maxie. When she found the page with Teeth's serial number again, she folded it up and put it into her coat. She continued to search the files.

Almost a half hour later, the voices stopped, and Hazel froze. A door opened and closed, and then Marie's heels walked all the way down the hall to the reception room. Hazel wasn't sure where Dr. Galton was, until she heard things being moved around and clanking in the exam room.

Every minute that went by, she became more jumpy. Hazel had searched every drawer except the three that were locked. She scratched her head… there must be a key some place. Probably in the doctor's desk across the hall. Hazel wrinkled her nose. *Bananas.*

The doctor and Marie were both in the exam room, from the sound of it. She had to act swiftly. She darted across the hall, opened the doctor's office door, and shut it softly behind her.

She let out a breath and wiped the perspiration from her forehead. Without wasting time, she rounded the desk and opened the drawer. She sorted through pencils and notepads, paperclips, a deck of cards fastened with a rubber band, and more pamphlets, encouraging people to do the right thing and help "cleanse the inferior races of man." In the far back of the drawer was a racy pin up picture of a buxom, brunette gypsy and a small leather coin purse. Hazel undid the clasp of the coin purse and found foreign looking coins and a small, copper key. *That's the ticket.*

Shoving everything back into the drawer, the key in her hand, Hazel's pulse thrummed. She paused at the door to make sure the hallway was clear. Marie's voice came from the exam room. "He has a younger brother as well."

"Right. Let's have a look at him too. This one will sleep a while. Could you hand me the needle?"

They were occupied. Hazel made it back to the file room and over to the wooden cabinet with the locked doors. Her hand trembled as she rushed to try the key. It slid into the keyhole and turned. She sighed in relief and pulled the drawer open. Her fingers crawled across the tops of the files, reading names as they flashed by.

Halfway through the second drawer, Hazel saw the name Maxine Washington. That had to be her. She pulled out the page, and her eyes darted across the form.

Negro woman. Aged 34. Skipping quickly past her residence and basic comments on her overall health, Hazel found where the doctor had scrawled some notes.

> *Pregnancy confirmed at 3 wks gestation*
> *Follow up examine upon discussion with Sinclair*
> *Intellect defective with melancholia*
> *Signs of mild skeletal malformation*
> *Possible candidate for bilateral salpingo-oophorectomy*
> *Family history of Thrombocytopenia*

Hazel had found it. This paper showed that Maxie had come into the clinic and was found to be pregnant. Something the papers never mentioned. Some of the words didn't make sense to her, but she'd worked with Dr. Galton enough to have picked up that thrombocytopenia was a condition of thin blood. This made the patient more likely to bleed out. Her mind flashed back to the time when she saw Marie mopping blood off the floor and dunking the exam table sheet into a bucket of bleach. She shivered in revulsion.

Hazel folded up the sheet and put it in her coat. She had to get this back to her father—he would know what to do with it.

She relocked the drawers. Putting the key in her pocket, Hazel tiptoed to the door. It was quiet. No voices or footsteps. Maybe they were treating a patient. Or giving someone a tattoo, she scowled to herself.

If she could just get back to the storage room, she was home free. Peeking out the door, the corridor was empty. Hazel stepped out, and to her horror, at the end of the hall, the storage room door stood wide open. Before she could think what to do, Marie stepped out of the storage room and stared at Hazel.

"Doctor!" Marie shouted, her forehead scrunching with anger.

Dr. Galton emerged from the exam room, wiping his hands with a towel, a look of alarm on his face. "What is it?" He stopped and took in Hazel, standing in the door of the file room. "What is going on here?" he sternly asked Hazel.

Her heart banged on her ribcage. No words came to her.

Marie stalked down the corridor, an approaching storm, pointing a finger at Hazel. "You came in through the window and have been snooping." The nurse's accent made her words come out like the crack of a whip.

"That. That's ridiculous. I came in the front and there was nobody there. So I knocked on the doctor's office door—and then I saw the light on in here."

Marie crossed her arms and sneered. "Oh, yes?"

Dr. Galton lowered his brows. "I was in the exam room."

"Was gonna check there next." Hazel's mind floundered. *Keep it calm, Malloy.*

Marie shoved past her and looked around the file room. She reached out and tugged on the drawers. Locked. By appearances, there was nothing out of place.

The doctor let out a sigh. "Clearly there is some misunderstanding. Hazel... why are you looking for me?"

"Oh." She recovered enough to remember what she had practiced in case this happened. She forced a grin. "My family and I would like to give you a Christmas present."

Marie came back into the hall, narrowing her eyes at Hazel.

Retrieving the check from her pocket, she held it out to the young doctor, and his face registered surprise.

"What's this?"

"Our support for the work you do in the community. You help so many people."

"I do what I can. Of course… sometimes I can't help." He blushed, taking the check. He unfolded it, and his eyes went wide. "This will buy a lot of supplies."

"Father wanted to be clear… this is not a donation for the clinic. Those are done through the Sinclair family. This is for you. Think of it as a bonus."

He rubbed a hand over his face and grinned. "Tell your father thank you. This is very generous." Dr. Galton was nearly breathless. For a brief moment, Hazel felt sorry for him, because maybe he was deceived. He lived simply, thought he was doing something good—wanted to be important. But he fell in with evil and was doing their bidding, unwittingly or not. She wondered how he had felt when Maxie died and how much he had to do with the cover up.

"You're welcome." Hazel smiled, her heart calming. Money was indeed a great distraction.

Marie snorted. Hazel turned to the tight-lipped nurse who had never been kind to her. Hazel had no pity for her and didn't believe for a second that she was deceived. Marie embraced the darkness. Hazel couldn't resist making things hot for her.

"Marie, I just don't understand your anger and paranoia. Why would you think I would sneak in here—through a window, of all things—the very idea." Hazel puffed out her chest, indignant, despite the fact that she was a champion window sneaker. "And that I would go through boring medical files? Why, the thought is bizarre." Hazel blinked. "Makes me wonder if you are hiding something." She squinted at the nurse.

Marie's mouth dropped open. "Ridiculous. Our patients have privacy we have to protect," she sputtered.

Dr. Galton made a noise in his throat. "That's enough, Marie." His face was tight with irritation.

"Furthermore." Hazel stood tall and raised her chin, summoning her inner debutante. "Have you any idea who I am? Who my father is? If my maid spoke to me the way that you do, she would be sacked."

Marie's face turned red.

Mortified, Dr. Galton, still holding the check in his hand as if it had just floated down from heaven, demanded, "Apologize to Miss Malloy, Marie."

"I—I beg your pardon, miss." The nurse scrunched her face up as if she had something sour in her mouth.

Hazel nodded. "Forgiven."

"I am so sorry, Hazel. I hope this won't make you stay away. We value your work here."

Hazel let out a tolerant sigh. "Don't think of it. No harm done. I know how difficult it can be to get good help." She shot a disdainful look at Marie.

"Thank you for understanding." Dr. Galton pushed up his spectacles, his handsome face tense.

"Merry Christmas. I'll be seeing you." Hazel straightened the fur collar on her coat and turned to go.

"Merry Christmas," he called after her. "And be sure to tell your father thank you."

Hazel hurried into the alleyway, relief rushing through her veins. She had the paper Arthur wanted that might help them find Teeth and the evidence that Stanley asked for. She'd done it. Henri loped toward her from where he had faithfully waited by the trash bin under the window, which was now closed. Hazel hunched down to receive his wet kisses on her face and to scratch behind his ears.

"I did it, boy. I did it."

Together they walked to the end of the alley. Before she rounded the corner to where Jennings waited with the Buick, Henri turned his head and growled.

Hazel followed his gaze. At the other end of the alley, silhouetted by the sun, was Marie, watching her go. From a distance, they stared at one another. A chill ran over Hazel's skin.

Even from where Hazel stood, she could see the glower and feel the hatred like heat waves through the December air. What a contrast to the love there was in the world. Now she did pity the woman. She wondered if she had ever been loved by anyone. But the moment of pity passed. In the end, some people, even ones with unhappy beginnings, lived on to bring goodness into the world. While others like Marie hardened into people willing to exterminate humans who don't meet their standards and ideals, unfeeling generals in a senseless war. Sacrificing as many lives as necessary to get what they wanted.

Standing tall, Hazel continued to stare back. She raised her arm and cut a salute across her forehead, then lowered her arms at her sides, dipped a curtsy, and stuck out her tongue.

She turned her back, and with her dog at her side, walked away from the hate.

CHAPTER TWENTY-ONE

Stanley laid his head against the wall of the trolley and closed his eyes. The rocking motion soothed him a bit, but not much. Everything was moving fast, and he felt like it was all out of control. But there would be no going back now. The fat, as Seamus loved to say, was truly in the fire now. And nothing would stop it. Not a damn thing.

Finding the train station confirmed all of his worst fears. It wasn't that he doubted The Winnowing was real, but seeing the train station, built some time ago, showed how long the VP people had been working to put their plan into motion. It showed the arrogance of money and power, believing their agenda could not be thrown off or stopped. Evelyn's murder showed that too.

Stanley sat up. But did it? Evelyn's murder seemed a bit too public with everything else he'd seen. He wondered if that was a mistake. No, not a mistake. Charles would not have been such a lunk head. He and Hazel walked up on him right before he could cover his tracks. They'd gummed up the works. The VP, or whoever, always wanted to work in secret until it was too late to do anything about it. And he and Haze ruined all that.

He smiled. Hazel was something else, all right. He and that dame could rule the world together, if they could get out of each other's way. No doubt, that dollface had a temper like Ducky from the Gas House gang. Yet, she could be soothing, comforting, and strong.

Shaking his head, he told himself to focus. He needed to find Seamus and tell him about the train station. Maybe he could do something, and maybe he couldn't. But at least it was worth a shot.

And Frisky. He needed to send her to Teeth. Maybe, somehow, she would be at mass. Sometimes she came, and other times she didn't. But it was Christmas Eve and that made everyone more Catholic. Well, if she came, she came; he couldn't go and find her just now.

He hopped off the trolley as it made its turn on Skinker Avenue. Walking fast, he found himself back in Dogtown and wound his way to his house. The whole block seemed to be celebrating Christmas, with loud singing, laughter, and conversations drifting out of the houses. And normally, he loved every bit of it. But tonight, he felt isolated and alone. No one at these parties knew what was going on in the city around them; at least, not yet.

Closing his eyes, he tried to pray, but nothing came. He didn't have any words. What should he pray? For all the people he loved to be protected? That seemed selfish. A lot of people were being hurt or missing their kids tonight.

He crossed himself. "Our Lord, help me to be brave and stand for what is right."

Stanley went inside and found Seamus dressed in his best suit. His uncle turned and faced him with a big smile. It transformed his whole face, and he no longer looked like the haggard, stressed-out police detective.

"Ah, boyo, best get ready for mass. You're serving all the…" He paused for a moment and then said, "Ah, look at you, like you've seen a banshee. Sit, boyo, sit."

Stanley sat down on the couch and took off his hat. He ran his fingers through his hair. "If only it were a banshee. I'd show her the crucifix and pray."

"Then what it is, boyo?"

He told his uncle about Lincoln, Mama Jefferson, Teeth, and the train station. When he finished his tale, Stanley looked up at his uncle. Seamus had bowed his head while listening to what Stanley had to say.

"Did you see anybody? More importantly, did anyone see you?"

Stanley shook his head. "No, I don't think so."

"Think. I don't like that word. I need you to know."

Stanley sighed. "Well, I got a little spooked and thought I was being watched, but I think it was just my nerves."

Seamus shook his head. "Boy, I know you're smart, God knows. But saints preserve us, you're not paranoid enough yet. How do you think I've survived with all the crooked cops? You don't trust any situation, not ever. Always have your eyes peeled."

"But come on, there wasn't anyone in that station."

Seamus arched his eyebrow. "You checked it all, did you?"

"Well, no, but…" Stanley's cheeks burned. "You're right."

"It's all right, boy. Chances are, they're following you everywhere. I think I need to go see this place myself."

"Oh. Why?"

"For many reasons. First, so Father Timothy can get a full report. Second, so I can look around the place and see something you didn't. I am the cop, after all."

"Seamus, don't go. I don't think it's a good idea. Let's go to mass and then have Christmas breakfast, like we used to."

His uncle grinned. "Get up, and let me have a look at you."

Stanley stood and towered over his uncle. The little man looked up at him and smiled with pride. "You're a fine man."

"Then let me come with you…"

Seamus put his hands on his shoulders. "I'll be fine, lad. Really. If anyone asks questions, I'll just show them the badge, and give them the usual bull about how they need to vacate the area."

"I don't like it. What if one of Legion comes around? They're not gonna run and hide just because they see your badge."

Seamus smiled again. Stanley had never seen so many smiles in one evening. His uncle was in a fine mood but seemed sober as a stone.

"I'll be down and back in time for midnight mass, just under the deadline. And then sure, we'll have breakfast together in the morning. I'm actually way ahead of ya. I bought all the stuff today. So be ready to eat like a horse. But then, you usually do."

Seamus laughed at his lame joke and then put his hands on either side of Stanley's face. "I'm proud of you, lad. Proud of how you turned out. Don't think it had anything to do with me, but I'm proud all the same."

They stared at each other a moment. Seamus's eyes watered as he said, "Your da would have been proud of the man you are and the one you're becoming. Cannot think of anything better to say than that."

He gave Stanley's cheek a few firm pats. "All right, enough of this woman talk. I'm off. I'll see you at mass."

Without another word, the detective grabbed his hat and was gone.

Stanley stood in his living room. He felt frozen and locked by all the emotions pouring through him. Watching Seamus crack open right before his eyes, well, that was something. It must be because the truth about Peggy was out. The burden of secrecy and raising Stanley alone was over. Stanley wondered how different things would have been between them if his uncle had displayed that kind of emotion on a regular basis.

Stanley went upstairs, took a bath, and dressed in the suit that Mr. Malloy bought for him. It wasn't like anyone would be able to see it under his server robes. But it made him feel more the man. He started to whistle "Jingle Bells" and then reached for his shoes.

The touch of leather reminded him of Vinnie's swinging body, and he dropped the shoes to the floor. How, how could he wear these when they'd been with his best friend at the moment of his death? Maybe he should just throw them out or burn them.

Stanley stared at the shoes for a moment and then picked them back up. No. He wouldn't throw them away. Instead, he would wear them in honor of his friend, and maybe Vinnie would send some prayers his way. He'd hallowed them with his death, and they were holy shoes now. In them, Stanley would walk forward in life—and grow old for the both of them.

He put them on, tied them, and said, "All right, Vinnie, if, somehow, you ain't in purgatory right now, I need your prayers for protection, you big, Italian idiot."

Making sure to lock the door, Stanley walked the few blocks to St. James's parish. Before he headed to the sacristy to "suit up," as Father Timothy liked to call it, he decided to check the sanctuary to see if Frisky was there. Something told him that she would be.

Looking out from the side door, he saw the familiar tangle of red hair bowed in prayer amid some other people at the altar rail. He knelt by her and crossed himself.

"Hey Frisky," he whispered.

No reply from the tangle of curls.

"I really need to talk to you."

"I'm talking to someone else, Lord Stanley, who has a bit of a higher claim than yours," Frisky said without moving her head.

Sighing, Stanley said, "This isn't about me; it's about Teeth."

She looked up, eyes wide. "You found him?"

Somebody shushed them and it echoed in the church.

Stanley ducked his head. "Nah. Lincoln found him, and he took him to Mama Jefferson."

Frisky frowned and whispered, "Who is that?"

"You'll meet her soon enough. Meet me at the boxcar later, and I'll take you there."

Frisky didn't say anything for a moment. "He's alive. He is actually alive. I need to go home and get some things for him, his little teddy bear..." She got up, crossed herself, and started to walk away.

He caught her elbow and said, "What about mass?"

Frisky smiled. "Offer it up for me."

With that, she strolled down the aisle and out the door. Stanley smiled a little. Teeth would be spoiled rotten with Mama Jefferson and Frisky looking after him.

CHAPTER TWENTY-TWO

When Hazel got home, Roberts greeted her at the front door. "Your father has gone out, and your mother is waiting for you in the living room."

"Thanks, Robbie." Hazel gave him a wink and walked across the parquet floor to the living room, with Henri at her heels.

Mumsy sat in the settee, gazing at the Christmas tree, a cocktail in hand. "Hazel. At last. I just can't seem to stay out of this room today. It's a grand tree."

"It is."

"So… mission accomplished? Your father said you were after something in the clinic that would expose some lies the hoity-toity crowd has been handing out." Mumsy reached down to pet the dog.

"Yes. I got what I went for." She pulled out the page from Maxie's chart and Teeth's sheet with his serial number. "Here is the proof that they took Stanley's little pal, Teeth. And that number is how they categorized him. I can't read German, so

I'm not sure about the rest of this. But I'll bet there's a page like this for each of the missing people in St. Louis. They didn't even bother hiding this stuff. They have a cabinet full of the city's citizens."

Mumsy gave the sheet of paper a look of disgust. "Sorted and filed like so many objects."

"You got it. And this proves that Maxie Washington went to the clinic and found out she was pregnant … and from what Gabriel tells, Mr. Sinclair is the father. I know this word means thin blood." Hazel pointed to the word *Thrombocytopenia* on the chart. "Not sure about the rest."

Mumsy wrinkled her nose. "I always knew that Woody Sinclair was a wolf."

If what Gabriel said was true, Woodrow Sinclair was perhaps the most wolf-like man that Hazel ever knew.

Her mother took the paper from Hazel's hand and squinted at the doctor's notes. "Hm… here's a term I recognize even if I can't pronounce it." She pointed a long, painted nail at the words *bilateral salpingo-oophorectomy.*

"What is that?" Hazel raised a brow, curious how Mumsy would know.

"That's having both hens removed…" Mumsy rolled her eyes at Hazel's look of confusion. "The egg factory…"

"Oh. Your ovaries? Mom, I'm sixteen. I've learned the terms in school." Hazel pursed her lips. "So that means getting your ovaries removed."

"Yes…" Mumsy fished the olive out of her drink and popped it into her mouth.

Hazel cocked her head at her mother with realization. She often wondered why her wild, flapper mother would ever opt into motherhood at all but had always wanted a sibling. "You had it done."

"I did," she said, chewing the olive and swallowing. "You were born and, hell, what a tough act to follow. You're perfect." Mumsy grinned and gave Hazel's cheek a pinch with one hand while the other held the martini; it sloshed a little onto the settee.

Hazel smiled back. Maybe her birth was an accident… and maybe that explained her parent's unlikely union. She wasn't sure of the timeline. Or maybe Mumsy thought she could do it—marry a responsible man and settle down—but found that it just wasn't in her. That's why Peggy was around. Hazel decided not to ask. Mumsy deserved to have her own reasons and anyway, Hazel couldn't fault her for trying. Besides, having both Mumsy and Peggy in her life had turned out just fine.

"Well, that certainly points to a botched sterilization," Hazel said.

"I'd say." Mumsy shook her head. She let out a dramatic sight and gulped down her cocktail. "Enough of this dreary business! It's Christmas Eve. Let's forget all of this… how about you and I have a lovely dinner together? Your father will not be home until late—but there is no reason why we can't celebrate Santa coming like the good old days."

Hazel grinned. "That would be swell." Yeah… maybe it was a good idea to take a break. There was nothing more she could do tonight.

"Hi-de-ho!" Mumsy stood up with a flourish of silk. "Why, let's have old Peggy along. What do you say?"

Hazel clapped her hands. "Could we?" Having Peggy along would make it extra special. Mumsy was the only dame on Lindell who would invite her maid on an evening out with her daughter, and Hazel loved her for it.

"You bet."

Henri wagged his tail as if he could tell something exciting was happening. Hazel couldn't bear leaving him behind on

Christmas Eve. She'd become quite attached to her goofy, formidable, guard dog. "Can Henri come along?"

"Sure. We'll get him a big, juicy bone someplace."

After Peggy recovered from her surprise, they called for Jennings and were soon off into the crisp, December evening, with hair set and red lipstick on. As Mumsy put it, "Max Factored" and ready to paint the town. Henri sat at Hazel's feet, tongue hanging out happily.

A quaint, Chinese restaurant on the edge of the high end of town served up some simply divine noodles and dumplings. Henri curled up under the table with a duck that Mumsy ordered just for him. Somewhere between the chow mein and steamed buns, Mumsy and Peggy began to talk about Stanley.

"I always knew you had a child, but guess I never thought much of it. Thought maybe he'd died years ago. When you first came to work for us, you mentioned something…" Mumsy scratched her head. "Imagine my surprise when Nicky told me Stanley was yours."

Peggy nodded; she seemed ill at ease to be chatting as a friend to her employer. "Well, ma'am, I just needed to keep him safe. I always checked in on him and made sure Seamus had what money I could spare. But I missed raising the lad." She glanced across the red, enamel table at Hazel. "If it wasn't for your darlin' girl, I wouldn't have known motherhood."

Hazel's eyes glossed over with tears. She reached out and squeezed Peggy's hand.

"You've done a pip of a job, Peggy. Couldn't have done it without you. I know she's snug as a bug with you." Mumsy looked back and forth between them. There was no note of jealousy or wistfulness to be seen, just a satisfied smirk as if she'd figured out a trick to the system. Then her face brightened. "You know, I should return the favor a little." Her eyes widened, and Hazel knew the drinks had kicked in, and she was about to get a big idea.

"Say. What if I was Santa for your Stanley this year?" She grinned, and then she flapped her hands. "I know, I know! How about all his little Knight pals too? They dig in the trash to feed folks—even after we started donating food and cash... can't waste a thing. What if we filled their fort with food, and presents, and maybe a tree!"

Peggy let out a chuckle. "Well, now, ma'am I think that would be a welcome Christmas surprise."

"What do you say, Hazel? You know where their little fort is, yeah?"

Hazel was touched that her mother wanted to do something for her newsie friends, but she was hesitant about descending on The Castle unannounced. "Wow... that sounds grand..."

"Then it's a plan!" Mumsy crowed, lighting a cigarette. "Let's get Jennings to run us around to buy a few things."

The department stores were in a wild, Christmas Eve frenzy. Mumsy faced it like a general leading her troops to battle. Charging here and charging there. It seemed she had charge accounts everywhere. The Buick was packed to capacity. Mumsy bought piles of new clothes in approximate teenaged boy sizes, toys and games, and a few big boxes of canned food, bread, apples, and oranges. At one shop, she haggled with the manager to buy a small pre-decorated tree from one of the window displays. The poor man was so overwhelmed by the shopping rush and Mumsy's loud voice, he finally just gave in. Three red, Radio Flyer wagons were purchased to transport it all.

Jennings pulled the Buick up to the edge of Forest Park, closest to where the Knights' hideout was.

"Guess we gotta hoof it from here," said Mumsy.

They loaded the wagons with Jennings's help, and the four of them made their way into the park with Henri trotting along. They followed Hazel, who led with the beam of a flashlight the chauffeur took from the trunk. Henri loped ahead, knowing the way, then circled back as if to tell them to hurry before running ahead again.

"Isn't this a scream?" Mumsy laughed as they bumped along with their loads.

"A wee adventure, to be sure," Peggy chuckled.

It was a frosty night with a clear sky, and Hazel was filled with a sudden hope and euphoria. They were together, like a family, bringing Christmas to the boys. They would be so thrilled when they discovered it all. Even if they played tough, they needed somebody to look after them for once. She hoped Stanley was pleased.

They trudged on in quiet excitement. Hazel held the flashlight in one hand and had her other arm wrapped around the little Christmas tree. Stanley was probably there right now, typing away for the next issue of *The Knight's Voice*. A thrill went through her at the chance to see him, and with Peggy too. She hadn't seen them side by side since finding out Stanley was Peggy's son.

As they made their way through the trees, getting closer to the hideout of the Knights of St. Louis the King, Henri began to bark. It echoed low and continuous through the grove from up ahead. An alarm. Danger.

Hazel stopped. "Something's wrong."

The air became hazy, dancing with fluttering, small bits of black.

"Smoke!" Peggy cried.

"Ladies. Stand back—I'll have a look." Jennings abandoned his wagon and jogged ahead, swifter than Hazel would have thought possible for a man his age.

Hazel glanced anxiously at her mother. Mumsy stared ahead, biting her lip. "What do you suppose is going on?"

Hazel's gut told her it was bad. The jolt of going from high merriment to this left her unsteady on her feet.

Jennings reappeared with Henri behind him. The old man was out of breath. "I'm going back to get help. There's a fire."

"Where?" Hazel croaked.

"An abandoned train car, but it is catching the trees as well." Jennings disappeared in the direction they had come.

"Stanley," Hazel whispered. She dropped the small Christmas tree and ran toward the now apparent orange that glowed like a sunset through the trees.

Mumsy and Peggy cried out behind her, but she didn't look back. Her feet pounded the ground with Henri barking at her side.

She stumbled into the small clearing where a few homeless people stood, watching the red boxcar engulfed in flames. The surrounding treetops had caught fire, and smoke billowed all around. Burning copies of Stanley's writings lay scattered on the ground and drifted through the air.

The door to the boxcar hung open like a screaming mouth as flames devoured the inside. Hazel's heart seemed to explode. "Stanley!" She lurched toward the boxcar. A strong hand gripped her arm.

She turned back to see Peggy and Mumsy lit up by the glow of the fire. "Hazel. There's nothing to be done. You can't run in there," Peggy said, releasing her arm.

"Stanley!" Hazel sobbed.

Mumsy put her arms around Hazel. "Oh, baby. I'm sure he's safe. He's a tough kid."

"That's right, lass. I'll go and find Seamus. I'm sure he knows where Stanley is. Don't you worry."

Hazel pulled out of her mother's arms and grabbed Peggy in a fierce hug. "I hope you're right," she wept into her maid's shoulder.

Peggy lifted Hazel's chin. Her familiar and beloved face was creased with worry, but her eyes glowed with love and strength. "See now, my girl. No matter what happens, you've got the strength. Do ya hear me? You're a Malloy. You've got the Irish fight in you."

Hazel sniffed back tears, the heat from the fire on her back, smoke blurring the air. "I can't lose him, Peggy."

"I know, I know. Losing William almost killed me. And giving up Stanley nearly broke my spirit. But I went on."

Hazel looked into Peggy's face, wanting her strength, but her whole body trembled. She swallowed. "You'll find him."

Peggy nodded, though Hazel saw the doubt on her face. The fire was no accident. Whoever set it may have killed Stanley before setting the boxcar aflame… Hazel shut her eyes, trying not to imagine a hooded figure creeping up behind Stanley as he hunkered over the small typewriter, tapping away.

"I'll be off now. Stay with your mother. Wait for news … I love you, sweet girl."

Hazel nodded, trying to hope. "I love you too. I'll be strong. No matter what." Hazel raised her chin, trying to be brave.

Peggy smiled and winked. "That's my girl."

Mumsy put her arm through Hazel's, as Peggy passed through the smoke and disappeared into the trees in the opposite direction they'd come.

Hazel and Mumsy distanced themselves from the flames, watching the red boxcar become surrounded. Something nagged at the back of Hazel's mind. Perhaps as a distraction from the painful thought that Stanley could be gone. But she had to know who did this. Needed someone to blame. Obviously, the Veiled Prophet would want to destroy Stanley and the work he was doing. This could be a direct retaliation to what Arthur had done at the ball.

Arthur.

Anger sparked inside of Hazel. This was all his fault… and maybe… could he have done it? He was so keen to burn things up that were in the way of him getting his revenge. She remembered the look of hatred on his face when Stanley had wrestled the gun away from him the night he tried to shoot the VP. Then he'd quit the Knights. She shuddered. It was possible.

"I'm sorry, Hazel…" Mumsy said, clutching her arm. "What a crummy thing to happen on Christmas Eve."

Yeah. It was no party. Henri let out a sudden growl.

"Hazel? That you?"

Hazel whipped around at the sound of the husky voice. It was that redhead. "Oh…"

"Frisky Jones? Remember me?" She had a knapsack slung over one shoulder and was dressed like a boy.

"Sure."

"Frisky? That's a hell of a name." Mumsy eyed the girl warily.

"That it is. You must be Mrs. Malloy. Can you believe this?" Frisky watched the fire spreading, the flickering lights on her face and red hair made her look like a part of it. She let out a deep breath. "I sure hope nobody was in there."

Hazel examined the girl she didn't know. Arthur's sidekick. "Yeah… where's Arthur?" She seemed like a tough tomato, but Hazel thought she noticed a tear.

Frisky pursed her lips and stuck her hands into the pocket of her trousers. "Been looking for him. No sign yet."

Hazel wasn't sure if that was true. "The Knights are going to be crushed about this," she said.

"That's for sure. I guess when you mess with a snake, you're gonna get venom." She shook her head at the fire, an expression of regret on her face.

Hazel scowled. "They were doing their best to help people."

Frisky raised her hands in apology. "I know… just made some big enemies. But if I know Stan and the boys, they'll just find a new place to gather."

"Do you know where Stanley is?" Hazel hoped.

"Nah. I don't. Altar boy was serving mass earlier… said he was going to meet me here later. Maybe he's on his way." Frisky chewed her lip.

"He was going to meet you here? Oh no…" Hazel stared at the collapsing boxcar, her heart aching with worry.

"Say, I'll go see if I can track him down." The look on her face was stoic, as if she was forcing herself not to panic for Hazel's sake, and it made Hazel more unhinged.

"You think maybe he didn't get here yet, right?"

"Sure, he could have gotten held up someplace. I'll round up the Knights and see what we can find out about all of this." She ran a hand through her wild, red hair.

"Will you let me know, please?"

"You bet." She turned to go and then looked back. "Hey. It's going to be okay." Frisky forced a gap-toothed smile and darted away before Hazel could respond. Sometimes when people said that it just meant, "even if it's not okay, you'll survive."

Mumsy led Hazel away from the snapping and crackling that marked the end of an era. Hazel thought back on the first day Stanley had brought her to The Castle and all of the other times they'd gathered there with the Knights over the past few months. The last time she'd been inside, Stanley had held her and kissed her on the old sofa. It was all ashes now.

They wove through the trees and past the wagons of Christmas presents that were now surrounded by shabbily-clothed people, adults, and children, picking through them. They needed this stuff more than anybody. One small boy held the small Christmas tree in his arms, a look of glee on his face.

"Did Santa leave this?" a small, scrawny girl asked her dad.

The scruffy man in the flat cap grinned at her. "I think so, pumpkin. He must have."

Mumsy tightened her arm around Hazel as they skirted the group of desperate people. "Merry Christmas," she called out as they drifted away.

"Merry Christmas," many of them answered automatically.

The scream of fire truck sirens came through the darkness. Hazel fought back tears. There was nothing merry about it.

CHAPTER TWENTY-THREE

Stanley sat in the pew and absorbed the peaceful atmosphere of the church. The altar candles burned brightly, casting dancing shadows all around the sanctuary, as if all the dead saints in heaven were celebrating Christ's birth. He sighed, breathing in the incense Father Timothy had used. After four masses, the smoke floated all around the church, glowing in the candlelight and tickling his throat.

Everyone had gone home after midnight mass, and Stanley decided to stay for a bit. Seamus hadn't come to midnight mass, and that worried him a bit. If he got home and his uncle wasn't there, he would have to go find him. But for now, Stanley wanted to assume everything was okay. He had told Father Timothy about the train station, and he was going to send people to explore it too.

If it was up to him, he would just fall asleep here in the church. Father Timothy had given him a key and told him to lock up. For just a moment, Stanley closed his eyes and felt peace in the quiet of the church.

O, Holy Night.

But he did need to go and see Frisky at the boxcar. Sighing, he stood up and locked the two side doors to the church. As he turned to walk down the aisle, Stanley stopped. Peggy stood at the end.

"Peggy, you missed mass." He smiled as he walked toward her.

"Oh, Stanley, you're alive." She raced down the aisle and gripped him in a fierce bear hug.

"Easy, you're gonna crush me to death before we spend Christmas together."

She sobbed into his chest for a few moments, and Stanley held her.

"Oh, Hazel is going to be so happy. She was beside herself."

"What's this all about? Where is Hazel? Is she okay?" His nerves were on high alert.

Peggy looked up at him, eyes swollen from crying. "Can I sit? I've been on my feet all night."

Leading her over to the nearest pew, Stanley sat down next to her. She grabbed his hand and held it so tight that he winced.

"When we saw the fire, we thought ...well, we thought you were inside."

Stanley's skin tingled, and he knew. "The boxcar. They burned the boxcar."

She nodded. "That they did. Right down to the ground. We, well, Mrs. Malloy, Hazel, and I came to bring you and the boys Christmas presents."

Smiling, Stanley said, "No fooling?"

"Not a bit. I believe that girl has it for you something fierce," Peggy said, patting his hand.

"Well, ditto. I think I love her," Stanley said.

"You're such a man; of course you do, dear. And she loves you back, you know. So, if you hurt her, I'll box your ears, you can count on it. You've had no mother to teach you how to treat ladies, but now you do."

"Now I do." He smiled, exhausted.

"Well, now what's to be done about your boxcar?"

"I knew they were going to come after the boxcar eventually. Something told me they would after what happened at the ball. They always knew where it was. That's why I hid the typewriter back at the house and anything else valuable in there too, like our maps of the city, and all that business."

"You've got *an da shealladh*. The Second Sight, lad. Sure as your grandfather did."

"Grandfather …"

"To be sure. My father could see things… sense things before they happened."

Stanley nodded. Seamus had often said he had a gift, and it was becoming clearer to him that it was true.

"I wish it did me any good."

"These are dangerous times… St. Louis isn't safe for you. You need to go. Get out of here," Peggy said. "Your father and I didn't leave soon enough, and look what happened."

Stanley sat for a moment and didn't reply. He didn't want to tell her about his constant dreams of fleeing west, or the recent feelings of foreboding that more terrible things were coming.

"Did my dad run?" he said with one hand clutching the back of a pew. "Did he run when people needed him?"

Peggy sighed. "No. But we were both young and foolish. And we had you. We should've been more responsible, that's for sure."

"But there were people dying and who needed help. So he stayed."

"To take care of our son, to raise him and protect him, that would not have been runnin'. We'd already fought well, and no one could object. But we kept pushin' ourselves, thinkin' we were the only ones fightin' evil in the city. And that's just not so. Someone else would have stepped up. Someone always does, sure."

Stanley walked toward the altar, as if approaching the answers he had always sought. "Maybe I am a someone... I don't have a kid. I'm not married. No one relies on me. So my time to fight is now. I thought about running west or something. But something tells me I can't run from this."

He reached the altar rail and turned to face her. She stood in the middle of the church, hands at her side, watching him.

"I know you think you must, but Father Timothy and Brother Martin have things in hand. Not to mention the whole Order of St. Michael. They might be small, but there is power to do something, especially with Mr. Malloy pitching in with his money," she said, wiping away tears.

"You could run yourself," Stanley said.

Peggy bowed her head "No. No, I won't."

Stanley spread his arms. "Then, how can I?"

Peggy shook her head. "It's different."

"How? How is it different?" he said, a bit louder than he intended, and his voice echoed through the church.

"Because you're my child—all that I have left of William... And I don't want this life for you. It destroyed mine."

"It's already destroying mine. They won't let up, and they would find me if I went west, or joined the army, or got lost in the mountains. Because they're spreading. If they are not stopped, no place will be safe."

Peggy stared at him, and the silence grew. "Please. Stanley. Please." Peggy wiped tears from her cheeks.

He looked at her and said, "I'm a grown man now. I'm staying, and that's it. Besides, someone needs to stay and take care of you in your old age… Ma."

Peggy smiled and took a step toward him. "Son."

A loud cracking sound echoed through the church, and Stanley winced, covering his ears in confusion. Peggy cried out, and he glanced up. She'd dropped to the ground, clutching her chest.

"Ma. What happened?" Stanley sprang toward her.

She stared blankly at him and held up her hand, covered in blood. Without a word, she tipped forward and fell to the floor.

"Ma!" Stanley froze, looking down at her lying so still.

"Say goodbye to mommy, Fields," someone calmly said from behind him.

The last thought Stanley had was that he'd heard that voice before.

CHAPTER TWENTY-FOUR

Hazel paced the front yard, hoping for some message from Frisky. Her breath came in white blasts in the frigid, night air. Where was Stanley? Her stomach roiled and turned with worry. She thought she might throw up. Why was it that just when life seemed to inflate with joy and possibility, when even the dangers and problems seemed for a moment to be surmountable, that something cold and merciless gleefully blew it all to smithereens?

Mumsy was inside waiting by the phone in case Peggy or Seamus called with any news. Hazel's father had come home, heard what had happened, and rushed back out again. Heaven knew what was going on. Hazel had never felt so alone. Even Henri had retired to his doghouse. There was nothing to distract her from the anxiety clutching at her chest.

What if Stanley's body had been cremated in the red boxcar? What if he was gone forever? Panic surged through her.

Where was Peggy?

A specter materialized out of the darkness, moving slowly, deliberately toward her. It paused just out of reach of the porch light.

"Who is it?" Hazel backed away, a chill crawling up her back.

The flick of a match lit up a familiar face. Arthur lit his cigarette and strolled closer, smoke trailing behind him like he'd just arrived from the furnaces of Hell.

"People are looking for you," Hazel seethed.

"No joke," he said out of the side of his mouth.

"He's been with me." Sandy appeared from behind him in a black, fur coat, her scarred face ghoulish in the dark.

Hazel let out a breath. "Of course." Sandy had been hiding him this whole time. A second of hope jumped into her throat. "Have you seen Stanley?"

"Nah. I ain't." Arthur blew out a stream of smoke. He seemed to mull over something he needed to say.

"So I guess you know about the fire." Hazel put her hands on her hips.

"Yeah. I heard." Arthur hesitated and removed his bowler hat, tapping it against his leg.

"Well? What have you to say about it? The Castle is gone, Stanley is missing—maybe burned to death!" She hadn't meant to lose control, but the words came out in an angry sob. "It's all your fault! Did you start the fire? Because even if you didn't, you caused it just the same. You declared open war on the VP at the ball, putting us all in danger!"

Arthur came closer, his eyes narrowing. "My fault? You shoulda let me burn that clinic down when I had the chance. I was gonna slow down their snatch and grab program. Now—"

Sandy put a hand on his arm, and he stopped talking, his chest heaving with anger. She leaned close to him. "Not like this, baby. Don't tell her like this. It isn't her fault…" Hazel's best friend gave her a look of pity.

Hazel's heart dropped. "What! Tell me what? What's happened?"

Arthur replaced his bowler hat and pointed a finger at Hazel. "You want to protect these people so badly? But you'll wish you never did. The church was crawling with cops, and one of my pigeons got the skinny. Your maid, Peggy, was shot like an Irish dog by the altar. That's the kind of people you're protecting."

For a few moments, his words didn't make any sense. Hazel blinked, staring at his mouth and how smoke puffed out as he spoke. When understanding finally clawed into her brain, Hazel let out a shriek. "No! No, that isn't right. I don't believe you!"

Arthur frowned, and Sandy pushed him aside to grab Hazel in her arms. "It's true Hazel. I'm so sorry."

Hazel shoved Sandy away. "You. Both of you. You did this." Her whole body shook; tears streamed down her face.

Sandy's face hardened. "No. They've been getting away with this for as long as this city began. The poor have suffered all along. Now it's touching the fancy edges of your kingdom, and you can't face it."

Hazel stared at her best friend, not recognizing her. The ragged scar crinkled on her face; the shadows under her eyes and blunt cut of her bangs made her look like mugshots she'd seen on wanted posters. Hazel covered her face with her hands. It was too much. Peggy couldn't be gone. She'd been there Hazel's whole life. A giant hole opened up in the ground and Hazel felt herself being sucked into it. There was no bottom to it and no coming back.

"No… Not Peggy." It was not real. Hazel could see Peggy's auburn hair, her dimpled smile… the sparkle in her eyes when she'd tease… the warmth of her hugs. She had counted on her for her comfort and wisdom… she needed her. The world would never keep spinning after this.

Sandy let out a sigh. "I know… how you feel."

Hazel uncovered her face. "Nobody does! Peggy and maybe Stanley in one night," she choked. "I can't…" She clapped a hand over her own mouth, willing herself to stop. If she kept talking about them being gone, then it would be true… and she would fall into that hole and be lost forever.

"Stanley… he ain't dead." Arthur reached into his back pocket and pulled out Stanley's cap. The one from his father that he always wore.

Hazel's heart leaped, she grasped at the remaining sliver of hope, wiping her face. "Where did you get that?"

"The steps of Saint Michael's church—one of my pigeons nicked it before the cops got there. Stanny must've been there with Peggy. They got him, like Teeth… like the others."

The thought of Stanley being at the mercy of those hooded monsters made something snap in Hazel's head. He had fought them so hard. It seemed impossible that her tall, strong newsie, who seemed to be able to take on the world, could lose a fight.

All feeling drained out of Hazel, and sounds became muffled. Her own voice sounded distant and monotone. "They took Peggy from me. Now they have Stanley… he's a page in their file cabinet now."

Hazel stared at the cap in Arthur's hands. He held it out to her, and she stepped forward and took it. She pressed it to her face and breathed in the smell of Stanley's hair and sweat. The scent of a living, breathing boy. Hazel set the cap on her own head and pulled it down snug.

Her mind wandered and seemed to grasp at thin air. All she could think about was Peggy and Stanley. Then Hazel thought of the page with Teeth's serial number. That thing would probably lead them to wherever they had taken Stanley.

"The clinic. They took him there to give him a tattoo and serial number," she said.

"He's gone by now." Arthur spat on the ground.

"It will be empty…" Hazel said.

"We figured." Sandy reached into her big, fur coat and pulled out the bottle that Arthur had with him the day in the alleyway. "You in?"

Hazel's pulse hummed. "Yes."

Sometime later, Hazel stood with Sandy and Arthur outside the tavern up the street from the clinic, in a crowd of drunk people who had gathered on the sidewalk to watch the Family Care Clinic burn to the ground. The firefighters were too late. There would be nothing left.

"An eye for an eye," Hazel said, a mixture of rage and grief blistering her insides and scorching up who she used to be.

"That should slow them down a bit," Sandy said.

"This is only the warm up. Just wait 'til we get to work." Arthur flicked his cigarette to the ground and stomped it out.

The people around them shouted and hollered. Many of them lost interest, and laughing returned to the cozy embrace of the tavern. "Santa Claus is Coming to Town" played in jaunty rhythm from inside. The smell of whiskey and tobacco mingled with the smoke of the burning building. The world had ended, and the party went on.

Hazel clenched her fists. She felt the cold of the Joan of Arc medallion at her wrist. She rubbed it between her thumb and finger. *Give me strength.* What would Stanley do if he were here right now…?

"Gather Frisky and the Knights," she said, straightening Stanley's cap. "And let's find someone who can read German. We have work to do."

"I'm way ahead of you, swell." Arthur's dark eyes met hers, but instead of feeling the usual fear, Hazel saw a reflection of her pain there. "We'll get Stanley back," Arthur vowed.

"I'm counting on it, street rat."

Arthur gave Hazel a crooked smile, and Sandy took his hand. She reached out for Hazel's hand too. Hazel took it, feeling nothing. She just needed something to hold on to.

The clickety-clack sound of a train woke Stanley up. A swirl of sights and sounds overloaded his senses, and he tried to order them in his aching head.

"Welcome back to the land of the living dead, white boy."

"Lincoln?" Stanley said and tried to raise his hand.

"Easy, pal. We're chained together."

Stanley felt the cold metal against his right wrist and shook the chain. He looked around and saw other pairs of young boys chained together, sitting on the floor, and leaning against the walls in the darkness. Only the dim light of a single, swinging light bulb in the ceiling revealed the huddled captives. Some looked asleep, others had looks of absolute terror on their faces.

"Where the hell are we?" Stanley said, knowing the answer.

"A place you should be familiar with; a boxcar," Lincoln said. "As to where we're going, I have no damn idea. My guess is wherever that train station was designed to take folks."

A cold chill ran up Stanley's spine. The Winnowing. He looked at his left arm and saw the black, numbered tattoo on his swollen, red skin.

He racked his brain, trying to remember the numbers in Evelyn's diary. Stanley realized the first numbers meant he was not going to be exterminated. At least, not yet.

The smell of sweat and urine permeated the boxcar, and Stanley coughed.

"Keep quiet, you filth," a voice said from the other end of the car. The young boys across from him cowered and whimpered in fear.

A man emerged from the dark, wearing a black mask with only eye holes. He carried a wooden stick, lifted up.

"What are you gonna do with that?" Stanley said.

"Shut up, man," Lincoln said in a low hiss.

"I'm going to knight you, Lord Stanley."

The stick came down on his arm faster and harder than Stanley expected. Pain shot through his arm, but he gritted his teeth. He would not give this bastard the satisfaction of crying out.

"Enough, Legion. This dog requires stronger medicine."

That voice. The one he heard in the church before he blacked out. And the one that haunted his dreams.

"Charles Chouteau."

"Very good, Fields. I've enjoyed watching all the hero attention you've been getting. It's very amusing," Charles said as he emerged from the dark. A long, ragged scar marred his otherwise flawless face. Stanley couldn't help but smile. Artie did him a good one.

"But too bad you didn't know when to quit. And what a shame little Artie is not here with you. He's a slippery, little fellow."

Stanley wished Arthur was there too. The kid would go savage on this goon, chains or no chains.

Charles walked over to the boxcar door and opened it. The dark landscape rushed by as the wind blew into the compartment.

"Ah, what a beautiful night for a hanging, wouldn't you say, Fields?"

Stanley tried to stand, but Lincoln jerked him back down. "Don't man, not now. He just wants an excuse to do something," he whispered.

Lincoln was right. But it made Stanley crazy to play by this loony's rules. "If you're gonna kill me, Charles, do it, and spare me the evil villain speeches."

Charles laughed. "No, Fields, you've not earned your death yet. But your Dad did. Your smelly, Italian friend did. And poor, little mommy."

Stanley growled, "You… piece of garbage…" He squeezed his fists together, remembering how Peggy had fallen to the ground.

"Oh, pardon me, I'm forgetting someone," Charles went on, ignoring Stanley's outburst.

He walked into the dark at the other end of the car and brought back a hooded figure. The other captives in the boxcar scrambled back against the walls. Stanley's heart thumped hard when he saw a rope like the one that hung Vinnie, encircling the figure's neck like a leash.

"Speak, you Irish dog," Charles said, jerking the rope.

The figure shook his head. Wind swirled in from the open door, and the sound of the tracks seemed to grow louder.

"Tsk. Tsk." Charles took out something from his pocket and stuck it in the person's arm. A sharp cry of pain echoed through Stanley's brain.

"Seamus. No. No. No." Stanley lurched forward, but Lincoln had gone dead weight, pinning him down.

"So you recognize the prisoner. Good. Makes things so much easier. Now, Fields, I want to know who is supporting this paper you've started and who is opposing us. And, for good measure, I want the diary of that piece of filth, baseball slut."

"Don't get them anything, lad. Not a damn thing," Seamus said with a muffled voice.

"Typical hero response. But Stanley gets the final say," Charles said, as he took the end of the rope and wound it around a steel bar near the open door of the boxcar.

"So, Lord Stanley, Pendragon of the Order of St. Louis, if you don't give up everyone, you'll kill off the rest of your family tonight. And Detective Seamus Fields will no longer protect and serve the good citizens of St. Louis again."

Stanley stared at Seamus, the man who raised him. He could not give up the Order, Father Timothy, Brother Martin, or Mr. Malloy. But he couldn't commit Seamus to a horrible death either.

As if reading his mind, Seamus said, "Lad, I'm prepared. I went to confession before mass."

Charles hit Seamus on the head and pushed him to the edge of the boxcar. "Last chance, Fields." He raised his voice over the sound of the speeding wheels on the track.

Stanley steeled himself and tried to empty himself of any emotion. He wondered if Charles was bluffing. But then he remembered the caves. Swallowing hard, he said, "Go to hell."

Charles stared at him for a moment with a blank expression. And then said, "Well, according to Seamus, he confessed and was absolved. Let's test to see if that will keep him from Hades, shall we?"

With that, he leapt into the air and kicked Seamus in the back. His uncle stumbled through the door and into the rushing air. He flew outside, and the rope pulled taunt. The body beat against the metal side of the boxcar with loud thumps as it continued to bounce in the wind.

Stanley let out a deep scream of rage and horror. The train whistle joined him as he screamed. "By all the saints in heaven and on earth, I'm going to end you!"

Charles whipped out a long, curved knife, went over to the rope, and cut it. The body gave one last bang and then the train left it behind, speeding mercilessly into the night.

"We will talk more, Fields, when you get to the island."

ACKNOWLEDGEMENTS

Writing a second book in the world of Stanley and Hazel was like traveling to a familiar place and hanging out with old friends… except that people were dying and the world was catching on fire. I'm grateful for good kombucha and dark chocolate to get me through the long nights, dodging Legion and prowling the streets of 1934 St. Louis on my keyboard.

It was a challenge to finish this book amid my college courses, job and being a mom, but I had a lot of support and love to keep me going.

Huge thanks to Jonathan Weyer, who helped create it all and gave me half his brain to use. Thanks to my kids and my huge family for their support as I devoted so much time to telling this story. To Katie Jarvis, and Jessika Stephens for reading early drafts and making it all seem possible and to my famous uncle Mike Guido for making me feel like a big deal. Also to my uncle Paul O'Connor who reads my stuff with enthusiasm and gave me Irish cred for Seamus and Peggy.

Thank you to my parents who love me and my writing despite any shortcomings. Special thanks to my sister Ali Durham who helped make my first book launch a blast. To my niece, Eden Durham, who is my Hazel and Colin Weyer for being the OG Stanley.

Forever grateful for Jennifer Jenkins, Margie Jordan, Lois Brown, Tahsha Wilson, and James Lewis, who are the best writing group ever.

I'm indebted to the works of Frank Capra and Cole Porter, and to the silver screen legends I loved to watch as I grew up.

Especially you, Clark Gable.

JO SCHAFFER LAYTON is a native of the California Bay Area now living in Texas. She is an author, speaker, screenwriter, TV/film producer, and is a Taekwondo black belt.

She is the author of YA novels *Against Her Will*, the Stanley & Hazel trilogy, and the forthcoming *Badlands*.

Jo is a co-founder of the nonprofit Teen Author Boot Camp, one of the nation's largest writing organizations for teens, with an annual conference and regular programs that support literacy, authorship, and provide books to underserved populations.

She is passionate about community, travel, books, music, healthy eating, classic films, and martial arts. But her favorite thing is being a mom to her awesome kiddos and wife to her hunky husband.

Find Jo at www.joschaffer.com.

#STANLEYANDHAZEL
#THEWINNOWING

www.ingramcontent.com/pod-product-compliance
Lightning Source LLC
Chambersburg PA
CBHW030808200726
48285CB00015B/1844